Karmafornia

Karmafornia

NC WEIL

Fool Court Press, LLC

Cover by NZ Graphics
Book design by Nita Congress
Printed by Lightning Source

ISBN-13: 978-0-9834893-0-6
LCCN 2011930567
First Edition
Published in the USA
Fool Court Press, LLC

http://FoolCourtPress.net

ACKNOWLEDGMENTS

MANY PEOPLE ASSISTED in my journey from ideas plus words, to this finished novel. First and foremost, thanks are due to my mate Tim. Writing feedback and advice from Richard Peabody, Lorine Kritzer Pergament, Bettina Lanyi and William Stromsen gave me valuable perspective. For fact-checking of Berkeley history, thanks go to Patrick McClintock; for Dead Kennedys references, thank you Jello Biafra; for a closer look at the Jonestown tragedy, I thank Anne Levy-Lavigne for a copy of Stephen Stept's documentary *Witness to Jonestown* which aired on MSNBC in 2008.

The quotations from the Robert Hunter-Phil Lesh song "Box of Rain" are included with permission from Ice Nine Publishing.

Karmafornia is a work of fiction; other than historical figures, any resemblance to actual persons is purely unintentional.

PART ONE

The Best Intentions

CHAPTER 1

Snowed In

December 1977

"Why's California trying to kill us?"

"It's just a snowstorm, Walt."

"Right where the Donner Party got trapped—"

"So who's gonna be the cannibal, you or me?" Laura laughed.

Walt didn't find their predicament funny—he was only here because of her, and California seemed to have decided he didn't belong. His Opel had barely begun climbing the Sierras out of Nevada when this blizzard swept in; soon the car was skating on white pavement, dense wet snow cramping the wipers. He pulled to the shoulder to put on chains, but before he got his door open, a snowplow thudding up the road raised a wave-curl of white that hit the little car hard, gravel staccato in the heavy *whump* as snow plastered the driver's side. No sooner had the reverb stilled, than another load buffeted them, smothering the rest of his view. Just like that, they were buried—and in a white car—whatever wasn't covered was invisible anyway.

He cut the engine. His door wouldn't budge and Laura's opened only a couple inches before hitting snowbank. She snaked out her window

3

and up, looking over the roof. Though of average build she was narrow front to back; her brown hair done in a single braid reached her shoulder blades. She had last summer's tan, a straight nose, eyes more turquoise than blue, smooth fingers ringless despite his efforts.

"Yikes!" She ducked in just before another slap of snow. "Let's get out of here," her voice panicky. "The next plow could hit us. As soon as the coast is clear, we can climb out on this side."

"And go where? In the forest they won't find us till April, and on the road we'll get run over. Makes more sense to stay put." He sat back. "We're equipped, right? Food, water, sleeping bags, batteries for the tape player— and you and me," running his knuckles alongside the buttons of her flannel shirt from throat to jeans. "Close your window—these horses ain't gonna freeze," patting the dash. His calm damped her alarm.

"A couple inches for air," she said, rolling her window higher.

He started Hendrix's *Axis: Bold as Love* on her portable cassette deck then got out his antler pipe and film-can of pot. They'd agreed not to drive stoned, but this car wasn't moving anytime soon—

HE POINTED OUT a perfect snowflake resting on the sleeping bag nylon— outside Laura's window airy clumps were floating down, but this one had made it through the gap solo. She admired its symmetry and kissed him for showing her, but he was too easily impressed—her aspirations reached well beyond the house-job-companion setup he found sufficient. He'd be a good plant, content with sun and rain to nourish him. Hendrix was singing "If Six Were Nine"—Walt's mantra, but not hers.

According to him, life was a river, and opportunities arose naturally; being rigid and goal-oriented only inhibited success. Finding their apartment was a case in point: once they'd decided to live together, he figured with weeks till their leases ran out, something would come up. Not willing to "leave it to chance" she pursued dead ends and argued with landlords—then when she'd worked herself to a froth without finding anything suitable, a guy in one of her classes offered his apartment, the inexpensive upstairs of a small house in downtown Boulder. "Trust the

Flow," Walt chided, and she had to admit the place was perfect—but she wasn't prepared to drift through life just because that turned out OK.

She defined *homo sapiens* as the dissatisfied animal. Cave-dwellers found out meat was easier to digest cooked than raw, but someone took the unnecessary next step, learning ways to make it delicious. Civilization accreted from a thousand such discoveries, and owed its glories to the recurring "That's OK but—" of generations. Walt with his freshly minted BA showed no interest in serious work, a career—he was content with a job that barely covered his bills. She however intended to make her mark; with another semester to go, she'd already been accepted to grad school.

California'd thrown a storm at them, but this wasn't the 1840s and she was no Donner Party *naïf*—she itched to be moving. Cranking the passenger window halfway down she stuck out her head again—wind carried the throb of engines laboring up the grade, rhythmic grinding of tire chains, the scrape of plow blades. But the fresh wet smell and fat snowflakes cheered her in spite of herself. Slipping back in, she patted hair and face dry with her bandana, then turned—that glint in Walt's eyes—"What?"

"Remember that acid Tom gave me? We've got time, music, noplace to go—let's trip."

What if it got weird? When they met she'd felt comfortable with Walt at once, as though the groundwork of finding out who he was had already been done; they'd shared the apartment a year and a half with no major hassles. Mom and Dad meeting him this week liked his polished manners, he looked presentable—on the tall side of average, friendly open face, warm hazel eyes unafraid to meet anybody's, bushy hair sunbleached auburn on top, cut recently enough not to give them pause. Beyond sharing a kitchen and bed she'd neither given nor sought commitment; as far as she was concerned they were just hanging out, their pleasure one element of the good life. She'd planned to mention her grad school application to Berkeley, but why would that even matter? They were too young to think long-term. Besides, she might not even get in.

Then in October her acceptance letter came—time to 'fess up. Shocked, he just took off, and showing up hours later with a look of cold concentration, hustled her into bed, commencing an extraordinary bout of sex and struggle. She hadn't thought he cared so much; pretty soon she realized she did too. But about the time it dawned on her their union went clear to the bone, he'd leaned back, looked her dead in the eye, and said, "You think you're leaving me to go off to grad school but that's not true. *I'm* leaving *you*—now."

Good-natured Walt, so calculating? He seemed to know exactly how bad she was going to feel, which she did, plunged in an instant from bliss to wide-eyed broken surprise. But he hadn't factored his own feelings into his equation, and before long their misery matched, offering her surge of fury no proper target. Arguments flew:

What's wrong with coming to Berkeley with me?

Why would I want to play sidekick to your setup?

I never promised—

You never told me—

They'd accused and apologized and loved, days slipping by uncounted during their sexual duel till they compromised: instead of her sending an acceptance check, they'd visit Berkeley together over winter break.

"I just have a reservation," she said. "I haven't committed yet."

"No, I'm the one with reservations," he'd said, exasperated. What business did a word have, answering to opposite meanings that way?

She felt queasy—his car might turn into a cage if that came up while they were tripping. "Tell you what—we'll share one hit."

WHERE THEIR STEAM had frosted the windshield he drew a huge truck bearing down on a tiny car—I-80 in Wyoming, both lanes jammed with semis, everyone but him picking up speed down the hill—going flat-out he couldn't pull away from the one behind—on that radiator she'd counted tattered wings of eight butterflies and moths, a perfectly intact damselfly and over a dozen bees by the time the trucker jockeyed an opening in the left lane and swept out to pass, blasting his air horn—she swore even the car jumped. Now she could laugh, and while Walt scratched DEATH on the trailer she gave the car wings, then spots on its back—and it became a ladybug. The acid coming on made their windshield etchings more intricate. He drew a Greek temple, she decorated the slopes below it with olive trees, and gradually she could read his thoughts and he could hear hers in his head. Meeting, their eyes crossed centuries.

"Kallia," finding her Athenian name on his tongue.

"Phoros," she greeted him, and they opened the curtain of time, those lives waiting beyond it like scenes in a play. Here he was embracing her in an almond grove, the cloud of faintly pink blooms lighting the dusk, her sweet skin competing with the subtle fragrance; another time she met him in the *agora* and pulled him to the back of a stall where she laid him on stacks of rough folded cloth, the merchant out front oblivious till she could no longer stifle her groans and cries—how they laughed when the indignant old man chased them out. All was rapture, centuries-old love binding them to each other—till the warrior Arkhilos attracted her. Phoros saw them together climbing the slope to Aphrodite's temple, offerings in their hands.

"I thought I pleased you," he told her, next time they met.

"Arkhilos pledged me honors—will you?"

Kallia expected them to meet in combat so Phoros accepted the challenge, but his rival was taller, quicker—when Arkhilos's sword lay at his throat he asked for death—who would live dishonored? As his spirit slipped free his final sight was his beloved extending her hand to his slayer—Walt stumbling out of mental darkness perceived Laura. "You owe me."

"There's more to who we've been," she said, and they flew together, the heat of dragons in fierce copulation. He bit her neck with his fangs the way some poisonous creatures mate, repaying sex with death. She loved him violently, scorching his face and horns with her breath, accepting the mortal wounding he'd dealt her but entangling him till her last pulse. And when he struggled away drunk from her sulfurous heat, scales broken by the lash of her tail, deafened by her roaring agony and blinded by the triumph of instinct over what in his corrosive heart passed for love, he was an easy kill. The spearman's arrogant laugh was the sneer of Arkhilos.

Those dragons no more cruel than the world celebrating their destruction, woke Walt and Laura to a past not behind them but lodged within. "You've hurt me too," she said. "Don't sit around resenting my ambition."

"I just feel like you're way out front," considering she hadn't even left a Berkeley course catalogue anywhere he'd see it—no clue whatsoever till she dropped her bomb—her thinking was 100% Laura. He'd initiated their sex marathon in anger, but under that energy was a spreading shame, making him first melancholy then defiant, trying to drown it in sweat and semen. When his hostility backfired he'd flinched under it, taking refuge in her embrace, hoping he'd never wake from the warm asylum of love. Now it was obvious why they'd found each other—their souls were trying to get it right—again. "Why won't you stay with me?"

"I *am* with you, silly." Their love strobed, bodies alternately furnace and freezer, threaded through with ecstasy that trickled along their nerves like ice melting, metal liquefying, frost forming. The air in his lungs was partly her exhalation and therefore partly her, seeping into him the way cold crept into the car. They were one substance—was separation possible? This Walt Sanders identity was a single chip in a great mosaic, their multiple lifetimes creating the complete image. He'd seen enough fragments—he longed to break out of this skin for a glimpse of the whole.

"Being part of everything isn't imprisonment," she said, knowing his thoughts.

"This existence is a limit—I want the history of my soul to flow through me and take me along."

"There's as much infinity between zero and one, as between zero and infinity," she observed. "Whatever your soul knows, is here. Every wail of birth and ash of scattering is in you now." Fingers light on his temples, rubbing little circles, she said, "You're thinking so furiously your head's all tense—let go."

Under his skin he followed her touch, each muscle going fluid with joy, every cell smiling as thoughts bounced telepathically, faces stretched so far it seemed their lips would split. Laura started the Grateful Dead's

American Beauty in the tape player; voices and guitars circling like a net gathered them up to be reborn in light, the whiteness of this snowbound car. Intricacies of frost had decorated their drawings on the windshield, acid's brilliant blues and pinks edging the crystalline feathers. Music rose in spirals visible as their breath, teasing every receptor to shrug off habits of perception—the world was incomprehensibly rich, and now they were awake to drink it in.

Whether they spun inside the notes of a song or walked among olive trees hand in hand, each minute was its own experience without accumulating into hours—trip-time was elastic, all-encompassing—and exhausting. When she thought to open the passenger window to angle upward into the snowfall, the road was a gray blur, occasional headlights going by. The whiteness dimmed, the storm continued. Some time later the acid relented as though they moved in a comet's elliptical orbit, zooming back in then receding, each journey releasing them a little further from its grip. At last they put on long underwear and cuddling heart to heart, sank into sleep, the vast silence punctuated by snowplows.

At Sue's Christmas party in Carling, people were packed tight as calves in a loading chute in the hall and doorways of her two-bedroom apartment. Walt was dosing the bean dip with cayenne when someone called into the kitchen, "Hey, Incredible Eddie's here—come see."

An excited buzz replaced Neil Young and Crazy Horse's *Rust Never Sleeps*. Walt and Laura pushed forward till they could see an absurdly tall figure in a military greatcoat gesticulating, patting his bulging stomach.

"Eddie how'd you get so big?"

Balancing on one high rubber boot he pulled off the other—stuffed with rags. Gesturing grandly and waving his stocking foot well above the floor, he stomped back into the boot then with a flourish unbuttoned his coat, flung it off and pulled throw pillows from front and back of suspendered pants, pitching them to clamoring fans—then he spotted Laura.

"Reiner!" he cried dramatically, arms outstretched; as his audience parted he lurched closer, burying his right arm to the elbow inside his baggy pants. His left hand slipped down giving her breast a tweak, then leaned firmly on her shoulder. Someone shrieked with laughter, pointing at his fly where a thin blue balloon was emerging. Walt despite irritation at his rudeness had to laugh as the balloon kept poking out, longer and longer; Eddie looked down and gave an exaggerated jolt as it continued to grow. By the time it was nearly a yard long people were grabbing at it so he twisted, teasing it away while he showed it off, then pulled his hand from his pants, spread his arms wide to gasp and moan, then squeezed his legs together. The balloon popped, he clumped backwards, hovered over the couch then dropped with a long sensual "ooohhhh." Everyone applauded as he lay gasping.

Laura leaned over him, laughing, "The climax of the party."

"Ah yes my dear, I just had to come. Now if you'll avert your gaze I need to remove a certain sharp object taped to my thigh—its purpose has been served."

Once he waved the thumbtack, she sat beside him. "Quite a performance."

"Thank you Reiner. Just walking into a party doesn't suit me, you know. I have to make an Entrance. Hope I didn't embarrass you back there," miming his pinch.

"Ordinarily I'd have walloped you, of course, but as part of your act—"

"But I meant it," leering.

Walt stepped up. "May I introduce myself?"

"Oh Eddie: my boyfriend. Walt, the one and only Incredible Eddie."

"Mmm, are you two—" Eddie spread his hands and one up one down, end-to-end, merged them, middle fingers back-to-back poking through wiggling.

"Yep," said Laura.

He sighed. "Monogamy's an antiquated concept: people forfeit their evolutionary potential. Even you?" looking disappointed.

"It just happened—I haven't analyzed it."

"No, that's the trouble. Situations arise, people go along without thinking—no reconciliation with long-term ideals, no experiments. We're so ingrained to think of one-on-one that when it happens we stop looking, close our minds. The first possibility becomes It. Life shrinks."

"Could be. So far no shrinkage though."

"Oh, it's subtle," wagging a finger at her. "By the time you notice, you've lost a lot of ground."

"What makes you the expert?" Walt asked.

"I've had the dubious privilege of observing my mother married first to my father, then to a second husband while she had a lover on the side—the only time I can recall her acting both contented and alive—otherwise one seems to preclude the other—then divorcing the second, marrying the lover—another mistake—and leaving him. Soon there'll be someone else, but in all that time, having two men at once made her happiest—but she said that was wrong and she'd never do it again."

"So you're prepared to shoot down an institution that's lasted millennia—"

"Violated for millennia—all through history you'll find men and women not content with a single partner—" and with a shrewd nod to Walt's simmering annoyance, "Jealousy's also outdated—obsolete as slavery."

"What's it got to do with—"

"Quite a lot actually—owning someone, controlling that person's behavior. 'Man and wife,' as they say—person and possession. Even in our supposedly enlightened age it's almost impossible to convict a man of raping his wife."

Walt thought anybody that glib was probably venting a lousy sex life. "'Scuse me while I get a beer." He swam into the kitchen where more people occupied less space than in any other room, then bottle in hand returned to the stereo to play DJ—out here he could actually sit, his back to Laura and Eddie. They were old friends, welcome to solve the world's problems from the vantage of a couch—but he'd skip the lecture. He put on *Workingman's Dead*, then as he watched the rhythm of "Uncle John's Band" invade people's movements, a hand pressed his shoulder—their host Sue. She sat on the carpet, offering a joint; they smoked half then passed it on.

"So," she exhaled, "What do you do?"

"I'm a projectionist."

"What a great job."

"Yes and no—I can't just watch—if I miss the reel cues, that screws it up for everybody else. If I want to see the movie I go on my day off—not too many rate that."

"After half a dozen showings you must know all the weak spots." She retrieved her wineglass and took a sip then rolled the stem between her hands, the burgundy's oscillations leaving a scalloped edge an inch above the wine. "Wow, Berkeley. That's so cool, that Laura's accepted. But grad students stay pretty busy I hear, between classes and work."

"Guess I'll have to hang out for both of us."

She nodded solemnly, blessing their union. "Shows you make a good couple—it drives me crazy when two perfectly interesting people get tight then try to do everything together, think the same thoughts, read the same books. Pretty soon they're bored out of their minds."

"If I was that in love with myself I'd line my room with mirrors and to hell with other people."

Her smile creased the bridge of her nose. "I hope to spend some time out there—I've applied for a research fellowship and that's where several of my sources are."

He liked Sue—the way she moved, her balanced energy—if he wasn't already involved he'd give her a kiss and see what happened. At least talking with her eased his mind about this upcoming trip, their future.

BUT WHEN HE and Laura visited Berkeley, walking the campus and neighborhoods populated by a mix of students, former students and the radical elements who gravitated there, he experienced a visceral dislike of the place. People were aggressive and self-righteous, on the fringes those who'd cracked under the pressure: wild-eyed street people as hostile as they were deranged.

LAURA'S FRESHMAN ROOMMATE offered them floor space—Diane had transferred to Berkeley, finished her BA in botany early, then moved to San Francisco. She and Laura were two of a kind, smart and competitive—she bragged about beating out seventy other applicants to land a job caring for exotics at the Arboretum in Golden Gate Park. Still, in her high-powered way she was friendly, and it was good to have a place to crash while they explored the Bay Area. They helped prepare for her New Year's party: cleaning up her apartment, assembling platters of vegetables, fruit and cheese, making a run to a crowded liquor store for beer and wine. As people arrived she made introductions.

"Laura and Walt, meet my fellow student Cob." He was two inches taller than Walt and leaner, with dark intense eyes under a strong brow and broad forehead. His broken nose, veering left, dominated his face above mobile lips. He wore his smooth black hair parted in the middle and banded at his neck in a three-inch ponytail, and when they shook hands, Walt's vanished in that big palm with long dexterous fingers which nevertheless pressed so faintly, it hardly seemed they'd made contact.

His gaze was already on Laura. "Know what a cob is?"

As Walt intook breath to speak she said, "A male swan."

His eyes lit, their heat for her only. "That's right. Most people say 'corn on the—.'"

"I'm a biologist—I'll be doing my master's at Berkeley on wetlands ecosystems."

"Yeah?" His eyes glowed warmer. "That's what I'm studying—how come I haven't seen you?"

"I start this summer—I'll get my bachelor's in May."

"We'll be classmates," nodding approval, then turned to consider Walt. "Who's your friend?"

"My boyfriend. We're checking out the area."

"What do you think?"

"I like it," she smiled. Wow, this guy set her nerves tingling.

"Seem like a lotta burnouts in Berkeley," Walt said. "Wandering the streets arguing with themselves."

"Yeah, there's paranoia. Check out the phone book—in the residential listings you'll see last name, first initial, no address. Every place has some, but Berkeley has a lot, and those are the people who refuse to spring for an unlisted number. Why should you pay every month when they only print the book once a year?"

"What's your alternative?" Walt shrugged.

"That's the phone company—'We don't care—we don't have to.'"

Laura's dad was a career man with Mountain Bell—he viewed phone service as a utility like water or electricity, but she guessed Cob would see him as a stooge, lending his competence to an organization that deserved to die. She'd hashed over the phone company's violations too many times—she'd rather find out more about this new guy: they had mutual interests to explore. "How'd you get the name Cob?"

"Guess I don't look like a swan, with my wings covered up," giving her the kind of look Walt often did—hungry and touched. "I'm named after my grandfather Cobham. First name's Allen but my dad goes by that, so I've always been Cob. Cobham seemed pretentious."

So does Cob, Walt thought, and as though he'd heard him, "So what's Walt short for—Wallet?"

He deflected the dig—no point starting off antagonistic with Laura vibing on the guy so strong. "If it was, maybe I'd have more money."

"Money," with a snort. "Money's shit. The more you have the more it stinks."

"I must smell good then. Know what it costs to get dug out of a snowbank after the plows bury your car for thirty-six hours?"

"How much?"

"Three hundred fifty bucks. Not including my cracked windshield."

"Did you get to pay that?"

"No, the California Highway Department picked up the tab, since they buried us in the first place."

"Good of them."

"Good to be alive to thank 'em."

"Ah." Cob's face opened, giving Walt too a glimpse at a formidable mind sorting details, making assessments. That heavy brow and skewed nose should look threatening, but his curiosity softened the effect. "Tell me about it."

"Want a beer?" Walt suggested.

"I don't drink beer, and it's early for wine—I'll have water, and comfort myself knowing I don't go to parties much—tap water's toxic."

"Doesn't taste good—"

"That's all the chemicals and crap. I drink filtered water—it's pure."

Again seeking neutral ground, Walt asked, "Where you from?"

"Nebraska. Man I couldn't wait to get out of there. I figure in twenty years I'll go back, give those assholes that used to pound me time to get fat and lose some hair, their wives to spread, and I'll show up with a beautiful woman on each arm and laugh at 'em."

"They won't break just your nose," Walt mused.

"Hm? Maybe not. But the thought cheers me up." He grinned.

"Find your beautiful women yet?"

"They're everywhere—haven't you noticed?" Cob made every state-ment a fact while treating Walt's comments as opinion—hard not to be defensive talking to him.

"Where's yours?"

"You mean ownership?" shaking his head. "Fly free, that's me."

"That works till you find someone you love."

"I love 'em all," Cob said, his eyes on Laura.

WHEN EVERYONE HAD gone and they'd spread out on their sleeping bags, Walt folded his hands behind his head and looked up into the dark.

"Maybe we should get married."

"Is that a proposal?" Laura asked, surprised.

"An idea. What do you think?"

She laughed. "You're asking because Cob was coming on to me—you think if we're married he won't. He would anyway—doesn't respect No Trespassing signs."

"What signs? Didn't see you setting boundaries."

"I didn't. And I don't, and I won't. If you want to own somebody, keep looking."

"Laura, marriage isn't ownership, it's partnership: one person means more than the rest. You can be friends with everybody, just not lovers."

"I'm not ready for that." All she could think of was Cob, the tactile intensity of his gaze. "If I want a guy I'm not going to put him off for you."

"No? What about Onion in the snow?" He'd named the car to commemorate the layers they had to hack through and their resulting tears from exhaustion and snow blindness in the storm's dazzling aftermath. "Didn't tripping mean anything?"

"We're connected Walt, but I'm not ready for monogamy. Don't ask."

"When can I?"

"When I have my degree. Far as I know you're still hedging about Berkeley, but I'm sure—it's the next place for me."

"That crazy guy who accosted us near campus felt like an omen. And you'd already decided."

"Walt, I kept an open mind, I really did—I looked around and asked myself, 'What if I studied with these people? What if this was where I woke up every day?' And my answer was: I like it—this is right for me. And I wish it was for you."

"Our future—"

"I've got exploring to do. I want some space. Don't live in Berkeley if you hate it."

"I won't—but I don't want your space, I want you."

"Careful," she said in that way she had of pinning down each conclusion as though she was arranging embalmed butterflies. "The leading edge of jealousy's desire, but the rest is chains. Don't be a jailer."

CHAPTER 2

Anticipation

"Careful of my wings."

Laura touched the jut of his shoulder blades—were they? A cob was a swan, after all. The faintest breeze carried the green smell of water up the bank; light of the high half moon between sycamores spread across the wrinkling surface of the Feather River. They were TA-ing Bio field studies in summer school, his emphasis plant life, hers zoology. Their students clustered around a campfire fifty yards away in the clear night, the prof talking about riparian ecosystems—standing on the periphery Cob had gestured with his head for her to join him. His kisses tasted like maple syrup; in moments she'd freed his hair from its ponytail and they were sitting below the crest of the damp earthen bank, bare to the waist. "You really have wings?"

"Sure—fly with me?"

"Where?"

"Hm," sounding amused. "Use birth control?"

"I'm on the Pill."

"You should get a diaphragm—that's better than disrupting your hormones."

"It's not your body—why do you care?" She'd debated her choices freshman year—failure rates, physical effects, hassle—and concluded the spontaneity and low pregnancy risk of the Pill were worth its impact on her health.

"I can feel the difference. It's like you're in a chemical jail, and I'm trying to love you through the bars."

"Oh, it's not as bad as all that," undoing the top button of his jeans; he put his hand on hers.

"Clear your system first."

"What?"

"Takes about three months for your body to purge it out."

"Three—" She was ready now. "What happens in the meantime?"

"We'll just wait." He sounded so cool and casual. "Didn't you ever wait for something you wanted?"

Dubiously, "Yeah."

"Didn't you want it more?"

"Either that, or I changed my mind."

"I'll take my chances," that certainty making her gut contract. She could practically hear Walt saying "What a crock," but she was curious. "Anticipation's a powerful aphrodisiac," he murmured. "Close your eyes, sit perfectly still—I'm going to touch you, but you don't know where. Wait for it." She let down her eyelids, heard the high whine of a mosquito and moved to swat it, but he caught her hand. "There's no malaria here. Let him have dinner."

"That's—"

"If you don't scratch 'em, the bites hardly itch—forget the mosquito. Pay attention to what I'm doing." His absoluteness mesmerized; she let awareness spread into her exposed skin. Something slid against her foot, she involuntarily pulled back. "No Laura. Still." She made her leg relax, her whole body alert now. As minutes went by her mind wandered and the touch on her throat sparked, she flinched. "Wait," he breathed. She calmed again to sense his approach, heard then missed the gurgle and wash of the river as she ordered her fingers not to respond to one itch after another. His touch traced the lower edge of her rib cage in front, disappeared. Again she waited. Warm breath focused over her kidney, she suppressed the urge to put her hand there. Time. He drew a thin wet line from neck to shoulder—his tongue?—she sat straighter. His fingers closed around her right nipple kneading it; as they finished, fingernails drew furrows up her inner thigh. Her vulva pressed against her jeans, cool breath followed the drying line on her shoulder raising goosebumps. A quick downward stroke on her spine made her arch away, his mouth surrounded her left nipple, sucking it, gone. She was turned on now, but nothing touched until as her skin began to relent he pinched her mons between his knuckles. She gasped, not sure if his exhalation was laughter.

"Eyes closed, that's right," just as she was going to open them. He touched the crown of her head, moving his finger in a tight circle through her hair like a fork gathering spaghetti, nerve-prickles spreading across her scalp sending waves of chills down her arms and spine. When those had nearly stilled, a finger traveled from her knee to an inch short of her meeting thighs. "Open your legs," he breathed, and she shifted them apart, pulse strong against her jeans, but as she waited for another touch there it came on her lips instead: a kiss, so unexpected she nearly choked. His mouth was cool—hers must be hot. "Purify your temple so I can worship here," and he was gone.

The privacy she'd felt behind closed eyes dissolved—the moon bright as a bare lightbulb left nothing to his imagination—while he was turning her on, what was he feeling? Wanting? Skin gone cold, she quickly pulled on her t-shirt.

During the day Cob was Mr. Information for the undergrads, full of suggestions, and every twist of his lips had her heart racing, but talking with her he showed no interest beyond the work everyone was doing. She noticed him coming on to one of the sophomores, a good-looking blonde with no bra, their private little smiles excluding her. But every night he sought out Laura, with her shirt off performing his ritual of random touch—except it wasn't random: it was studied, and it worked—she wanted to coil around him and soak up his heat.

BACK IN BERKELEY she had a diaphragm fitted, and practiced inserting it in before putting away the kit. She liked her new home, shared with four housemates: a two-story house clad in dark cedar shakes, its full-length front porch piled with abandoned bicycle parts, boxes of weathered textbooks and a long sagging couch draped in mold-speckled sheets. The front door's oval beveled-glass inset, along with the walnut wainscot in the foyer, hall and living room, hinted of statelier times. The doorways into kitchen, living room and downstairs hall were arched, the walls lath-and-plaster carefully patched except one deep floor-to-ceiling crack—the back of the house had settled, perhaps in an earthquake—Jack's room had matching damage. His bedroom and Petra's were separated by a half-bath off the short hall left of the front door, just beyond the stairs which in a pair of flights arrived outside Laura's room. Upstairs Steve's room was to the left, Beth's to the back. On the right was a bathroom with stained chipped tub and pedestal sink, already jammed with towels and toiletries; Laura kept hers in her room.

Since her big window viewed the walk and street, she placed the overstuffed armchair where she could glance out, stacked cinderblocks beside it to support her tall gooseneck desk lamp, and set up brick-and-board bookshelves. The mahogany-stained bureau was marred, its mirror clouded; she made up her mattress with graying sheets and her childhood blanket. Her deep narrow closet had a row of hooks handy for hanging camping gear—she didn't want things piled on her down sleeping bag.

The large square living room had pine floors covered by a rag rug, the duct tape scuffed where separating loops had been repaired. Armchairs and couch were sidewalk rescues, Indian-print bedspreads hiding holes and suppressing dust. Steve's stereo system, raised to thigh height by a pair of sturdy plywood boxes packed with LPs alphabetized by group, drove two big forty-watt speakers in there and two smaller ones in the kitchen—the one by the arched entry was their phone stand. On the walls bearlike apparitions were faintly visible, like cave paintings not quite effaced by smoke and damp.

In the kitchen, off the foyer to the right, the table was a varnished slab of plywood on steel legs. Its maker had done a good job—bolts were countersunk, edges and corners rounded. On it stood a toaster, a shotglass of salt, a soy sauce cruet and a bottle of Szechuan hot sauce. Two of the half-dozen chairs were rickety wood, heavily duct-taped and creaky, but the other four had sturdy tubular legs and bright green plastic-covered seats and backs. The room was decorated with mutilated examples of dining hall cutlery: Jack would curl down three of a fork's tines leaving the other upraised in a middle-finger salute; holding a spoon he'd say "I'm Uri Geller—don't interrupt me I'm concentrating," while bending its handle into a loop. Beth thought that was funny and tacked them to window frames—Laura counted a dozen.

The fridge had been painted royal blue though not much was visible: Petra had posted the chart from *Diet for a Small Planet* showing which vegetarian combinations yielded complete proteins; Steve put up a list of national, state and local politicians with their office addresses and phone numbers—he was out at meetings two or three nights a week, often till two A.M. Jack contributed an R. Crumb cartoon: *"Mr. Natural's definition of karma is 'He who shits in the road comes back to flies.'"* Beth's tutoring schedule was marked A for "away" or H for "here"—she preferred to work in the living room, setting up a small chalkboard where her tutees worked problems. With a BA in math she was slowly earning a master's in education, her high school students taking university-level calculus just as she had ten years earlier. Laura taped up UC Berkeley's Fall 1978 calendar.

Petra worked three days a week in Sausalito doing layout and paste-up for *CoEvolution Quarterly*, publisher of the *Whole Earth Catalog*. She'd cobbled together a degree in Sociology studying utopias and communes, and she'd bring home thrift store silverware stamped Oneida, admiring that group. Jack made a point of throwing away any that bled rust, not really caring how that pissed her off. At first Laura found his abrasiveness disconcerting but everyone else ignored it—including Petra after she'd yelled at him; Laura learned to shrug it off too.

The fridge was packed—her allotment was a crisper drawer plus space on the tall top shelf; she crammed her overflow wherever it would fit. Her first lesson in food storage came soon after moving in—she'd put her banana bread in the pantry, and Steve discovered tiny ants thick inside the bag, their trail out the painted-over window.

"So where am I supposed to store bread?" Within moments of his giving her the bag she felt them advance across her hands. "The plastic didn't keep 'em out."

"They're sugar ants—make sure sweet stuff's cleaned up and air-tight—Beth uses Tupperware." This was like the tropics—palm trees, purple and orange bird-headed flowers, eucalyptus trees—California was different all right—she had plenty to learn. She took her banana bread, ants and all, to the alley. The small dirt patch had succumbed—oil and transmission fluid spills kept even weeds from growing.

When she yanked the tight cover off the trashcan, she saw skittering: rats. Dropping in the infested loaf she pressed the lid down firmly and went back indoors, brushing off stray ants. She'd intended to plant a garden, but this yard was a man-made desert—like most of them. According to her theory, desert cultures—Egypt, Mesopotamia—hadn't started out in barren places; overgrazing, pollution and destruction of native plants created them, same as the Dust Bowl.

Despite morning fog it didn't rain. Beth explained that coastal California had climate not weather—a wet season roughly November through March then dry the rest of the year, seldom freezing. Laura'd missed the weeks of April and early May when the mounded hills were pool-table green—now the grass was tawny. The ridge east of the city, streets winding to the top lined with expensive houses, was dense with trees and shrubs thanks to regular watering.

HER THIRD WEEK in her new home, Cob showed up, finding her in the kitchen stir-frying rice and vegetables. "Are you vegetarian?" he asked.

"I have nothing against meat, I just don't eat it very often. What about you?"

"I'm fruitarian—I don't eat slaughtered food."

"There's nothing dead in this."

"Harvesting rice kills the whole plant—I eat things that didn't have to die."

She looked at him, puzzled. "Like what?"

"Fruit, nuts, some vegetables—peppers, eggplant, green beans and pod peas, squash and cucumbers, broccoli, cabbage. No root vegetables— no carrots, onions or garlic, no potatoes or peanuts. No grains except corn, no leafy greens."

"What about eggs or dairy?"

"Eggs that aren't fertile are OK, I can eat cheese, yogurt. Milk'd be fine if I wanted it. No sugar—I sweeten things with honey."

"So you don't want any of this."

"No. Got an avocado?"

"It might be ready." She put it in his hand, he wiggled the stem like a loose tooth.

"Yep. Lemon?"

"In the bowl on top of the fridge." He sliced that, then halving the avocado struck the blade into the pit, lifting it out and with a hard flip of his wrist hurling the large round seed across the kitchen where it thwacked into the trashcan. He winked at her, polished a spoon on the inside hem of his t-shirt, squeezed lemon juice into the hollow in half the avocado, sprinkled on salt then scooped out a bite. Beckoning with his eyes he leaned against the counter, feeding her the spoonful.

As she stood waiting for another he said, "Don't burn your dinner." She hurried to scrape her now-scorched onions, zucchini and rice into a bowl. Splashing soy sauce she saw him watching as she set down the cruet.

"Let me guess: none of this either."

"The soybean plants had to die, didn't they?" arching an eyebrow as though she ought to be more considerate.

"Must be hard to be so pure," she said sarcastically.

"I try," he said mildly. "But I'm not out to be holier-than-thou—I just don't feel clean if my food's been murdered. You'd taste so much better without death on your breath." His look electrified her—laying Walt meant friendship and the communion of hearts, but Cob's desire felt conditional—she'd assumed that once her body was prepared they'd fly together—how humiliating, if after months of waiting he didn't want her.

BY AUGUST SHE'D dropped twelve pounds, some from going off the Pill but more thanks to constant nervous energy that made her hollow and restless. Her favorite foods—bread, carrots, rice stir-fry, salad—weren't part of her new fruitarian regimen; her appetite disappeared. Cob's touch governed her thermostat, now sunny, now a cloak of ice—when she dreamt of him she'd wake up sweating, but most of the time couldn't get warm. Three months: she looked at that late September Friday with yearning.

Shortly after Labor Day a chatty letter came from Sue: she wouldn't know till spring about that research fellowship but she had hopes, asked about Walt and how they liked Berkeley, filled her in on Eddie's latest antics and apologized for not writing sooner. Laura sat down to reply, but descriptions of her courses seemed anemic, *Walt lives in Santa Cruz* cried for elaboration—she and Sue had been confidantes—she should say what was really on her mind, or not bother answering. She wrote about Cob, how after long anticipation the payoff was within reach. But rereading she thought she'd misrepresented him—it was hard to explain to someone who'd never heard his voice or tasted his kiss. She couldn't send this letter—she buried it among papers on the end of her shelf—after they flew—

BUT BY THAT Thursday he hadn't said anything, leaving with his usual quick kiss despite her rising frustration. The next night she called him—she didn't know where he lived and the phone book listed only "A. Dunn" and his number.

"Oh hi Laura, what's up?"

"Sort of thought you'd be coming over—I've been off the Pill three months now."

"Mm. Feel better?"

"Yeah, I can tell what it was doing to me. But weren't—"

"A friend's here from Nebraska. We were tight in high school, y'know?"

Yes she knew.

"I'll come by when she leaves," then paused. "If you want me to."

"Yes!" which came out as a dry hiss. She controlled herself. "Yeah, come over. Next Friday, you think?"

"Well, I don't really know—she said a week." He chuckled. "Don't worry, I haven't forgotten you. We're gonna fly aren't we?"

"Yeah," her throat so tight the word barely got out.

After he hung up she slammed the phone down—she could tear herself into pieces and fling them everywhere, she wanted him so bad. The night crawled by while she thought about him with his visitor, and in the morning on impulse she called Walt—he'd given her maximum space, leaving it to her to initiate contact.

"Hey listen," he said, "I have Tuesday and Wednesday nights off—want me to bop up and see you?"

"Yeah, that'd be good." How would she get through the week otherwise?

While she was grading papers in her armchair Tuesday afternoon she heard a car door and glancing out saw Onion, Walt heading up the walk whistling.

"Door's open," she yelled. Bounding upstairs he dropped his knapsack by her mattress. She squared her papers to set aside and stood into his hug. He tasted sour and stale compared to Cob but his kiss wasn't a tease—he gave her all of it unthinking. Stepping back he looked her over.

"Wow, what's been going on?"

"I lost some weight," she said coyly. "What do you think?"

"Um—there was nothing wrong with you before, but— But you—" Rumpling his brow he studied her. "Are you doing a lotta drugs?"

"No. I haven't even smoked pot for months."

"You look—needy."

She glanced off sideways, saying nothing. She *was* needy.

"Whatcha been up to?" he asked lightly, as if she was too fragile for real questions.

"Nothing—went off the Pill," adding, "I got a diaphragm."

"You like it?"

"Haven't actually tried it yet," she confessed.

"We'll break it in." His smile faded. "Thought you were seeing Cob."

That's what she'd told him, halfway through summer. "I am—we're waiting."

"Lady you're on fire."

STANDING CLOSE WITH his hard-on between them, why'd she hesitate, wrists covering her breasts: reluctant? Or ashamed? "Hey," he said gently, stroking her ribs that used to ripple and now stood out like corduroy. His heart constricted—of course she'd change, living in Berkeley doing the grad student thing, but this happened so fast. It hadn't been easy to stay away—without their acid trip he could never have done it, but he trusted their connection to bring her back when she was ready—if he pushed she was likely to shut down their future.

Almost from the moment she took him she was groaning and shaking—she came and came, as though he'd provided the final degree to set her boiling. "I'd like to think that was me," he said wryly, "but I know better. Tell me?"

Still wound tight, she frowned as though he was prying.

"I'm not out to pass judgment, OK? But nobody here knows you very well—I'm your ground, your reality check."

"I know, Walt, I'm glad you're here. This week's so long."

"Why this week?"

She spun some flimsy story about purifying herself, building a new level of energy and awareness. He listened, meeting her eyes whenever her gaze wandered back from her Klee poster, the bar of sun crossing armchair and floor, the cracked plaster on the ceiling.

"All that teasing—don't you see? He's enslaved you."

"He has not."

"Sure he has—you're afraid to even tell me about him. And he'll know I've been here too—I blew the lid off his pressure cooker. Bet you something."

"What?"

"He'll make you wait, maybe another three months, to build you up to a state of need so when he does finally come through you'll be helpless. He must have a lotta self-control, or else a lotta women, to hold himself back like that."

"He's with a high school girlfriend this week."

"Ah, the longest week—just when you think you'll get some, he pulls it again. You let him do that?" Laura, the original No Bullshit lady?

"I'll have huge orgasms."

"And they'll all belong to him. What's his thrill?"

"We'll fly together."

"We did, remember?" nuzzling her. "I love you Toots. Lemme stay a couple days—you'll be glad."

"I'll take you out—got a preference?" They stood in her kitchen.

"I—don't go to restaurants."

More Cob. "What do you want then? We'll eat here."

"I'm fruitarian."

Knowing that if he rolled his eyes she'd slam a door he wanted open, he nodded while she recited what her diet allowed and eliminated. "So no beer. What about wine?"

"I could drink wine."

"Is it OK to smoke pot? You said you haven't."

"*Sinsemilla*, I guess—buds."

"Fresh out, but at least you have good taste. And you taste good," kissing her. "That must be behind this—Cob's molding you into someone he can enjoy."

"Hey, I'm benefiting—"

"In some ways maybe. But you're wound tight as a druggie—"

"No judgment, remember? You don't know him."

He wanted to tell her the guy was power-tripping like Charles Manson, but words wouldn't convince her. Maybe love without strings would give her perspective. "Can you eat soufflé?" His specialty.

"I think so—eggs and cheese are all right."

He assembled ingredients. "Tell me your schedule Toots."

"I have a class at eleven tomorrow, then I teach my recitation at two, Thursday I have a three o'clock. I've got papers to grade, reading, lab, and I have to review before my recitation—usually I do that in the grad lounge after my eleven o'clock. I can't just fool around—what's your plan?"

"Walk, hang out. I don't mind, long's I can see you," putting butter in the saucepan to melt.

"Oh, you're using flour in that aren't you?"

"I don't know how to make a *roux* otherwise. Three tablespoons won't blow your diet will it?"

"Could you try cornstarch?" She sounded pitiful.

"That'll ruin it." Turning off the burner he came over where she counted out eggs at the table, and stroked the backs of her arms, eyes on hers. "I won't make soufflé if you feel wrong eating it. Frittata's OK."

"I—"

The hooks of obligation—to her new diet, to Cob—were sunk deep.

"Do a frittata," she said.

He continued to look at her, concerned.

"Thanks Walt."

The dish wasn't as tasty as usual—she wouldn't eat onions—and he wanted toast with it but she wouldn't eat that either; he warmed corn tortillas, and they had wine. Her housemates showed up—Beth, with a fifteen-year-old girl she was tutoring, then Petra who offered to share her salad. Walt would've but Laura declined so he did too. Steve and Jack came in with a few groceries they packed into the fridge.

"Windfalls again?" Jack teased. Laura went red.

"Yeah, whattaya call that—the nuts diet?" Steve asked.

"Give her a break," Walt said. Why be mean?

"Who're you?" Jack asked.

"Steve, Jack—my friend Walt."

"'Friend'?" Jack probed.

"We used to live together."

"New to California?" Steve asked.

"Since June."

"Didja vote?"

"You mean against Proposition 13? Didn't move here soon enough to register. How much difference will it make?"

"We don't know yet, but if schools and public spaces are funded by property tax, and they roll it back and freeze it, you can guess. They'll cut salaries for profs, and the good ones will migrate to industry—that already happens, but it'll get worse. Probably start charging tuition."

"You don't pay tuition?"

"No, the UC system's free for Californians—that'll change. And the secondary schools will get screwed—that's our future."

"Well, housing's really expensive—people on fixed incomes—"

"That's a pretext—the guys who pushed it through ain't hurtin', they're just selfish. And people are hypocrites—if you ask if they want good schools, parks, rec centers where kids can stay out of trouble, they all say 'Of course,' but they don't wanna pay: 'Gimme more but cut my taxes.'"

"Yeah, that's—"

"Magical thinking—two minus two equals four. The public has the civic-mindedness of an infant."

Jack rolled up his flannel shirt sleeve, groping deep in the fridge. "Want a beer?"

"No thanks," Walt said, "I'm trying her diet, just to see what it's like."

"It's simple," maneuvering his hand out gripping a bottle horizontally. "If you want it you can't eat it."

"This is pretty good," gesturing at the remains of his frittata.

"I don't get it," Steve said. "Why are eggs and dairy all right, but not rice?"

"Have Cob explain it," Walt said; Laura winced.

Jack squinted at him as though he was a complete fool. "You know Cob?"

"I met him."

"Later," Steve dragged Jack to the living room, in a moment Bob Marley's *Exodus* came on the kitchen speakers. Maybe tomorrow Walt could catch up with them—he had questions.

Nashville was showing, so he took her. He'd seen it already and loved the epic sweep, the idealist candidacy playing backup to personal stories of love, fame and selfishness. The hopeful was a Kennedy-like figure whose message of unity was undercut by his campaign manager's empty promises. At the end his assassination launched a singer's career, as though Altman saw politics as just another flavor of show business. But Laura didn't get caught up in it—she was all over Walt, worse than ever—their major point of friction was movies: he liked to disappear into the story, she wanted him conscious of being next to her in some theater seat. Their first cinema date, she'd declared, "Movies are escapist drivel like TV—an amusement park for the eyes and ears that's making somebody else rich. They're the opposite of live music—I'd rather dance any day." He'd hoped *Nashville*'s songs would soften her attitude—no such luck.

BACK IN BED, his affection sparked irritation—sitting through that long movie had exhausted what patience she had, and now every move reminded her how different he was from Cob. When he first got here she'd welcomed the familiarity they enjoyed in Boulder—not anymore.

"You wound up all the time?" he asked as she deflected a kiss.

"When Cob's here I pick up on his energy—he's so clear."

"Really?"

"He is," she insisted. "Everything must violate him. I had you skip the soufflé because he'd know if I had even a little flour."

"Your guilt would tell him, whether he's sensitive or not."

"His body's so clean—even his sweat—he smells like a baby almost."

"Wow—he must have women all over him."

She flinched.

"Who else is he seeing, while he's stringing you along?"

"I don't know," trying not to think beyond the Nebraska girlfriend. She'd spotted him at a distance leaving the Bio building with that blonde, his hand playing with her hair, her body tilted toward him like a heliotropic flower as they walked. Another time she'd seen him kissing a petite woman who carried herself like a dancer—he lifted her to sit on a retaining wall so he didn't have to bend down, her bare feet curling to hold his hips while tanned graceful hands cupped the back of his neck. Even recognizing she'd lost her rationality didn't help—she should tell him to shove it, but instead all she could think was how happy those women looked—

"While you're waiting for him to come over," Walt pressed, "he's balling his brains out, right? Not just this week? Is that OK?"

"What do you expect me to do?" she flared.

"Be honest with yourself. You were surprised when I said you look like you're using, but one glance in a mirror should tell you that."

"He said we'll fly. I want to, and going halfway won't—"

"That's true. But don't give up your sense, OK? Don't let him tell you what to think, or to stop thinking."

But she was withdrawing, trying to limit how exposed she felt. What did Walt know about hoarding energy? She was on the verge of learning something powerful—once she knew, maybe she could explain.

NEXT MORNING WHEN she went to shower he lay back thinking about her, how Cob with a farmer's instinct was watching her ripen, timing his harvest. But she'd chosen to live here and he'd refused—he'd squandered his option to be protective. He joined her in the bathroom.

"No more sex now. I can't take out my diaphragm and change the gel till six."

He made a scolded-puppy face.

"Do what I have all summer—wait." She might not be turning it on Cob but she sure had a honed edge.

"I've been waiting—haven't seen you since June."

"But you're seeing somebody."

"Tom's friend Opal." Tom being his best friend in Boulder, who got him started as a projectionist. When he found out Walt was moving to California he encouraged him to look up a lady he'd met at a Rainbow

Gathering: "She's such a free spirit, I know you'll hit it off." Walt hadn't planned to start anything but she immediately invited him all the way in, which felt completely right. Their mutual affection for Tom made intimacy emotionally straightforward: she knew he was already involved elsewhere, he understood her love for Tom. "We're not out to prove anything," he told Laura, "we just get it on."

"Well, fooling around seems like marking time to me—I'm learning something."

"Hope your new education isn't too expensive."

"Thanks for your concern Walt." His signal to can it. In the daylight of his love she was bound to glimpse something unwelcome.

Back in her room they combed out their hair—hers had always been long but he'd stopped cutting his and now it hung almost to his shoulders, thick as a mane, bleached gold from all the time he spent in the sun. He'd tried a beard but it looked patchy so he shaved every couple days with his electric razor—he ran that now while she put on jeans, bra and t-shirt, a flannel shirt over those, and packed her schoolwork. He dressed and came downstairs where she was bagging almonds and raisins.

"No breakfast?"

She grabbed a banana. "Want a bite?"

"I'll find something." He rested his hands on her hips, beaming love into her through his eyes. "Thanks for the invite. It's so great to be with you."

"Sure," already steeling herself for the day—for seeing Cob, he supposed. Well, maybe she'd notice how uncomfortable that made her.

He was idly opening cupboards when Jack came in. "Hey Walt."

"Say, what do you know about Cob?"

"Really want to know? How tight are you with Laura?"

"Someday maybe we'll get married. In the meantime, no strings. Tell me."

"Well, the first thing I noticed was his harem. Beautiful women, won't go with any other guy. I asked Laura what's the attraction, she said he tastes good. Does she—?" extending his mouth into an O.

"I didn't ask," Walt said curtly.

"They're like a cult—the death-free diet." He snorted.

"She's healthy."

"They say sperm's nutritious," Jack said slyly.

"Don't make me punch you out, OK?" But was it Jack's disrespect that made him want to belt the guy, or the likelihood that she—? It was her body, her business, but—

"Sorry," Jack said. "But she's really under his thumb, y'know?"

"When's he come over, and how long's he stay?"

"Two, three nights a week, half an hour tops. Usually less."

"Ever talk to him?"

"I can't stand that opinionated bastard. Everything's a conspiracy, history's fiction, on and on and on. If you let him start you can't shut him up."

"Yeah, that's the guy I met New Year's. He said he wasn't into ownership though: 'fly free that's me.'"

"Bullshit—I've never seen a guy string along so many women." Jack cocked an eyebrow. "He may not like you bein' here."

"Laura invited me."

"Well, good luck buddy. Far as I can tell, they come but they don't go."

Walt remembered breakfast. "Can I bum a couple slices of bread?"

"She'll taste all that dead wheat—you sure?"

"I taste that way anyhow."

As Walt ate his toast he wondered whether he could ever tease anyone at such length no matter how ecstatic the payoff—seemed wrong. But if she didn't lay the guy, the missed opportunity would poison her affection for him.

Cob was in the Bio grad lounge jotting on note-cards for his recitation. She sat on one of the sprung couches, pulling her backpack onto her lap to open it. He shifted to the adjacent chair—every hair on her arms rose at his proximity.

"Hey Laura, what's up?" His standard greeting had an undertone of interrogation, as though he detected Walt's fingerprints even through her clothes.

"My boyfriend's visiting a couple days—just like your old friend from Nebraska."

"Oh… right, right," nodding, and it stung her—there was no visiting girlfriend. "So you're having sex," he said.

"Yeah." Daring him to say she shouldn't.

"Well, you know what that means."

"No. What's it mean?"

"We have to wait. That intensity we've been working on, that sensitivity? It's all blown. Have to start over."

"What if I don't want to?"

"Don't wanna fuck me?" he shrugged. "Hey that's easy—don't."

"Don't want to wait."

"But that's how it is babe. I know no other way, to fly. But tell me," drawing his finger down her neck inside her shirt, then lifting it off and blowing on the tip like a gunslinger who's just won a shootout, "Even with him, wasn't it better? You probably came half a dozen times, didn't you?"

As though he'd mapped her sensations, pinpointing every heartbeat and thrill, he'd staked his claim to her desire—refusing him was denying herself. "Yeah, it was good."

"We'll fly so far," he promised, sincere and hungry. "If you still want to."

"I want to."

He smiled but as their lips touched he pulled back suppressing a grimace. "Maybe next week I can kiss you again," looking at her with regret. "When's he leaving?"

"He has to work Thursday evening."

"So if I come over Friday or Saturday you'll be free?"

"Yeah." That reminded her of weeks of flipping ahead to September, looking with such longing at last Friday, which he'd pushed up to this week, only now it was—December? His lack of guile was what trapped her, she decided after he'd left the lounge. She had no problem spotting phonies—he wasn't. He could taste Walt in her mouth, and to him that was foul. And she did want him. She wanted him now but he was in charge, and if he said they had to wait, she would.

THAT EVENING WALT let her fix dinner, saying he'd use some forbidden food. "So how'd it go with Cob—wish I hadn't come?"

"Well, you were right—he put me off again."

"If you're not half outta your mind, he'll be just another guy."

"I don't think so."

"But you're never gonna find out, are you? He won't let you." What would it take to draw her away from this fascination? Something he lacked, apparently—all he could claim was that cosmic vision of their future. When his friends were smoking pot in high school he'd refused, contending stoned experiences weren't "real"—in college someone argued persuasively that everything was real, even dreams—since then he'd welcomed altered states of consciousness. But at this point his abstinent position was making more sense—tripping, his link with Laura through time had blown him away—but now that it counted, that didn't inspire loyalty?

"Go ahead and fly," he said. "You'll come back. Birds have to land sometime. Even that SAC B-52 that flies over the Bay Area night and day and refuels in midair, lands sometime. Call me."

SHE'D ALWAYS PUSHED herself. Some friends were content to hang out in low-wage jobs after high school, others settled for second-tier colleges—not Laura. When her parents said she had to stay in-state, only University of Colorado would do. Conceding that some departments and some teachers were better elsewhere, she knew a degree from CU meant more work and a better education. Eddie'd accused her of snobbery but that wasn't it—assigned a paper in the seven-to-ten-page range, she'd push the ten-page limit, and in the process learn more. Cob, inquisitive and hard-working, was a kindred spirit. They'd have gravitated to each other in this program regardless, pursuing not credentials but the learning those represented. Walt was wrong: she wasn't enslaved. She'd willingly absorb the lessons of anyone with greater knowledge—that's all she was doing now. Cob knew what she'd feel—she was waiting to find out.

CHAPTER 3

Argo

When Cob bumped into Laura out walking and saw her button

I = Initiative

J = Jive

he smiled cynically. "Think that makes a difference?"

She was wearing it because Steve had pushed the household to get the word out—I, the "Renter Property Tax Relief Initiative" was drafted by Berkeley Citizen Action with tenants in mind, while J, the "Proposition 13 Tax Benefit Ordinance" was the business-oriented mayor and City Council majority's effort to co-opt it. Students usually ignored local politics, but measures involving their money might get their attention.

"You don't vote?" she asked.

"Does it matter if I do?"

"I've seen just a few votes swing an election."

"Politics is noise—true power's based on human energy."

"Explain," she said.

"Let's sit someplace—ever go in Argo here?"

"No—too many smokers."

"It's a great coffeehouse—I'll buy."

The two-story box had a front wall of partitioned glass through which they could see a crush of small round tables and narrow chairs. The blondes of California were elsewhere—these twenty-five to sixty-year-olds, gaunt intellectuals with dark oily hair, would look at home in European cafés. Some read, others wrote in journals, small groups leaned together talking intensely—about a third were smoking. The hours on the door said 7 AM–2 AM. A few dismembered newspapers were scattered among tables but there were no vending racks or freebies inside. The haze collecting against the eighteen-foot ceiling formed a plume drawn toward the back wall where high up an exhaust fan chattered—Laura was pleasantly surprised at how the coffee aroma overpowered the cigarettes. The shaded lights hanging on long cords were turned off—a benefit of all those windows—and the white walls were undecorated except by scuff marks, the brown tile floor worn shiny around the counter, elsewhere dulled by accumulated grime. A stocky Mexican circulated with a gray tub, collecting cups and emptying pressed-foil ashtrays into a coffee can.

A matched pair of gay guys—same build, same faded jeans and snug t-shirts, black bomber jackets flung over opposite shoulders—were in front of her, hands in each other's back pocket. When the cashier announced their total in a Mediterranean accent and extended her long fingers to collect, each grabbed for the other's wallet, laughing and twisting away. One bumped into Laura, and with a little moue said "Thorry thweetie" while his partner taking advantage of his distraction fleeced him of a five, handing it off to the cashier then dancing out of range.

At the big stainless-steel espresso machine a lean black man moved fluidly to knock out wafers of expended grounds, press in new, crank them onto the machine, flip switches and turn dials, blasts of steam rising around him, a Hephaestos of coffee at his forge. He wore a Soviet Army officer's cap over a short natural, his face a blue-black folded terrain of muscle and bone—he could be thirty or fifty, Laura couldn't tell.

She was next and his eyes drilled her, recognizing her first visit—like a lot of people in Berkeley he didn't meet her gaze so much as confront it. As Cob ordered espressos she put on her don't-mess-with-me face but the barista saw her uncertainty beneath—her wish to fit in—and narrowing one eye as if he found that amusing while appreciating her looks, he turned back to his task. His work was unhurried but a steady flow of drinks went up on the counter, his gravelly voice sing-songing the orders—"dub shot, cap, two spress." His glance flicked some signal of male collaboration Cob's direction—he must've seen him here with other women.

Cob with their cups nudged past empty chairs, squeezing over to a spot by the windows, shifting the ashtray to an adjacent table. "Not very crowded today—I've been in here when there wasn't a vacant seat."

"Doesn't seem like a student hangout."

"Not undergrads—no room to study, no food. Somebody's always asking the owner to sell snacks, but then he'd have to worry about the Health Department."

"And clean the floor?" she laughed.

"Not likely. He has all the business he needs—why change anything?"

"So, what were you saying about power?" she reminded him.

He closed his eyes, holding his drink just beneath his nostrils, inhaling long and slow like a professor ready to begin a lecture. The self-importance he projected would make Walt bolt for the exit, but she'd chosen Berkeley imagining this—discourse, insight, an intellectual atmosphere. Just for a moment she experienced vertigo—for a kid from Carling this place was mythic: former university president S.I. Hayakawa, SDS leader Mario Savio, the great anthropologists Kroeber and Kluckhohn had all made their reputations here. Desire to win renown on that scale focused her restless mind. This bitter espresso seemed the very essence of challenge and discovery—already her palate was learning not to crave sugar to counteract its bite.

"When you give up control over your life," Cob began, "you allow others to tap that energy for their own uses. Sometimes those are good—or start that way anyhow. Reverend Jim Jones for example—People's Temple had a positive impact in San Francisco for years, opening clinics and soup kitchens in poor neighborhoods, and politicos cultivated him because he could deliver thousands of votes. But power went to his head—he

pressured followers to pony up for his new operations in LA and South
America—some even sold their houses to finance him. He got paranoid,
stonewalled reporters, and after an article came out a year ago charging
him with faking cancer healings, he moved to his compound in Guyana—
called Jonestown, in case you're not sure whether his ego's oversized. The
faithful went with him."

"Why'd he go there?"

"He can keep a low profile, do things the way he wants. I've heard he's
running an experiment in mind control. A woman who left last summer
told reporters there were armed guards, public beatings—virtual slave
conditions."

"I don't know that much about him I guess—"

"Living here you have access to stories you won't hear across mainstream America—underground papers and radio stations offer a version
of what's going on that doesn't bow to wishful thinking."

"Does that mean they're right?"

"Who knows? But if they were off-base, why would the government
be so eager to shut 'em up? I'm always suspicious of the compulsion for
secrecy."

Which made her recall looking up Cob in the phone book. He seemed
open, and spoke with conviction about things he believed, but—"Where
do you live?"

"Got an apartment—why?"

"You always come to my house."

"You don't really want to be walking around after I visit, do you?"

No, she couldn't even deal with her housemates then—she couldn't
imagine facing the aggressive burnouts so abundant on the streets. Just last
week a panhandler had followed her a block, hissing that only children of
Satan refused to help, and when she continued to ignore him, he spat at
her. When she felt vulnerable she kept a low profile. "What makes people
want power, anyway?"

"Testosterone. Castrated men are docile. The success of any political system is built on castrating the majority. The power elite buy off

the rich, promising they can thrive if they stay out of the way, and keep the poor working so hard for the basics they don't have energy left for dissent. We're the dangerous ones—young enough not to've bought into the system, not burdened with families to support. Educated, skeptical. Remember COINTELPRO?"

"The intelligence operation that infiltrated antiwar—"

"Oh, you think because that war's over, those guys all went home?" He laughed.

"No, but—"

"Not at all—they're still among us, deeply embedded—you might be reporting to someone, for all I know."

"Or you might," she said.

"You can't tell I'm independent? Every political system's parasitic and coercive. I respect life. You bought into the mentality that it's not murder to eat bread."

"And you didn't?"

"I used to, sure, but the more I learned about living organisms the less I wanted to kill anything just to get by. Death systems desensitize people—if you can kill plants, you can kill animals, people included. We're killing this planet too. I'm less bothered about some wrongheaded tax initiative putting a few bucks back in my pocket, than about the corruption of children. If schools have less money, they can't do such a good job of indoctrination."

"Cob, that's the most twisted argument I ever heard—better funded schools encourage imagination and curiosity—instead of reading outdated biology textbooks, kids can go on field trips and observe stream ecology first-hand."

"Not that they do now, in most schools. Anyway, politicians are impotent—Governor Moonbeam opposed Prop 13 from the minute Jarvis and Gann started collecting signatures—until the polls said it'd pass. Then all of a sudden he's saying 'Well, I think we can work with this.' He's just a surfer—he may look good hanging ten on the crest of events, but he has no effect on the waves."

"He's appointed some good people."

"In a few years that'll be undone—I know, you wish an election actually made a difference. Doesn't really."

"What will then?"

"Change of consciousness. People walking away from the machine, seeing the futility and opting out."

"Alternative communities?" thinking of Petra's obsession.

"You don't think those get bogged down in politics? Summer before I was a junior I lived in a fruitarian commune. I was thinking about dropping out of school—we had the same philosophy, right? They had some property in Paradise—"

She began to laugh.

"No really, there's a town called Paradise on the edge of the Sacramento Valley. There's all kinds of orchards—almonds, walnuts, every fruit you can imagine—the soil's incredibly fertile. The Pickers had a pretty nice setup. When I showed up in late May they wanted money, but I convinced 'em I was a hard worker so they let me donate energy instead. I was there about six weeks—quite the eye-opener."

"What happened?"

"Well, there was this couple who basically ran it—it was her land— her parents' actually—and she was tight with this guy Ross who liked conformity but didn't have a strong enough personality to impose it—he was more like a yappy little dog going for your ankles, hassling people to not only eat the same things but think the same way he did. Know anything about goats?"

"Not a lot—I'm from cattle country."

"The commune kept goats—tree crops are seasonal so cheese-making was their steady income. Like any dairy, they'd breed the herd to keep 'em lactating, then raise the female kids and sell the males. I think they'd saturated their market already because nobody'd buy this half dozen, so there was this crisis over what to do. A butcher offered to buy 'em. That was out, so Ross decided we should let 'em go."

"Wild? Is that a good idea?"

"That's what I said, but they were 'out of sight, out of mind.' I said they should sell 'em to the butcher because at least he had a use for 'em. Just turning 'em loose was deferred murder."

"Bet that went over well."

"Oh yeah," he laughed. "So the big day came, and the people chosen to free the goats—you'd think they were political prisoners—were Jeff, the worst driver I've ever been around, and Cindy, this very skittish girl. The plan was pretty simple—they'd drive up to Red Bluff then east till they hit National Forest, and park the truck and let 'em out." He shook his head.

"So what happened?"

"Well, the truck-bed had plywood sides and chicken wire on the back and top, and while they were driving one of the goats got a leg caught in the mesh. Cindy told Jeff to stop but instead of picking a nice flat spot he freaked out and pulled off the road right there—the shoulder was sloped and the truck tipped over. They got a little banged up but the plywood splintered and the goats got tangled in the chicken wire, and by the time Jeff and Cindy got back there, those billies were in bad shape. A sheriff's deputy stopped and radioed for help; he had some pliers so he started cutting, then the first goat took off. The deputy started to chase it but Cindy told him not to worry, they were gonna release 'em anyway. Wrong thing to say.

"So here we are waiting and four hours later they show up in the back of a cop car with the goats in a truck right behind, but no sign of the commune's truck. Jeff and Cindy and the woman who owned the property were charged with animal cruelty and abandonment while those cops were looking around, thinking we were all pretty weird. But Ross, who made that decision, never said a word, took no responsibility, and later at a group meeting—"

"How big was this group?"

"Ah, there were—a dozen maybe? Anyway, Ross reminded everyone I wanted to sell the kids to the butcher, then all their frustration came down on me. That was a trip—so much like high school—"tapping his broken nose, "except the Pickers wouldn't hit me—they verbally abused me instead. So I left. A week later a girl told me the sheriff came back with a search warrant and busted half of 'em for pot—they thought I narc-ed—I'd become their scapegoat, if you'll pardon the pun. That's the last time I thought an ethical slant made one person better than another—they assumed because I disagreed with 'em I had no integrity." He snorted. "Those life-respecting fruitarians didn't respect mine too well, or face the consequences of their livelihood."

"You think there was no other solution, besides butchering the kids?"

"Not in the long run. Large numbers of male goats are useless, just like bulls. No dairy farmer keeps male calves past veal age—they eat but they'll never produce—might as well be food."

"How's that square with being fruitarian?"

"If somebody else eats animals, I can't control that, can I? And I wouldn't anyway. Maybe it's cruel to harvest fruit—is that really different than slaughtering baby goats? Do we know what trees feel? If one has five hundred peaches, does that mean it can't care about 'em all?"

"Cob, nobody knows stuff like that."

"But shouldn't we even think about it? Shouldn't we doubt who we are and what we're doing? Why respect the life of a rice plant, but not the children of a fruit tree?"

"Or maybe we live in a murderous world," she said, "and we're complicit no matter what we eat. How do you make any choices, if you don't differentiate?"

"My body feels cleaner and my spirit clearer, if I don't slaughter to eat. But that's just me. A squirrel can live on nuts but a mountain lion can't. There's not one right way for everybody to act, or think, or believe."

"So do you care if I'm fruitarian?"

"Only because you taste better—you're the one who has to decide what it means to your psyche." He grinned. "Maybe I'm just another California wack job."

She grinned back. "Maybe."

As they left she asked, "You're so into purity—why do you like this grungy smoky place?"

"It's the coffeehouse in its purest form—no music or décor. Argo has such a strong personality, all the CIA and drug agents who hang out here are being corrupted by it, their faith in the system continually undermined." His eyes danced with glee.

"How do you know?"

"Don't you think so?" He was always turning her questions back at her. She'd played tennis one year in high school before giving up—the guy who taught her, instead of playing at her level so they could get a volley going, had her dashing from one corner to another so she either missed the ball altogether or lofted it to set him up easily. After forty-five minutes she'd be soaked and stumbling while he'd barely broken a sweat. Unable at sixteen to separate her resentment of him from her frustration over her lack of skill, she quit the game—now she felt as though she was back on the court chasing well-placed shots. Cob thrived on debate, his arguments accurate and devastating as smashes. When she had the energy to return them she didn't mind, but she felt her curiosity droop and plod, her sense of wonder inept, her instinctive trust setting him up for the point.

FRIDAY BEFORE THE election was her birthday—she got a card from her folks with some sentimental verses and a twenty, and Walt sent a newspaper photo of the Santa Cruz Pier amusement park, decorated with colored pencils and glued to a 4 x 6 index card, with a note on the back:

> Dear Laura, at 23 you're in your prime, indivisible, unique. Have fun on your special day. At exactly 5 PM I'll send you a birthday kiss—open your window so it can get in.
>
> Love, Walt

But Cob came over at quarter to five, and she forgot. He'd said something scathing about astrology when she asked his birth-date months ago, so why would he be interested in hers? If she mentioned it now, he'd give her a "think you're special?" look as though she was angling for a favor. So if she wouldn't tell him, why bring it up to anyone else? Who cared enough to ask her? The day passing unobserved by those around her made her feel prime all right, unique. Alone.

That night she dreamed a cecropia moth was bumping at her window, but before she could let it in a blackbird caught it and flew away, one tattered maroon wing twitching in its beak. She called "bring it back," Cob's voice in a blackbird's trill said "see you at Christmas," and the moon which had watched the whole episode said, "that's all the birthday you get—hope you liked it."

A cecropia—when she was nine she'd discovered a large cocoon hanging from a plank of their backyard fence, and every day she watched, one late afternoon in high summer rewarded by the sight of a sleek wet head squeezing out the bottom. She sat transfixed while the moth emerged completely then a pair of small wings unfolded from its long fat body like Japanese fans. As it spread and slowly waved them its abdomen pulsed and shrank, pumping into those wings till they were smooth and flat, close to five inches across. While the moth clung to the empty cocoon its coloring intensified. Everything about it looked soft: the delicately furred surfaces of its wings, the tiny red hairs clustering where they connected to its body, its feathery antennae. Then and there Laura decided to be a biologist—this busy Earth must be crowded with marvels—as though they were extended family she wanted to meet them, discover their histories.

The dream made her feel unlucky, and puzzling over it she remembered Walt's note. Part of her defiantly stated, "I told him not to expect anything," but she couldn't shake her guilt—how much had he asked for? A minute of her time, so despite the miles they'd be together? His gift was his affection, and she couldn't be bothered.

HER HOUSEHOLD HAD a party while they listened to election returns— voters sent Ron Dellums back to the House and confirmed Rose Bird as Chief Justice of the California Supreme Court. The capital punishment initiative went down but so did J, while Initiative I passed by a wide margin. Steve bought champagne out of deference for Laura's refusal to drink beer, and they danced to Talking Heads, but their sense of triumph was fleeting—tenants getting some of the tax rollback didn't help the treasury. The university president had released a report on the effects of budget cuts of 5%, 10% and 15%, and some of it was scary—10% would mean a 25 to 35% hit in salaries for faculty and staff—with TAs taking the first hit, of course—and about half the general fund support for UC Berkeley. What good were slightly lower rents if pay rates dropped more?

Saturday two weeks later, Beth listening to the radio called everyone together. "Listen," she said. "The People's Temple in Jonestown? They all committed suicide today."

Laura went cold—she'd only recently heard of the group, and now— She felt ignorant for not knowing more, or sooner—as though her awareness could have prevented such a thing.

Beth went on, "Nine hundred people lined up and drank cyanide-laced Kool-Aid."

"Everybody cooperated?" Steve doubted that.

"No, apparently some people were shot. And get this—Leo Ryan was shot too."

"Congressman Ryan? Why?"

"He went down there to find out why they wouldn't communicate with families here, and his group was ambushed at the airstrip when they were leaving, and five of them were killed—the mass suicide was right after that."

"That's just nuts," Petra said—she'd followed the group's charitable work locally, donating money because their track record reaching and helping the desperately poor was better than official city services.'

When Laura called Cob he said, "CIA."

"But Jim Jones died too."

"He took cyanide?"

"I think so—the reports are sort of garbled."

"No shit," he said sarcastically. "He might've had a double—"

"What's a—"

"Somebody who looked enough like him, to pass when they did the body count. He could be someplace else by now."

"Is any theory too extreme for you?" she said.

"Sure was convenient it happened in the jungle, wasn't it? Not a lot of people running around asking awkward questions. Bodies rot fast in the tropics—bet they have a mass burial in the next couple days and take names off a list. If the numbers don't match, they'll say they recruited natives, or some followers ran off—there's a million ways to hide the truth. Laura, whatever you're most afraid of, somebody's out there doing it. Nightmares reveal what our conscious brains won't accept."

"You think dreams just pluck information out of the air?"

"Kind of—psychic pain has a story to tell. Our subconscious is harder to fool than our logic circuits—as long as we think everything fits together, we'll buy it. Buddhists say the whole world is like that—an illusion maintained by our need for it. Once that falls away, everything changes."

"Oh, are you enlightened?" she said acidly.

"Come on Laura, don't shoot the messenger. I've never made a claim like that, I'm just a skeptic. Doesn't make me smarter or more right, but it gives me a perspective on things we'd like to believe—that powers-that-be want us to believe."

"You think they made up that Jonestown report?"

"I'd bet those people are dead. How and why, I doubt we'll ever know. The mainstream press will broadcast whatever crap they're given, and everybody'll eat it up."

"You must think anyone credulous is a fool," she said.

"Why trust a con man?"

Why indeed? He hadn't set a date, she'd lost another four pounds along with way too much sleep—

"Hey, want to join us for Thanksgiving?" he suggested. "A bunch of fruitarians are getting together—we can eat anything on the table, won't that be great?"

She laughed with him—she'd been dreading the day, figuring she'd spend it walking, or in her room—couldn't stand the thought of being around all the foods she loved that she wasn't eating. She got the phone number of the woman hosting it.

Tina sounded glad to include her. "Bring three bottles of sparkling apple juice."

"Sure," then hazarded, "How do you know Cob?"

"Oh, he and I—"

"Yeah. See you Thursday." It was easier when her mind had no identities to latch onto—was Tina the blonde, or the dancer, or—? She had a surge of nausea—being with Cob one-on-one was so good, but at a gathering where he could've laid every woman? She wasn't some damn groupie. But Walt said she was keeping the truth from herself—that was cowardly. She'd go.

CHAPTER 4

Counting Coup

When Cob visited Monday of Thanksgiving week, he spent longer than usual stimulating her, then kissed her eyelids to signal he was done. "Friday?"

She blinked. "However you want to do it." Resigned to waiting, she wouldn't permit hope or anxiety—her feelings were too raw.

"Carte blanche, how trusting you are—I'm always surprised."

"You must be an old hand at this," picking up her t-shirt, looking for where he'd tossed her bra.

"How else would I know what's possible?"

"How many women are you seeing now?" Not that she really wanted to know…

"You. Here we are, me and you."

"Concurrently. This fall."

"Mm. Why's that important? When I'm with you I give you my undivided attention and affection," adding, "Don't I?" with rhetorical-question confidence.

"You're not answering me."

"You want specifics? Names, bra sizes—want to see their driver's licenses?"

"No I don't." And where the hell was her bra anyway? She'd scanned as much of the room as she could from where she sat—nada. "But are there two others, or a dozen?"

"That's the right range." He combed his fingers over her knuckles. "Look Laura, I never pretended to be monogamous. We're about to fly—don't you want to?"

"Yes." Her heart clenched. "But why me?"

"You should think better of yourself—why not you? You're smart, you have great self-control, you're beautiful, you taste so sweet... You like sex," his voice a kiss. "Want me now?"

Her breath snagged in her throat, she had to force air in then out. "Really? Now?"

"You've been thinking about it too much. Impromptu's better." And he was taking off his shirt, standing to undo his jeans; she could only sit astonished as he stripped. It dawned on her he was waiting; she rocked back to slide off jeans and undies, then remained on her mattress prostrated by the racket in her brain, as though ten weeks' worth of lectures were all babbling at once while she was trying to take notes—her paper was blank, her pen wouldn't write, her memory didn't recognize a single word. All she was aware of physically was the sting where she'd scratched near her navel getting her clothes off—the rest of her had vanished somewhere.

HE LOOKED HER over—his creation, this body he'd sculpted with desire. When he was in high school his sister had come home from college mid-semester, broken-hearted because her boyfriend had laid her then ditched her for someone else; despite her humiliation she was still in love with him. For weeks Minta hardly ate; longing reshaped her face and body. One day Cob was lying in the grass listening to his radio when she came out with a basket of clothes to hang on the line, her skin semi-transparent in the sunlight—in maybe a month she'd gone from pretty to truly stunning. In this culture females were governed by their looks but mostly dissatisfied. If he could set up that yearning and a woman was beautified in the process, she'd appreciate that—and him—wouldn't she? A college campus was a good place to practice—someone who in ten years might shed her baby fat naturally would lose it fast with proper motivation, and in Berkeley it was easy to find willing sex partners—the scientist in him formalized his approach, with method and libido dovetailing flawlessly. "Don't forget your diaphragm."

MAYBE I AM *hypnotized*, she told herself—his reminder parted the chaos in her head as though all that other noise was a background hum. Abruptly she was standing, rummaging in the drawer where she'd stashed her kit, and once the soft rubber cup was in, straightened wiping her fingers. She felt stronger being ready, and sought his eyes—unfocused—he was already in a pleasure state where she was about to join him.

"Climb aboard," flexing his legs, fingers waving invitation.

Stepping over his thighs she hooked her feet around his shins, but as soon as she slid onto him tears started from her eyes—she'd ceased to believe this would happen. Wanting him had become a reflex—

"Not *cry, fly*," running his fingertips under her lashes to collect what gathered there. He licked them, then put his mouth on hers so she could taste her own salt—sharp, but under that his sweetness summoned her. She locked herself against him, all the flowers of months of waiting bursting into bloom one after another—

She'd seen *Swept Away…by an Unusual Destiny in the Blue Sea of August* with Walt. She was indifferent to most movies, but that one infuriated her—how dare a woman contrive her female lead to gladly subjugate herself to that puppy Giancarlo Giannini? Lina Wertmüller mixed sex and politics into a Molotov cocktail she hurled at dogma, appalling the feminists who'd thought up till then she was one of their own. Right now Laura was ready to detonate all the ideals she'd identified with—having Cob finally inside her was better than freedom.

No longer touching the floor she didn't know where it was—he was gravity. Her muscles going stiff then watery as thrills surged through her, she thought she was falling, his palm spread on her spine the only thing suspending her, then the mattress was against her back, his weight splaying her hips, her slickness conducting electricity—if she had hundred-watt bulbs in her hands they'd be at full brilliance. He was panting, licking her face with great swipes of his tongue, his hair sweeping her cheeks in rhythm with his thrusts. She grabbed handfuls of skin on his back only to have them flatten out of her grip when the muscles under them tensed.

He rolled her on top, his long middle finger slick with Vaseline probing her ass. "Relax, baby, you can't fly if you're all tense." As he kneaded her buttocks with his other hand he pushed his finger further in, rocking her, feeling the wave when she came, counting, but she was conscious only of how his touches communicated through her flesh. Once his finger was deeply planted he flipped her under, laughing as she came a fifth time. He was going for a record—they were only getting started. Her kiss was fresh—fruitarians tasted so good—and so hungry. He leaned onto his side to free his hand, smeared his finger again then rested it where her ass folded together. She pushed.

"Like that?" he teased. "Say please."

"Please."

"Want bigger?"

"No. Just come in."

Later. She was willing. Finger back inside he wrapped the rest of his hand tight to her curves, she clenched it with her buttocks. His other hand moved up to roll one of her nipples while he took its mate in his mouth—she was coming again—six—the night was young. She could probably get the same thrills solo—gratifying she wanted him to take her there. He kissed her dry mouth, sucking her tongue to wet it—she tasted of tears again, her sweat and funk accumulating like fog.

SHE WORRIED ABRUPTLY how he felt—when she and Walt were loving they were in close harmony. But Cob was separate—maybe the force of her appetite kept them apart—he couldn't possibly match this desire. She was using him for her own pleasure—they were making orgasms but not love. Was this a con, after all she'd invested physically and emotionally? Strangled howls broke through the tears flowing down her throat—wrong, all wrong—flying was a bliss-state—how could you achieve that alone? She could hear her lab prof saying "Assume your testing method introduces bias. Instead of denying that, identify it."

By the time he disengaged, her body was a drum from waist to knees— stretched, echoing, thudding.

"Should I leave?" he murmured.

"No. Sleep with me please," pressing her back into his warmth.

"Can you sleep?"

"Float. Fly. Don't go." This was the first time he'd embraced her—why didn't he offer affection? Plenty of guys just wanted to get laid—from Cob she'd expected more—was that naïve? Holding his arms around her she dozed, half-waking when he left the bed, but as longing pierced her she heard the door, he flung blankets around till they were covered, the soles of his feet cold on her ankles, his chest and belly snug to her spine again.

"See why I can't give women my address? But when I visit, I'm all yours." He put one large hand across her abdomen, down approaching the zone of her bonfire; she groaned, leaking when she moved. "You know about the famous swan of myth, right?"

"Which—"

"There's only one—Zeus took the form of a swan and fucked Leda, who gave birth to Helen, whose beauty started the Trojan War."

"Oh yeah—that poem by Yeats."

"Good enough to start a war, isn't it?"

Or else it was the kind of sex that did, the king of the gods parading his firepower for some mortal who had the misfortune to catch his eye. She just grunted.

"But I'm not done—you've only come ten times. Think of how long you waited—shouldn't you have one for every week?" He resumed, his thumb riding in the juice between her legs, and pretty soon she was shaking and gasping again. By now she was curious, lost on some frontier where she'd never been—might as well look around—she didn't expect to be back. Her body was having orgasms like hiccups, and she observed dispassionately how nerves and cerebral cortex activated in turn to flush and chill her skin, tense and unstring her muscles, the process bypassing her heart completely—she was reduced to a physical entity, not animal even but robotic, recording rather than feeling these waves. Was Cob studying her reactions too, or was he getting off and she was the only one shortchanged?

"WHAT CLASS ARE you missing today?" he asked in the morning.

"I'm not—it's at three. I'll be there."

"No you won't," fingers on her vulva very lightly, counting as she hit it again. Deciding that might be sore he slathered her ass, the thought of her surrender raising his hard-on. "Easy easy," pushing his way gradually in, back out for more lotion then way in, touching her mons with one fingertip—fifteen now.

"Keep 'em coming," he breathed, rocking against her, and she obliged with another burst, her mouth working like a landed fish. "Fly with me to the outer limits." She was tumbling through space, heart emptying and filling with yearning not blood—sex should be an antidote to isolation not its epitome. He was squishing inside her as though she was a pair of sodden shoes he was walking around in; she became conscious of creases in her sheet, a mattress button biting her rib, her damp bedding cold when she shifted. Still joined he pulled her to her knees and bent over her, a hand on each breast, pinching her nipples then releasing them, letting her wavering wail subside then doing it again, using his fingernails now, the orgasm jarring her.

"Seventeen girl, come on. Didn't know you could fly so far, did you? Feel my wings beating behind you? I'm a swan, a large powerful bird," and she felt the rush of air—he was flapping the sheet, still in her ass, hurting now if it hadn't hurt all along but her body didn't understand how to stop, like a person who's been up too many hours to sleep. He slipped out, squeezing her buttocks between his hands which made her come again, then slid his thumb in that slipperiness, and her shaking thighs gripped and released and she came. Words floated into her head in groups, shook their heads at her and left unspoken. A channel ran up her spine between the blaze in her ass and the fire in her skull, waves bouncing back and forth. An image of Walt pinged into her head like a submarine sonar noise, and she cut loose sobbing, slobbering, feeling hideous, her sexual parts swollen, drenched in sweat that smelled like maple syrup. Awareness fled to her extremities—her fingers felt her jeans on the floor beside the mattress, her other hand found Cob's palm and clenched, and she was still coming like a car out of control on a long steep hill.

"That's twenty-two. Must be a record. Want to stop?"

She could only croak.

"I think we better stop. Lie still now."

She woke feeling she'd been painted with glue, opening her eyes to the light of midafternoon. She was one giant throb. Cob was gone. She was missing class. She wanted someone to hold her—her mother, or Sue, or Walt. Someone who loved her. Not Cob. She'd never let him touch her again.

She hauled herself slowly from the bed as though it was giving birth to her, she was so sore and her skin so strange, and stumbling to the rack pulled on her bathrobe, not finding the other armhole, finally figuring out she'd put her right arm in the left sleeve. She tried again, then about to wrap it, glimpsed the mirror and shrugged the robe to her elbows, turning to see. Her nipples were red, so was a spot on her rib, but instead of glowing skin she looked the way she felt: dull, not the smallest residue of ecstasy. What a waste.

She winced at the shower spray—why'd her nipples hurt so bad? Soaping her hands she tried to wash her crotch but it was raw—she just let water sluice off the fluids that had mixed and dried all over—her inner thighs clear to her knees glistened with rehydrated slime on its way down the drain. Back in her room her shaking hands couldn't manage buttons so she pulled on her oldest softest turtleneck and a long skirt, then rubbed her hair and combed it out, put on socks and took the stairs slowly to the phone.

"Hey Walt."

"That you Laura? You sound like a train wreck."

"I am—can I come for Thanksgiving?"

"Sure—it's my day off—sit tight—I'll be there in a couple hours, OK?"

She searched the fridge, wondering what she'd missed the most, finally raiding Petra's salad stuff, nibbling romaine like a rabbit—feeling like a rabbit ready to dart for hiding. She went upstairs to sit in her big armchair looking out her window at the bright afternoon, enjoying the crunch and sweetness of a carrot, enjoying too that it grew in the earth and died so she could eat it.

"We're one life now, carrot," pleased she'd conquered this obsession that had taken over her system, corrupting her rationality and vetoing her instincts. Cob spent all that time lecturing about independence while he was twisting her behavior to suit his desires—didn't the contradiction bother him, or was he too selfish to notice? She felt thirsty but didn't want to go downstairs again—someone was home now. Time hung in the air like the late-season mosquitoes in the warmth where the sun struck her window, but it wasn't till streetlights glimmered on that she saw Onion. Walt looked her way, she waved then raised the sash a few inches to holler, "Come on up." She heard his feet on the stairs, he advanced through the dimness to squat looking at her face, hand on hers on the arm of her chair.

Wow, THIS ROOM was skanky—must've had her Big Score. "You all right?"

She turned her palm to meet his and began to cry. He folded her into his arms and sat with her in his lap, stroking her hair, her back, singing the chorus from "Box of Rain" while she soaked the shoulder of his denim shirt with tears and saliva. At last in darkness she stifled it. "I don't know what hurt the most," she quavered.

"Shh, you don't have to talk about it." A year ago, comforting her in their apartment after his conquest had taken them so far into each other, wounding them both, he'd thought the purpose of love was to hold someone who'd fall apart otherwise—he'd been so ashamed of giving in to the impulse for revenge. That sealed their union: once you hurt someone deeply and acknowledged it, maybe you were linked by matching scars, a stronger bond than the airiness of generosity, the way atoms in a solid hang onto each other tighter than those in a gas. But if that was true, Cob would own her for the pain evident in her clinging—if he admitted he was wrong. Her emotions were all focused on Cob—if he'd stuck around to hold her, Walt never would've got a phone call. He felt like his ancient Greek counterpart Phoros, asked to do something beyond his ability: dishonored if he refused, dead if he tried.

But she did call, wanting him this much anyhow—his lower gut was clenched in apprehension he chose to ignore. Up on Donner Pass they could've been casualties like unfortunates before them, but instead the lucky circumstances of where he'd parked and her bright gold Gonzo Guilt t-shirt they'd used as a flag had provided an escape—not so Cob could prevail, surely? If love wasn't sufficient, what on Earth could be? He kissed her damp temple—her head was hot from crying.

"Want to eat?"

She nodded.

"Done with that diet?"

She nodded harder.

"Pretty soon I'll get you something."

"I want a haircut," she whispered.

"Opal does that. When can I take you home?"

"I have to teach my recitation tomorrow at two—after that."

"I'm gonna do laundry and round up some food. You be OK?"

"I can't sit here without you—I'll come."

Stripping her mattress he sensed the parallel reeks of sweat and longing permeating her bedding. At the laundromat he loaded a washer then they went up the block to a café, ordering salad, a basket of bread, and beer. Watching the time he rotated her stuff to a dryer, and on the way back the sight of her through the café window brought to mind pictures of Vietnamese women numb and hopeless beside the ruins of their huts—hoped she was strong enough to tell off Cob. They finished their meal and collected the hot laundry, Laura hugging the bundle on the ride to her house. While she stood watching he made up the bed, easing her trembling onto clean warm sheets then shedding down to boxers to lie behind her, turned so his hard-on wouldn't touch her, his arm across hers. She slept deeply, trustingly, while he jolted from a dream of being pecked at and clawed by a furious flock of seagulls that turned into one huge white bird slamming him with wings hard as baseball bats.

COB CAME IN the grad lounge, same as any Wednesday—Laura sat in the most comfortable chair. His sharp eyes tried to read her, but she was closed.

"Hey Laura what's up?"

"I'm wondering if I'll have four students today, or two."

He laughed. "I had six this morning, out of twenty."

"I'm giving an extra credit quiz, to reward the ones who stuck around."

"They'll appreciate that." He moved closer. "So what's happening?"

"I'm going to Santa Cruz for Thanksgiving."

"Oh, right, that's where your boyfriend is," with just a trace of a sneer—what boyfriend could match what she'd just experienced? "I'm surprised to see you today—thought you'd be in bed," an eager light in his eyes.

She glared back. "You set your goddamn record on my body. It isn't yours. Don't talk about it to anyone, got that?"

"I'm discreet." But she was resentful not modest. "Something wrong?"

"You asshole, how can you say that? You hurt me—and now I'm done with you. At least when I flew with Walt we could see where the hell we were going." Her voice chilled. "There's nothing personal between us anymore, got that?"

"This never happened before." He looked at his hands—his right middle finger, his thumb, his nails that had pinched her nipples so hard. "I'm sorry."

"Ever say that?" Still cold.

"No, I don't think so. Usually it works out—better." He'd strung her along five months—in retrospect, way too long—she'd been ready when what's-his-name showed up—stupid to give her that line about an old girlfriend but she seemed capable of going further, which meant more prep time. Tina cried but she was emotional anyway, Liss damn near perforated his wrists with her fingernails—wasn't that passion? They never said anything—

"I chalk it up to education," she said. "Makes me appreciate love—and Walt."

That stung—sure played this one wrong. Those other girls stayed conquered, but proud, distant, a warrior, Laura was back on her feet steeled to cut him to pieces, his equal or possibly superior—just when he should have the upper hand she was turning on him. *I'm better than that stoner you're in love with*, he wanted to say—but was he? "Better" was needing a new definition right about now—knowledge and dexterity weren't enough. *What's he got?* he wanted to ask, but it was obvious—he had Laura.

CHAPTER 5

Rusty

When Walt parked Onion in front of her house Sunday night she looked at him longingly. "Stay?" then gave him a very sweet kiss. "OK by me."

In Santa Cruz he'd taken her to the big Thanksgiving feast hosted by his housemate Ray's painting partners. The crowd ate three turkeys—one tofu—and tons of side dishes, everything from traditional dressing and mashed potatoes to fruit salad, sweet potato pie, curried rice and homemade cranberry ice—must've been thirty people there, including Walt's lover Opal. She was Laura's opposite, big and curvy, dimples in her cheeks, dark blue eyes and long thick black hair—and the capacity to share herself without getting bogged down in needs. She and Walt kept it light, rolling in her featherbed maybe once a week, happy to have met, requiring nothing deeper that would chain them together.

Walt introduced her to Laura, then Opal ended up spending more time with her than he did since he was screening matinees, evening shows and midnight movies all weekend. Laura read Vonnegut's *Cat's Cradle*, and Opal gave her a haircut that changed her whole look, completing her transformation from girl to woman.

They came to the midnight show of *Harold and Maude* twice, watching it in the booth with Walt Saturday night. Laura'd been too sore for sex till Sunday, but since then she'd been all over him as if to prove to herself conquest was different than love. Hence, her cajoling him to spend the night in Berkeley.

She woke him early Monday for one more before going to shower; he pulled her blankets around him watching her fluff her hair with her new brush, appreciating the countermoves her body made while she did that. She crouched by the mattress to kiss him. "Thanks for everything sweetie. I want some time with you, OK? You're on my schedule this week."

"I'll be here," sitting up to hug her. "I love you babe."

"I love you too Walt. One more kiss—I gotta go."

When she was gone he stretched back. In the crack patterns in the plaster overhead he could almost trace the arc of the Potomac River—been a while—nothing to draw him back East, but California felt like what rock climbers called a temporary hold, good for leverage as long as he kept going, crumbling away if he tried to stay put. Laura was all the home he had—in this place that didn't fit him at all. Saturday night he'd held her close, slow-dancing to Leonard Cohen's *New Skin for the Old Ceremony*— though they both wanted more she was still too sensitive—but she was so beautiful, not just her face and figure transformed but her presence, her self-awareness.

In high school he'd pursued a gorgeous girl who was always surrounded by guys outdoing each other to offer treats and trinkets, ask her out, do wild stupid things to get her attention—Walt was an also-ran but watching her respond to their overtures made him miserable—she should be laughing at his joke, going to a dance with him. Couldn't help feeling that way now—Laura appreciated him at the moment, but once other guys closer by started vying for her interest? He felt he was treading the thin ice of luck while the cold deep waters of inevitability waited just beneath his shoes to swallow him, drown him, freeze him.

Jolted from reverie by voices downstairs raw with panic, he yanked on his jeans and came out to the landing. "What's wrong?"

"It's insane—"

"What is?" He hurried down. Petra had the radio on, she and Steve were staring at each other and around the living room in shock.

"Mayor Moscone and one of the supervisors were shot this morning—"

"Killed," Petra put in.

"—at City Hall in San Francisco."

"Who? How—"

"Another supervisor did it—Dan White. Ex-Marine, hated gays, and he shot—who was it?"

"Harvey Milk," Steve said.

"First thing this morning," Petra finished.

"Early bird gets the bullet, I guess," Steve said. "If Willie Brown had been there he'd have shot him too I'll bet."

"No warning?" Walt said. "Why?"

"Guess we'll hear more, when they figure it out," Petra said. "Moscone's secretary heard the shots but thought they were a car backfiring, and when she went in his office, there was the mayor on the floor—by then White was shooting Harvey Milk."

"The Bay Area's starting to seem like those experiments with rats," Steve remarked. "Y'know, they put more and more in the cage, and when there's too many they start devouring each other."

Walt was glad not to live in Berkeley—or San Francisco for that matter—but he didn't feel shielded from this insanity—like Jonestown ten days ago it seemed part of the times, not a function of where one lived. Was it because of the loss of frontier, people inescapably crowded together lashing out? He'd read about a man in Tokyo driven crazy by a neighbor practicing the piano: in the confines of his apartment there was noplace to avoid hearing those stumbling chords and repeated notes; he killed him to stop the noise.

The whole drive home Walt thought about death—the loss of so many lives was more horrific in contrast to the beauty of sun on the waves, surf seething among the rocks—if Jim Jones and Dan White could have left the constricted world of their own heads to witness this day, maybe their homicidal urges would have shrunk to something momentary, forgettable. How could a man believe he was connected only to what he approved of, understood, controlled? Everything was connected—there could be no picking and choosing. To perceive Earth as a vast ball, its moon pulling the oceans into tidal sloshing as both circled the life-giving sun, was to watch one's self-importance vanish into the cosmic dance.

Walt parked, left his shoes in the car, rolled his jeans cuffs and waded in the cold water. If Jim Jones could've stood here with his thoughts silenced, surely this vastness would've conquered his mad urge, pounding his jagged edges into a piece of sea-glass incapable of cutting anyone.

What about the Jonestown children? Reports were still filtering out from the chaos in Guyana, but certainly they drank the Kool-Aid. Where were those souls now? Was it worse to die trusting, or by force? Walt wondered where his point of extremis lay, at which he'd choose not only to end his own life but to cut off a loved one's. If he was trapped and couldn't survive to protect them, he supposed he would dispatch his children first—but he'd flee if he could. The worst part of that whole tragedy was that the danger in Jim Jones's mind wasn't real until he made it so by dictating death for his followers.

And in San Francisco a guy doesn't like people he works with, so he kills them? He can't just talk about their disagreements—or even argue—but decides violence is his only recourse? Whatever was at stake must have loomed large in his own head, magnified past endurance. That supervisor let a few details of circumstance chafe till he lost all sense of proportion, then murder seemed the only way to assuage it.

And yet, the ocean rocked indifferent to the miseries ashore. Earth turned beneath the sun, creatures woke and slept, filled and emptied their bellies. Earthquakes and volcanic eruptions, blizzards and typhoons pounded home how small *homo sapiens* really was. A sense of wonder might be the best defense against the siren song of murdering one's problems. Being less than a blink—an eyelash—of cosmic time, how could anyone magnify outrage to the level of taking others' lives?

His jeans were wet past his knees, the cuffs heavy with sand when he finally churned across the beach to his car. He drove barefoot the rest of the way home, grit between his toes reminding him that he too was a fragment, swept from one caesura to the next by the wind of time.

"WALT, LISTEN, I'M up to my eyeballs—way more work than I thought." Tuesday night—he'd only gone home yesterday—

"You don't have time for me."

He'd done the Thanksgiving shuttle without a murmur of discontent though she'd been too sore for loving till the end—this visit was supposed to compensate but now her head would be complaining nonstop about her coursework. "I'll be buried for weeks—I can't wait that long. Come anyway."

"Will do." His doubt rebounded. "You sure?"

"Yeah, I'll fit you in."

"Somewhere close I hope. How you feeling?"

What a sweetie. "Good enough to make up for what we missed."

"Tomorrow night—about ten, OK?" She heard him kissing the phone as he hung up, and thought she shouldn't have insisted.

When she slogged home from studying he hadn't arrived. She took off her wet shoes, stood her sodden umbrella in a cake-pan by the front door, hung her parka to drip.

"Walt called about an hour ago," Petra reported. "Said he got a late start—due here eleven, maybe later."

"Wish he wasn't driving in this downpour."

Up in her room she unpacked her books—studying till he got here would buy them more time. But midnight passed without him—maybe Onion had conked out somewhere—what a night to be stranded. At two, nodding over her notes, she heard the telephone, scrambled to answer.

"Hey Laura." Walt sounded weak, wet, far away.

"Where are you? Are you OK?"

"I'm at a hospital in Los Gatos. Some asshole ran me off 17." She remembered California 17, twisting over the mountains between Santa

Cruz and the South Bay: steep, sharp curves, four lanes, people driving like maniacs. "Onion's totaled."

"But what about you?"

"I—ah—" he started laughing ruefully. "Broke my leg."

"Oh no."

"In two places. It's gonna be a huge pain, I can tell already. A cast from hip to ankle. I can't drive, can't walk. Shit, I don't know what I'm gonna do."

"Is the rest of you OK?"

"Well, my heart's broken too, that I couldn't see you."

Just like him, to apologize for that. "Walt that's terrible. How'll you get home?"

"Ray has a van."

"Then what? Your insurance covers accidents, right?"

"I have to phone the agent. He's in Colorado—I never changed over when I moved—probably give me shit about that."

"So what, if they'll pick up the tab?"

"I know. I'm just so—" his voice closed, she strained to hear "disappointed."

"I'll come see you this weekend."

"You don't have time."

"I will anyway, with all my books and notes, and study."

WHOSE CAR COULD she borrow? In the morning she called Diane, but she'd sold hers before San Francisco's hills could finish off the clutch. Petra needed hers to drive to Sausalito. Before class she asked another woman, who said no; Cob overheard her.

"I have a car—what's up?"

"You do?" He always walked.

"Yeah, drive just enough to keep it alive. Where you going?"

"Never mind—I'll figure it out."

Friday she was in the grad lounge discussing the Moscone and Milk shootings with another TA when Cob walked in.

"Seems so cold-blooded," Aline was saying.

"My theory," Cob weighed in, "is Dan White spent Thanksgiving with his family, or maybe in-laws, and they found out he wasn't getting reappointed and gave him shit—there he is, supposed to be having a relaxing holiday, and somebody's rubbing his nose in a prospect he's trying not to think about. Then they comment about all the queers running the city, and he decides he's losing his job because he's not one. By Monday morning he's hit full boil, and goes to City Hall to ask the mayor to reconsider, but packs his gun, just in case."

"In case what?" Laura demanded.

"In case he's right. So Moscone blows it, says 'well, Harvey Milk—' and White snaps—he shoots him, then barges into Milk's office, unfortunately for him he's there so he gets it too."

"On what do you base this theory?" Laura asked, but Aline was rolling her eyes, headed for the door.

"Thing about a long holiday weekend is, you don't have your regular routine to hide behind—your problems didn't go away, and being with people you're supposed to be close to, puts 'em front and center." Which was pretty much how his weekend had gone. After Laura confronted him last week he'd thought about his behavior and felt unclean, dishonest—reaping sweetness from Liss and Saffron and the rest, suddenly seemed part of an enormous deception he'd been practicing for years—he wanted out. If they loved him they were brainwashed; if they thought he loved them, well, that was his fault—when had he ever said otherwise? So he'd called each of them to come to Tina's early, before the other guests arrived; when they were gathered, he explained he'd lied. First they were nice about it, saying he was just depressed, then Saffron said he was more concerned with his own humiliation than with hers. She told him to go fuck himself, then like harpies they vented their hurt and surprise in a sharp rising clamor. Tina, a dancer whose agility'd always impressed him, leaped across the room to fling the door open; as soon as he'd stepped out she slammed it hard, clipping his heel.

Foot stinging and that bang reverberating, he walked bayward, under the freeway to an industrial section of town. The day was chilly and drab, rainy season hovering, picking its moment to begin. Traffic was sparse—people were with friends and relatives, stuffing themselves or groaning in front of TV sets. Thinking of his own family neutralized his hunger—all those dead things they were eating, to celebrate what exactly? Through a gap between two buildings he emerged at the stretch of muck that was Berkeley's beach, and squidged forward till nothing impeded his view of the shore. Leaning against a rotting piling he watched wavelets roll a drink cup to the water's edge then pull it back, over and over and over. A fringe of beer cans, orange peels, cigarette butts and chunks of Styrofoam marked the tideline, but the waves weren't dropping their load yet. He'd kept those women hanging on the same way, tugging them back and forth, not caring but not letting go. If Laura hadn't called him on it, how long would he have continued, unaware he was using them? He never thought he needed anyone to tell him who he was, that his own penchant for honesty was sufficient to keep him straight—just one more lie.

He'd never felt so alone since leaving Nebraska—in California relationships were fluid, people open to new influences—he'd been happy in the mix. He loved fruitarian holiday feasts: sharing food and kinship, being accepted. But that was over now—like his experience at the commune, his actions made him a pariah. Growing up, he'd bucked everyone and everything—if he'd fallen into apology and eating crow they'd have demolished him—arrogance kept him strong. Telling these women he'd lied was all he could manage—they had every right to despise him but he hadn't been deceiving them consciously, and once he saw what he was doing, he quit. If they wanted more contrition, too bad—he wasn't going to grovel.

Damn Laura anyway—he was willing to let her exercise power over him, just to help him sort out this faltering persona—but she wasn't interested. The price of hurting her wasn't only losing her, it was losing a large part of himself he'd invested time and energy into constructing and believing, that turned out to be bullshit. Sure, he knew where Dan White was coming from, suddenly having to reinvent himself, the lash of others' contempt driving him.

"He was a Marine," he said to Laura, "with a tough-guy image to maintain—was he supposed to accept getting publicly screwed?"

"So you approve?"

"Hell no—but it's hard being the outsider, people dumping on you."

"Outsider?" she exclaimed. "He personifies mainstream intolerance."

"Not in San Francisco—you have to see it in context—probably made him feel that much more oppressed, knowing most places he'd fit right in."

Laura looked at the clock—he could harangue for hours. "I have to get going."

"That's right, you wanted to borrow a car—still need one?"

"Not from you."

"What's it for?"

"Walt was in a crash and broke his leg."

"Bummer. So you'd like to visit him."

"Yeah."

"Well, you could always hitchhike."

"I EXPECT THAT's what I'll do," she looked out the window at perfectly vertical rain streaking the air like a million silver beaded curtains—from here she couldn't sense drops falling—it was just air full of water.

He squinted, gauging her determination. "Hitching in the rain's a drag."

"I've done it." Freshman year she and Diane had hitchhiked into the mountains to go backpacking, and had a great weekend till a cloudburst chased them the last mile to the road. Because they were soaked they didn't get their first ride for twenty minutes—to a junction only fifteen miles away. Diane was ready for a motel but Laura had a test Monday morning so they kept going, and by the time a succession of rides delivered them to the dorm hours later, they were so frozen they showered in their clothes till the hot water uncramped their hands enough for them to undress. But Laura, far from being put off by a bad experience, considered it a challenge she'd met: she'd been wet, she got dry—wouldn't stop her.

"Take my car," Cob said.

She met his eyes coolly. "What'll it cost me?"

"For this weekend, just gas. If you need it again I'll have to think about it."

"What is it?"

"A '50 Plymouth—good tires but the seat's shot—bring a pillow—you'll be sittin' on springs."

"Why have I never seen this car?"

"I don't use it. My dad gave it to me when I turned sixteen. It was old and tired then, and it's even older now. But hey, it runs. Every once in a while I need it." He smiled. "Like now."

"I don't know Cob—a favor from you—"

"You'd be charging the battery—you're the one doing the favor."

"Bullshit."

His mouth twisted as though he'd been caught out, and she saw a flicker of admiration in his gaze. "That's right. Borrow it anyway." He jotted on a corner of her pad. "Here's my address. I'll be home after four."

HE LIVED IN a two-story building divided into a dozen apartments, its sloped roof making it resemble a broad house, a breezeway connecting street to alley beside a set of stairs. She read the names on the mailboxes, pushed the buzzer for #7, heard a door on the second floor.

"Come on up."

She reluctantly climbed the stairs and paced down the hall—two low-wattage bare bulbs faintly reflected off the painted wood floor. At the far end a pair of doors faced each other, one ajar; she pushed it further open without going in. To the left stood his double bed mattress and springs, the metal legs of the frame showing below the droop of blanket and sheet. To the right was a five-foot-tall fridge with thick walls and rounded edges, beside it on crates a hotplate and toaster oven below a wall-mounted cupboard. A card table cluttered with papers and books was set up near them, a sturdy kitchen chair pushed up to it. Stepping in she saw a sink to her immediate left outside the tiny bathroom, straight ahead a big multi-paned window where Cob slouched in a wide legless armchair. She hesitated to come further into his territory but he rose at once, jingling a pair of keys.

"Chapter One was *Anticipation*," he said, "Chapter Two was *Cob the Monster*, Chapter Three was *I'm Sorry*. Chapter Four's *Let Me Help You*. All right?"

"Then what?"

He shrugged. "Could be *Cob's Not Actually a Monster*. But maybe not."

"I don't think I've demonized you, but you probably haven't taken your share of blame."

"Nah, I'm not into suffering."

"You could dish it out though." She cut short his apology. "If you're gonna lend me your car just do it—I need to get moving."

"Into this dismal weather."

"That's right. Walt's sitting at home in pain, depressed. Needing me."

He'd been pleased she showed up, but he didn't want her harping on how good she had it with some other guy. "Let me introduce you to Rusty," grabbing an umbrella and stepping into rubber boots on a wet towel by the door. Behind the building three cars were parked on a patch of gravel. He walked to the humped old car next to the wall, its paint chalky from decades of sun; raindrops gleamed on impact, the glint vanishing as they spread. Opening the driver's door he sat on the eroded seat, handing her his umbrella; she leaned in as he pulled a knob on the dash.

"This is the choke. Bring it all the way out when you hit the ignition—" he turned the key "and give it some gas." The starter skittered, the exhaust popped once as the car trembled to life. "Leave the choke open about a minute till the engine's racing then slowly move it in—if it starts to die, back it out and wait. Gas gauge doesn't work—it gets about twenty miles a gallon on the highway—just buy what you need—don't bother filling the tank 'cause somebody around here siphons it off. The gearshift is three-on-the-tree, reverse is up and toward you—drive a clutch?"

"Yep—how fast will she go?"

"Fifty. Bundle up—heater works but the weather-stripping's shot."

"So she leaks?"

"Rusty's male. Yeah, has a couple cracks in the floor too. Don't stomp hard or you'll hit pavement."

"Will this car really make it to Santa Cruz?"

"Oh sure, we've been to Nebraska twice, but you have to be patient—" patting the steering wheel. "Rusty doesn't like to hurry." He stood quickly, kissing her before she saw it coming, and while her brain was sorting out what to do with the umbrella in each hand, he prolonged it, leaning into her as she tilted back. "Before, I just thought I wanted you," he breathed. "Now I do."

Pushing him off with her elbow she slipped around him, letting go his umbrella and folding hers and throwing it onto the floor on the passenger side as she got in.

He bent toward her.

"Don't say you're sorry for that," she accused.

"I'm not. That's my favorite moment this week. Thank you."

"Don't thank people for what you take without asking."

"If I'd asked, would you have let me?"

"No."

"I rest my case. Only a fool always waits for permission."

"Or a gentleman."

"Is that what you want? Should I study to be a gentleman?"

"Wouldn't hurt," yanking the door closed. In the wallow of the driver's seat she couldn't see anything through the rear window but rain, even after she'd moved the bench forward. Squinting at streaks that might be obstacles behind her she tilted the inside mirror. The one on the door was dirty—she cranked the window down, wiping and adjusting. He reached in and pulled out the headlights knob.

"The brights switch is on the floor under the clutch pedal." She groped with her toe, pushed a hard protrusion, the lights brightened. "The wiper switch is next to the lights." She turned them on, the windshield smeared. "Turn 'em off a sec," pulling out a bandana and lifting each blade to wipe its length then moving back to rub the rear window—now she could see through it. "Let me guide you out—it's tricky."

He beckoned, she shifted into reverse and gave it gas as she eased out the clutch. It coughed. Revving to keep from stalling she leaned out.

"Where's the emergency brake?"

"On the left—squeeze the handle against the shaft and let it down—pull up to engage. The cable's new—you can park on a hill if you need to."

She released it and backed out slowly, hoping he was guiding her well because anything to her right was completely out of sight. The wheel-base was short, the turn tighter than she'd expected—she was amazed to get to the alley without hitting anything.

"Good job," he praised, putting a hand on her shoulder. She tensed, ready to raise the window on him if he tried to kiss her again. "The registration and insurance are in the glove box, but call me first."

"I hope I won't need to."

"There's no seatbelts. Drive carefully."

"I will. Thanks."

As she rolled up the window he said, "Someday I'll deserve your love."

"Don't bet on it," she muttered. With the rain shut out, the sharp dryness of the old car surrounded her, the split upholstery and roof lining leaking dust, and closing her eyes she was eleven, in a friend's backyard where an old couch stood outside their garage. One summer day they'd walloped the cushions for half an hour with a shovel handle, dust billowing out as thickly on the last blow as when they'd started so they gave up and sat, and when they stood, reddish-brown powder covered the backs of their legs and clothes, smelling just like this. Rusty seemed an inverse oasis—a small desert in this downpour, a transplanted piece of the dry high plains. Cob's frankness and sincerity were familiar too, Midwestern—he didn't know he'd hurt her because he'd never been in anyone's head but his own—his assumptions made him misread her signals, extrapolating where he had no information, no right to go. He'd probably think about that kiss all weekend, and be ready to try again when she got back.

"No," she said aloud, and drove home, collecting notes, books, a change of clothes, the seat cushion from her armchair. Jack walked in while she was adding sliced cheddar to the mashed avocado on two pieces of bread.

"Whose heap out front?"

"I'm driving to Santa Cruz for the weekend," bagging her sandwich.

"Junkyard having a sale?"

"Someone lent it to me because I need it," and slung her pack onto one shoulder.

"Someone has a piece of shit for a car."

On her way out she retorted, "It's better than yours"—his nonexistent wheels.

"Not necessarily," he yelled after her. If he was smarter his taunts might sting, but he was just annoying—by now she thought of him as a file, keeping her edges sharp.

She picked a lane and stayed in it across the Bay while rain battered the roof and bounced off the hood, a din so unvarying that soon she stopped hearing it, while the windshield flooded faster than the arthritic wipers could clear it. In a better car with bright headlights and seatbelts, rainy Friday rush hour traffic would make her impatient, but in this ancient boat, poking along stop-and-go was perfectly OK. No radio—she'd thought about bringing her tape deck but couldn't find any fresh batteries, so she sang water songs—"Ripple," "Box of Rain"...

Making the merge approaching Daly City where a single sign saying Route 1 pointed skyward into the downpour, she putted along in the slow lane, not even caring when buses stopped in front of her to discharge passengers who took their time, unfurling umbrellas as they stepped out. Drips coming in the upper edge of the door hit the shoulder of her parka, occasionally big enough to splash her cheek—hitchhiking she'd be drowned by now. Beyond the city Rusty rolled comfortably in thinning traffic, the brakes responsive to her tap after sluicing through a big puddle. When the road narrowed to one lane each direction she watched for a buildup of cars behind her, pulling over to let them by. The only indications of ocean fifty yards to her right were beach turnout signs. Visibility was nil—what did those drivers racing around her think they could see?

She passed Half Moon Bay, and later the turnoff to San Gregorio. La Honda was back in those hills, where the Merry Pranksters had hung out dropping acid and doing whatever occurred to them with whoever showed up. She'd been too young for that, but she could relate. After a long dark stretch on wet pavement, she rolled through Davenport. Another half hour, she reached the outskirts of Santa Cruz, trying to remember where Walt lived—the roads spiderwebbed between steep wooded hills and the Pacific. She found a pay phone; Ray answered.

"Oh hey Laura, where are you?"

"On Route 1 at the north end of town."

"West you mean. The ocean's south."

"West. How do I find you?" She repeated street names and turns while she drove, finally down a familiar street, and parked. But their house was in a lake. She peered across the street—how deep?—no cars in it. Seeing four front steps she tried to remember—were there six? More? Turbulence boiled in the middle of the pool—sea monsters! She began to laugh—Walt was stranded in a moated castle—where was the drawbridge? The porch light came on, Ray yelled over the splatter of rain, pointing around to the side of the house—underwater too. She loaded her books and notes into a trash bag, decided to wear shoes but not socks, rolled her pant legs. Halfway across the street she reached the edge of the flood. Ray was still on the porch and now Walt too, on crutches, his long white cast the brightest thing in sight. She waded carefully as water rose past her knees, cold turbulence thick with sand scouring her shins and packing inside her shoes before she stepped up on the sidewalk, a low-tide funk overpowering the rain smell.

"Come in through the back—it's not as deep."

She felt her way among submerged obstacles, at the back door pumped her umbrella and set her wet pack on the floor. Kathy hung her parka over the utility sink as she emptied and rinsed her shoes then set them upside down to drain.

After a hug and kiss of welcome, Laura sat with Walt on the couch. Propping his cast on a milk crate he drew his bone with a felt-tip pen on the plaster encasing his right leg, marking jagged lines for two fractures midway between hip and thigh.

"So, the accident—it was pouring, there was all this traffic, and a long line of cars was passing me on the grade. This van behind bumped me, I skidded and braked, he hit me again and off the road I went, watching a tree come at me—if I hadn't had my seatbelt on I wouldn't be here. The dashboard broke against my leg—the ambulance guys had to cut it apart to get me out. Took 'em forever to get there—I was caught, the pain was unbelievable, the windshield honeycombed and rain was coming in on me, and all I could think about was I wasn't gonna make it to see you. But a lady stopped, and held her umbrella over the hole in the windshield, and sang hymns to me while we waited for the ambulance."

"What about the guy who hit you?"

"A witness called in the company name painted on the side of that van—he's been charged with hit-and-run. I have to write—they might garnish his wages, compensate me a little."

"Does it hurt bad?"

"Worst when I'm upright, but sitting, lying down, awake, asleep—you name it. The hospital gave me pain pills, but they're not as good as pot."

"Car insurance paying anything?"

"The medical, yeah."

"Nothing for Onion?"

"I wouldn't get much—Blue Book's about three hundred bucks."

"So no car."

"I can't drive anyway. What were you getting out of, across the street?"

"Maybe in the morning you can see—an old Plymouth. Say, what's with this lake? I swear your house was on dry land a week ago."

He laughed. "Our neighbor told us when it rains a lot the storm-sewers overflow and this is where they back up. We've been flooded since yesterday."

"So there's no dry way in."

"Not right now."

"That's not good for your cast is it?"

He shook his head. "Not drinking water coming out of there."

"So what do you do?"

"Haven't gone out since the waters rose—perfect excuse actually. The union found a guy to take my shifts and I'll get some microscopic disability check for the next few weeks."

"A few— How long will you have the cast?"

"Two months, the doc said. But I can go back to work before that."

"How?"

"Ray and John labored long and hard to get John's car working, and John's wife Kara will drive me when they can't."

"Wow, that's really good. You're lucky to have friends."

"I could certainly be worse off." He sagged. "I could be dead."

She hugged him. "Onion saved you twice."

After a sweet moment he asked, "So who owns 'an old Plymouth'?"

"Guess."

"Not Cob."

She nodded, and right on cue his leg throbbed sharply. "You really borrowed a car from him?"

"I tried very hard to find another—"

He rubbed her arm. "Well, you're here." Only an ingrate would lay on the guilt when she'd done what she had to, to come see him. "How long can you stay?"

"Till Sunday night."

"I'll help you study—you need to do well."

They retired to his room where she helped him lever his cast onto his hip-high mattress, then joined him lying down.

"Call your parents?" she asked.

"From the hospital. Mom was really upset."

"Will they help you out?"

"Maybe," waving his hands, at a loss. "My brain's jelly—when I blow my nose it comes out grape."

"DID YOU SAY it doesn't have seatbelts?" Ray asked the next day when he and Kathy got back from buying groceries. "That's dangerous—that car's scary anyway. I have an extra from when I put another seat in my van—I'll install it today."

"In the rain?"

"It's letting up." Ray was a slim Chicano from LA with a pencil moustache and ready smile—at Thanksgiving he'd regaled her with house-painting stories: in one, he'd tried to talk a couple with volatile tempers into choosing cool blue or green for their living room and kitchen. The wife preferred a shrill yellow; he didn't want to contribute to their discord with such a jittery shade, but they wouldn't listen. "Wish I could pick the colors—I know how they affect mood. I can wake up bored people, calm the nervous ones, make little kids cheerful. They subconsciously want to maintain the status quo, even if that's negative, but if they were in a different space for a month I think they'd like the change—their whole lives'd be better." That compassion was asserting itself now.

He put on tall rubber boots and went out the front, Laura following to see how deep the water was. The bottom step was completely submerged. He waded out, when he stepped off the curb murky water rose close to his knees; he splashed to the lake's edge and over to Rusty. Poking around inside then underneath, he gave her a high sign then waded to the back-yard, emerging from the vine-grown shed with a box. In the kitchen he unpacked two lengths of webbing grommeted at one end, a buckle and release, and a set of sturdy-looking bolts with nuts and washers.

"Will those hold? The floor has cracks."

"Yeah, I saw those. I'll anchor it to the seat frame—that's pretty strong."

"I really appreciate this."

"Laura, if nobody works at it, nothing gets better. I can't change the world all by myself, but I can keep my little zone from going to hell. That's my revolution: fix what's broken, do my part where I am."

"Can I help you?"

"Look after this banged-up guy you came to see," he smiled, confirming that her visit was in the same category as installing a seatbelt.

CHAPTER 6

Karmafornia

Sunday morning the clouds were low and ragged but it wasn't raining, and the lake had sunk back into its hole. Walt's crutch-tips skidded in fine black silt on the bottom step, he skirted the hummock of sand caking the sidewalk above the storm drain—their personal beachfront. When they reached Rusty he began to laugh.

"This? You drove this antique?"

"This car's how I got here." Enough jokes—the more people derided it, the sturdier it seemed. She opened the back door and held his crutches, he extended his cast across then sat. In the driver's seat she put on the new seatbelt, adjusting the mirror to show his face. "Smile for the cameras," she instructed, so he did. "Where to?"

"Let's drive up to UCSC."

"In Berkeley they call it Uncle Charlie's Summer Camp."

"A university like no other."

She drove Rusty up a steep street, finally leaving houses behind as they came out onto table-land tipped toward the coast. Beyond the entrance sign the narrow road forked, the inland branch ascending a

bleached-yellow grassy field toward stands of redwoods. The only struc-
tures in sight were an ancient weathered barn and sheds.

"This is a campus?" she said. Where was the bustle, the hive energy?

"Classroom buildings and dorms are back in the trees—every college has its own cluster. The dropout rate's high—students don't feel like
they're in school, and pretty soon they're not."

"I'd quit too—this is ridiculous. Think of Boulder—all those people
in close quarters contribute to the ferment—ideas, politics. What do you
engage with here—grass? Trees?"

He laughed. "It's an alternative—the urban model doesn't work for
everybody."

Parking where they could look out at the ocean—what they could
see between clouds—she moved to the back to sit beside him. One arm
around her, he grew pensive—she was never talking to that guy again,
and now she was driving his car? "You're still seeing Cob."

"He's not invisible," in a tone that closed the topic. She kissed
him. "Come with, since you're not working."

That hadn't entered his mind. He had all these chores—letters and
phone calls about the accident. Though he could use her phone and
typewriter, he felt anchored with Ray and Opal looking out for him. "But
I'm home here."

"I'm not saying move—it's an opportunity for an extended visit."

An opportunity to be helpless, in the way? "You won't have time
for me."

"I expect to sleep every night, and if you're there—"

Right: her bedwarmer. The glow in her eyes should thrill him—he'd
been steadfast while she fooled around—so why'd his reward make him
feel like a piece of ass?

"A visit," she repeated. "If you come we could drive back sooner, in
daylight."

"You should anyhow—that'd be safer."

"Not without you."

His hand slid around, finding the smooth curve of her breast. She was wearing his undershirt instead of a bra—he reached further to touch her nipple beneath the thin ridged cloth.

"I feel so stupid," he mumbled, kissing her bare neck.

"Ten days ago I was the idiot."

True—he'd helped her through damage, now she was the nurse. But why'd she want him to come? Energetic sex would be excruciating, but cautious embrace in the shadow of pain was somehow worse. "Do you know how bad I feel, knowing I can't please you without the Revenge of the Leg? I should stay put."

"Depth sounding confirmed," she droned. "He's in the Pacific subduction zone, below the range of our submersibles—only love can save him now." She raised one eyebrow. "Come with. Please."

"Yas'm, Cap'n," sure it was a mistake. "How long?"

"Let's find out—we'll steal a little time."

As they passed the sandbank in front of his house at crutching speed, she noticed a gleam under the jasmine bush that filled the corner between porch and steps, and moving branches aside discovered a cardboard box—squat and square, for four one-gallon cans of paint—half full of rainwater. The clean still surface reflected jasmine branches and beyond those, clouds broken by hints of blue. The cosmos spoke through details, little reminders everything was connected—her discovery felt like a blessing. She took Walt's hand, they beamed at each other like the sun coming out.

"*It's just a box of rain,*" she said.

"*I don't know who put it there,*" he answered, starting to sing.

"*Believe it if you need it.*"

"*Or leave it if you dare.*"

"*But it's just a box of rain,*" together, "*or a ribbon for your hair. Such a long long time to be gone and a short time to be there.*" They hugged, the unity of acid returning, her cheek to his shoulder, his fingers in her hair, one smile on both faces.

IN HER KITCHEN, sitting tilted back with knees propped against the table, Jack and Steve forked ice cream out of cartons to the guitar brilliance of John McLaughlin. Jack dropped his chair's front feet to the floor when he saw Walt's cast.

"Hey, what happened to you?"

"I told you he broke his leg," Laura said irritably. "Why'd I bother?"

"So the bucket o' bolts made it," he went on.

"It was fine. Walt's here for a visit, since he can't work yet."

"Ice cream?" Jack extended his carton, in which fork tracks outlined lumps and craters of butter pecan—a half-gallon Zen rock garden.

"No thanks," Walt said. "I gotta sit."

"Oh, I have to get the cushion," Laura remembered. "But I should leave it there while I take the car back."

"Whose car is it?" Jack pried, a glint in his eye as if he already knew.

"Never mind," quickly, before Walt could speak.

"Why don't you call?" Walt said. "Take it back tomorrow."

"Yeah, good idea. I'll get the cushion. Can you do stairs OK?"

"I can't carry stuff except in my pack, but I can hop up." She went out while he began his ascent, returning as he arrived at the top. She put the cushion back, setting the orange-crate she used for laundry on end to prop his cast. Leg up, he sighed raggedly.

"Hurt?"

"Yep."

She moved his pack close, and a box of matches.

"Join me?" he asked.

"No, I have to study—go ahead."

As she went out to get his duffel from the car, Walt called down, "Hey Jack, Steve, care to smoke a joint?"

"Not now," Steve called, but Jack was on his way up.

"Hey thanks man." Walt fished one out and lit it while Jack sitting on the arm of the chair eyeballed his Baggie. "Lotta j's there."

"Painkillers. Another week I'll be needing more."

They compared accidents while they smoked—Jack had smashed up his VW a few years before.

Downstairs Laura phoned Cob. "I'm back—the car was fine. Thanks for the loan. Want me to bring it over now? When do you need it?"

"Whoa, slow down," he laughed. "You're back—good. Rusty behaved—also good. Must've been a nasty drive Friday night."

"It was. But I got there."

"Good."

"Walt's housemate installed a seatbelt—wouldn't let me drive back without it."

"Yeah? What do I owe you for that?"

"Cut the bullshit Cob. When do you want your car?"

"No hurry—it's not like I use him. But you're back early."

"Walt came too," but her reserve was thawing. "I didn't call to chat— I'm back, so's your car. Period."

"Fine. See ya." He hung up.

TUESDAY WALT WAS parked in Laura's armchair working on his claim letters when there was a tap on the door: Cob, with a smile or smirk twitching the corner of his mouth before he smoothed it away with his hand, like a conjuror's trick. "Laura said you're here."

"As you can see. What brings you?"

"I—ah—wondered," coming the rest of the way in. "She said your car's wrecked—need a replacement?"

"I can't drive at the moment—"

"When you can?"

"I suppose. I'm writing the guy that hit me, see if he's good for a few bucks."

"Well, if it wasn't your fault, why should you get stuck with the expense?"

"Why should anyone have to pay for somebody else's fun?" Walt met his eyes accusingly.

Cob looked away, his gaze falling on the rumpled bedding. "I apologized to Laura for how that turned out—don't know if she believes me."

"Not a matter of belief—something's gotta change."

"I know—I'm trying. I'll do whatever she asks."

"Except leave her alone," Walt said pointedly.

"Our karma's tangled now. Anyway," shifting from one foot to the other, "Interested in my car? Make me an offer."

"I'll give you fifty bucks for it."

Cob recoiled as if Walt had spat at him. "Rusty's a good car—he's worth more than fifty bucks."

"To you maybe. Blue Book on that car's gotta be zero."

"What do they know?" Cob snarled.

"Nothing. But that doesn't make it valuable to me. What're you asking?"

"I haven't decided. See, he's not just a car, he's a piece of my life—if you or Laura had him, I'd still be connected."

"Then no. Every time she gets in she'll think of you."

Cob smiled, a real smile this time. "Yeah."

"You like that?" queasy, the pain of his leg biting.

"I brought out her beauty, didn't I? Maybe she'll remember that. Before it was pain, she was in ecstasy. Maybe she'll remember that." Turning abruptly he walked out.

Walt sagged back—was this why he'd come? To have Mr. Brass Balls tell him how she felt, taunt him with his weakness? The pull Cob had exerted on her before was still there—this broken leg was the first salvo in a war he didn't want. He should leave—not just this room but California, their history. Karma, Cob said—Walt had barely given it a thought before coming out here but Karmafornia was where he'd landed. Berkeley, Cob, the van driver on Highway 17, even Laura were on the same wavelength: hurry up, push, go, trample. What was he doing here? He couldn't see his peaceable nature prevailing. Karma supposedly provided opportunities to fix past mistakes, to evolve, but Cob had already destroyed him twice—what was going to be different this time around?

He was getting mixed signals—that van running him off the road made it clear he was in altogether the wrong place, then Laura found the box of rain, as strong an omen as he could ask for, assuring him they really did have a future and he shouldn't give up. So on the strength of that optimism—and her steamroller will—here he was, where he had no business being, only to have Cob look him over as though to confirm his voodoo had worked. Laura's affection had snaked into knots so profoundly constricting he could hardly breathe—quite the opposite of what love was supposed to be, how it started out...

He'd taken her hiking up Twin Sisters, just outside Rocky Mountain National Park, on an April Saturday. There was enough snow on the trail to discourage most visitors, and they went up forested switchbacks to the summit at a brisk pace. At over eleven thousand feet, looking across the valley at the higher vertical east face of Long's Peak, she leaned on a rock and he covered her hand, she turned it over so their palms touched. Hers was vibrating from the exertion, slightly swollen from swinging at her side on the hike up. She looked at him warily, some wild thing that had come close to check him out—the slightest wrong move and she'd flash away— He held steady, nothing moving but the little smile inching across his mouth, and inside him the stillness was complete.

Her fingers were tapered, not vanity nails but clean and unbroken, only long enough to be useful, cuticles in good shape—he brought her hand to his mouth, ran his teeth over the pad of her middle finger—salty: the mineral deposit of clean sweat—he licked it then blew on the damp. She shivered; his heart was shivering too.

"It's cold up here," she said finally, hunching in her light wool jacket.

He offered his parka.

She laughed, "It's my problem if I didn't dress for the weather."

"I'm plenty warm," he lied, "go ahead," thinking if they didn't stay up on top too much longer, he wouldn't turn into the Human Ice Cube.

"Thanks." She accepted his coat. Despite a flannel shirt over his t-shirt the wind attached itself to his skin, so cold it made him feel naked, dizzy—but he was lightheaded anyway, from touching her. "Let's go down," she suggested, and once they were below timberline hiking at a good clip, his body heat recovered. They stopped down near the trailhead to drink icy water, and with cold tongues and warm lips shared their first kiss. What was memory but alchemy's lie, its inaccessible riches? That sweetness, innocent of events to come, turned this present and whole future to dross—the gold he had to close his eyes to recall, was gone. He could spend a lifetime chasing a moment like that and miss out on everything else: once he knew love was possible, how was he supposed to turn his back on it, even when it abused him?

The pain in his thigh heated up and he lay on the mattress, elevating his cast on a pillow for relief. When Laura came in he woke with a headache and sat up slowly, massaging his temples.

She was quick to notice. "Head hurt?"

"And my leg. Guess I should use those pills—can't smoke all the time." He got out the pill bottle and read, "'Take one tablet three times daily as needed for pain.' But they never tell you how to take it the second or third time."

SHAKING HER HEAD at his feeble joke she undressed, lying beside him to welcome his kisses, his touch trailing around her waist, desire choking off words then thoughts altogether. She helped him love her—when his leg was healed she'd dream up some acrobatic sex that would have them both seeing stars—and afterwards ran her fingers into his thick hair, sun-bleached twenty shades—here was the gold of California, in her hands—no amount of prospecting would turn up anything more valuable than this man's loyalty and kindness.

"Walt, am I making a mistake?"

"Everybody is, all the time—it's a wonder anything works."

"No, specifically—should I stay here in school?"

"Cob getting on your nerves?"

"Yeah. I can't avoid him—wish he didn't want me so much."

"You wanted him—it's his turn."

"But I was expecting a payoff. He is too."

"You didn't get what you were after, why should he?" He rolled up on his left hip to face her, wincing as he maneuvered his cast. "Laura, I came up here to be with you, but I'm not your protector."

"Your love is." She nuzzled. "Wish I could chase off your little dark cloud."

"See? I'm distracting you. Get up now—study."

She sat up and pulled on his undershirt, he ran his hand over it. She gave him a profile, the knit material riding her contours.

"I'd give anything to be this shirt," he murmured. "Do you know—" He rotated his palm over her nipple, moved his hand to see it stand out, then with a hopeless look slumped away onto his stomach as if he couldn't fall far enough. She kneaded his shoulders and neck, loosening him into sleep.

THURSDAY SHE CAME back after her three o'clock; his things were gone, a note on her chair.

Toots—

Sorry I couldn't tell you—I can't stay anymore—I'm worthless here. Sorry. You need to study without me taking up your time and mental space. I'll get myself home so you won't have to accept any more favors or whatever he calls them from Cob. I should've talked to you, but I know you'd bulldoze my resolve—it's not good for anybody for me to be here. I'm sorry. Walt

She put down the note, hurt—she should be apologizing, for everything she'd done since she applied here without telling him, but the guiltier she felt the more their friendship devolved into obligation, and she didn't see how to restore it. Back in Boulder when he'd challenged her intention to move here, he'd been strong, decisive—the whole time she'd sensed something ticking under the surface, a glint in his eye she didn't recognize—and finally, when she was full of semen and salty and purring, he'd said, "You're not leaving me, I'm leaving you—now."

He wanted her to feel good when he told her so the comedown would be further and harder and worse—and it was. Unable to shield herself she cried, then grabbed him by the hair and screamed at him. He confessed he'd hurt her deliberately—so contrary to his nature—then said that when he left the room they were finished. She didn't want that so he agreed to stay till he couldn't get it up anymore, and time went somewhere else while they had sex till they were just oozing, sweating, dripping, taken beyond pleasure and soreness into new unity. They declared their love and vowed to work it out, but maybe that had been a mistake: she wasn't willing to put the brakes on her ambitions just because his were nonexistent, and being here had swept her beyond him. Hard to say which of them had changed—both?—but their difference had intensified, and though part of her needed his grounded simplicity, love couldn't cancel out the way his hangdog expression undermined her respect.

Taking a long breath she pushed her quandary aside, thinking about what she had to do next. That damn paper—she'd given her experiment maximum time to run, figuring she could knock out the analysis and write it up quickly, but the statistics didn't match what she sensed was going on, and she couldn't figure out why. The Bio computer lab offered statistics help every evening till finals so she packed up what she needed, put on her parka and got her umbrella—not raining yet but the clouds were sinking.

Most of Bio's basement was lab space but one room had four computer terminals, a table and some chairs. The guy working tonight was a space cadet—he'd "helped" her before, then Dr. Dolph pointed out the flaws in her analysis, done according to the guy's instructions. She'd complained to the department, but jobs were by the semester—they wouldn't replace him before finals. She frowned watching him ponder her charts, correcting himself and changing his mind—she knew this better than he did.

"Type in your data and we'll have the computer crunch it," he concluded lamely. The room was hot—the building heated unevenly—and typing and feeling pissed off, she first unbuttoned her flannel shirt then took it off. She'd been wearing an undershirt with no bra since coming back with Walt—it turned him on, and she liked the way it hugged her skin. She felt self-conscious for a moment but as she resumed typing, forgot. Out of the corner of her eye she saw someone come in but kept working—had to get this done. When her last page was entered she turned: there was Cob sitting at the table, staring at her like his eyeballs were gonna fall out. Her first instinct was to grab her shirt, but an inner voice told her not to—*he knows what you look like. You're not ashamed are you? Of your shape, or desire you provoke? Don't hide.*

"What are you doing?" he asked tightly.

"Trying to finish this paper, but the statistics are hanging me up. And the help guy here—" lowering her voice, "is no help at all."

"I'm good with stat," he recovered his aplomb. "Want me to look at it?"

"Would you? It's due tomorrow, but I can't write anything till this makes sense."

He pushed his work to one side and she dumped her papers in front of him, dragging over a chair while he scanned her data. "You input everything?"

She nodded.

"Do the distributions yet?"

"I don't know which—"

"Run 'em all, we'll see what you've got. What're you looking for?"

She explained while he typed in commands at the terminal, then the printer began to chatter and the wide greenbar paper jumped out half an inch at a time. When it stopped he advanced a page and tore it off, bringing it to the table where she was going over the textbook for clues. The dot-matrix print was hard to read; he pulled out a pen and began to circle numbers.

"What this says is—" he launched into an analysis that was a lot like what she'd been trying to coax from it without success. She jotted fast while he talked, lettering the data-points and her notes so she could keep it all straight. As she leaned over the printout his hand brushed her breast. She yanked her chair a foot away and pulled the stack over, refocusing through momentary blur—his face was pinched, his eyes remote—just the way Walt looked this morning. How many times had he written "sorry" in that short note?

"Don't touch me."

"OK," he said hoarsely. "This help?"

"Yes—thank you. Now I can go home and write this miserable thing."

"With time off for good behavior?" His voice barely audible.

"No. No time off. Walt went home." Why'd she say that—was she sabotaging herself? What was going on here?

"Want to get coffee at Argo?"

"I don't have time—I'll make some at home."

"Could I—" He knew he was wasting his breath—"Could I come over? I have to study too. If the stat gives you trouble—"

"No."

"Well, if you get stuck, call me—I'll probably be up all night."

When she was two steps out of the lab he came up behind her.

"Why are you teasing me?"

"I'm not—"

"In that shirt? Come on." A plea not disbelief. "Punishing me now?" She looked him straight in the eye. "No Cob. Thanks for the help."

The rain wasn't hard, but enough to make her hurry. At home she loaded her percolator, washed her favorite mug—cobalt blue with a white interior, thick ceramic that kept a drink hot—and made a snack: a slice of dark rye, toasted then smeared with avocado, topped with jalapeño jack cheese. Carrying the plate and mug to her room she unpacked her notes, grouping information. She had her thesis statement—that was about it—but now the rest of that paragraph took shape. Her first cup tasted wonderful, the way coffee so seldom did, magnifying the burn of the jalapeño. Refreshed, she finished her outline, ready at last to turn it into an explanation.

At two thirty she was clicking along, feeling good, hoping she wouldn't be too tired to type it up neatly. She could hear Dr. Dolph: "You're not undergrads anymore. From now on your work should be professional. It's like dressing for an interview—on the job you may not need a suit, but you better look serious when you present yourself." And he'd glared at their patched, frayed jeans and shaggy hair as though he wouldn't hire anybody in the class, no matter how smart they thought they were.

But when she started the statistical analysis, the numbers just wouldn't support what they had earlier. She carefully compared the data to Cob's explanation but it didn't jell, and she spent forty-five minutes trying to find her mistake. The clock said quarter to four when she carried the phone into the kitchen on its long cord, closed the door so she wouldn't disturb her housemates, and punched his number. At the final digit she stopped—did she really want to call him? Well, she didn't, but she needed to figure this out and the lab wouldn't open till eight—too late, to turn this in at eleven. She pushed the last 3, he picked up on the second ring.

"Laura?" Who else?

"I went over the numbers twenty times and something's wrong. Could you—"

"Give me ten minutes—make some coffee."

She started a new pot, adding a drip of almond extract to the water, then cleared the kitchen table, piling dishes in the sink. Back upstairs as she crouched over her mattress to gather stuff, she heard a sharp rap on the front door glass and hurried down—there stood Cob, shivering and dripping, hair going four directions, cheek still creased from sleep. He hung his wet jacket on the back of a kitchen chair and accepted a cup of coffee, she poured herself another.

"Show me your data again."

"It just doesn't jibe," she complained, leading the way upstairs though that was the last place she wanted him. Half-awake, he read points from the printout while she checked them off, but even going through them together they couldn't find the mistake.

"Our analysis must be wrong then," he said.

"But it made sense before. What's different?"

"Must've missed something."

And halfway through, she saw—two sheets of greenbar had stuck together at the lab, and the apparent support of her thesis was based on misreading the data. She sat on her mattress, annoyed and discouraged. "Now I have to rewrite it."

"That's science," he shrugged. "Doesn't always tell you what you want to hear, but ultimately it makes better sense. You've heard of researchers who fudge results—the mice are supposed to have black spots only they don't, so the guy takes his marker—" cradling an imaginary mouse in his left hand, drawing on it with his right.

"I'm not doing that."

"Sure you are, if you insist something's true when the data say it isn't. The scientific response is to admit you're wrong and try to understand. If you twist your findings to fit a foregone conclusion, why do research at all?"

"Yeah yeah, I know. If I had this a week ago—"

"Dr. Dolph respects scientific honesty. Admit this contradicts your initial determination, make that last-minute discovery part of your conclusion. If you turn it in like this he'll butcher you for sloppy analysis."

"Ouch."

"I know; in the long run isn't honesty better?"

"You're asking me that?"

"I learned something. I wasn't straight with you—hey, I thought I was—"

"No confessions," she said. "I can't sort out your trip right now."

"Is this clear?"

"I'll redo my outline, then you can look at it. Sit down—won't take long."

So he settled in her chair where Walt had spent the last four days; she sat on the mattress amid her notes. When she got to the statistical analysis she wrote carefully, checking the printouts, confirming her data—but rereading, it was all gibberish. Cob tipped forward, drowsing. She nudged his arm with the clipboard, he jolted awake.

"Tell me if this makes sense."

He hopped a few times to get his blood circulating, then leaned close to the lamp and read. "You'll be OK—nothing makes Dr. Dolph happier than clear-headed analysis."

"How do you know?"

"I took this class last year—I was a hotshot so they let me in as a senior."

"You didn't tell me that."

"When did you ask?"

She turned back to her outline while he stood there like a parking meter ticking down on its last dime. "I've got it now—you can go."

"Dismissed huh?"

She looked up into piercing eyes.

"I was useful and now I'm not? How's that better than the way I treated you? At least I thought I was giving you what you wanted."

"After withholding it long enough to drive me nuts, you raped me—"

"Whoa—don't use that word—you wanted me girl." The backs of his hands went bloodless with the clench of his fists.

Between the chaotic images crowding her mind there was suddenly a still white space—Onion buried in the snow, the acid ringing like a bright-toned bell inside her, expanding, cooling this hostility that filled her room. She saw dazzling colors in the margins of the Greek landscape on the windshield, heard Hendrix singing "Castles Made of Sand." Throwing around charged words just made a bigger tangle of the knot this relationship had become—what was blame going to accomplish?

"I did want you," she said quietly. "Go now, before we hurt each other any more."

His hands fell loose, his face made an injured attempt to smile. "Be a good scientist. See ya." She heard him in the kitchen, the foyer, then the front door closed. She sat wideawake, riveted by this clarity, and began to write—it came together seamlessly. Even the conclusion was easy now—everything pointed to it, she understood, and she was able to discuss what the disconnect between the data and her thesis told her.

The rain slacked while she typed; by nine she'd finished. She'd pick up a report cover at the bookstore; as she assembled pages and clipped them then slid the whole thing into a 9 x 12 envelope, she congratulated herself.

COMING OUT OF class she walked straight into someone. "Excuse me," then realized it was Cob. "Oh it's you."

"So are you rescinding your apology?" he teased, eyes lively.

"No. I try not to ram into anyone."

He turned to walk beside her. "It's good, isn't it?" looking at her approvingly.

"Yeah—after you left it all just fell into place. Should get me an A in the class." Mischievously she asked, "What'd you get?"

"A B. He told me he wouldn't give an undergrad an A."

"The way the data turned out got me thinking—there must be more discrepancies where that came from, a whole different way things are knit together, than how we think of them—an ecosystem's an organism not a series of reactions."

"Right—the Gaia hypothesis—James Lovelock. The basic idea's simple—life and the geochemical and atmospheric systems of Earth don't simply coexist, they create each other. Earth makes life forms possible, life makes Earth hospitable. Earth really is our mother—it's all one."

"It is. That's what I saw last night."

"Now that you recognize the crack in how we've been thinking, hit it again—break that vessel and see what surrounds those contradictions."

"Too profound for how long I've been up." They'd arrived at the student union and he had the door open, heading in. She heard the din and smelled cigarette smoke, didn't want to be there. "See you later. Thanks." Giving him a small tired smile she wheeled 180° to head home.

CHAPTER 7

Mugging and Kissing

S aturday's mail brought a small padded pouch from Walt—a note and a cassette in a broken box. In the living room she popped in the tape—first was "I Want You," from the Beatles' *Abbey Road*.

Laura Laura—

In this tape my vacant time meets the space my head's been in since the accident—hope it doesn't bum you out, but it seemed like the easiest way to explain…

Love, Walt

Was that all he had to say—another apology? She sat with her class notes and let the tunes soak through as she studied—Monday she'd have a test, which the prof assured them would be difficult. They'd covered this last round of material so fast, she didn't know if she'd have it assimilated—to be ready for the final was challenging enough.

Two Jimmy Cliff songs—"The Harder They Come," then "By the Rivers of Babylon." Rebellion, slavery. In that order. The Dead, "Dire Wolf." She tried to think about symbiosis. Then it was Dylan, "Boots of Spanish Leather"—faithlessness. As she focused on plant cells, Commander Cody sang "Seeds and Stems Again Blues." Neil Young, "Cowgirl in the Sand"—disconnect, misery. Would he be in better spirits when she was done with finals?

Dear Walt—

Thanks for the tape. Wish I could erase these blues from your head & heart. I was surprised when I got home and you weren't here—guess I coerced you into coming but I thought you shouldn't be alone—was I wrong?

Is Opal looking after you? I know Ray is—what a good guy. Rusty's still sitting in front of my house—I haven't used it, Cob doesn't seem to want it back. If I wasn't so horrifically busy I'd be on your doorstep, even if it's underwater again—miss you babe. But now I'm in midnight oil mode— monster exams coming up, plus I have to write the final for my recitation, then after my last exam, grade them. Write me?

Love you, Laura

"What's on your recitation final?" she asked Cob in the grad lounge.

"Twenty-five multiple choice questions. They can prove what they know, guess if they want, and I can grade 'em fast. What about yours?"

"A combination—some people explain better than they memorize, so I'll give three topics—pick one for a short essay. Then I'll make 'em draw something, and throw in some multiple choice to finish it off."

His eyes warmed. "Sounds like a good test—mind if I take it?"

"With everybody else, if you want."

"And will you grade it?"

"How else will I know if you understand the material?" She wasn't sure anymore if she was leading him on or he was tailing her close, picking up every thought she dropped—or was karmic affinity striking these sparks? Again she thought she should get the hell out of Berkeley, move in with Walt. But he was so depressed. What would Christmas be like, with his broken leg and that deeper injury?

The last week before finals, when she hardly had time to think, his letter came. On her way to show the prof her recitation exam, she stuck the envelope in her backpack and went to his office. They spent a long time discussing her questions, made a few changes, then she went to the stat lab—she couldn't read her last printout so she badgered the guy, he looked at the faint broken lines and stopped the printer, going to find a replacement ribbon. Waiting she remembered Walt's letter.

> *Laura my Dear—*
>
> *The doc says my leg's doing fine. The pain's dull now, like stabbing me got boring—I'm supposed to say this is an improvement so I will. The tape wasn't intended to cheer you up—probably shouldn't have sent it—what do you need my downer for? But you said to share...*
>
> *My great-aunt died so my mom's giving me her car and they sprung for a plane ticket to DC. My brother wants to see California so he'll drive us out, then fly back before his semester starts—he's a freshman at Maryland. My flight's from San Jose the 20th, I'll spend Christmas with the folks, then Grant and I head west. He's jazzed because now that he's out of the nest he's starting to open up—we'll have time to talk. Tom's still coming to Santa Cruz—he and Opal both want to see you, and Ray's going to LA and Kathy to Spokane for the holidays, so you and Tom can look after the house.*
>
> *I know I should've talked to you but this came up really fast and it seemed right. I'm sorry Toots, but with this $&^% cast on I can't love you right anyway... I'd rather see you when it's off, if you don't mind waiting.*
>
> *Hooowwwwlllll Walt*

She was absorbing the shock of his change of plans when the lab guy came back with a new ribbon. She knew he was going to load it wrong and wreck it so she helped—one of the clip-catches wouldn't release and they had to poke around with a pen to open it, then the new ribbon had to be woven through forked slots—they were both getting ink on their fingers. He ran a test page, the ribbon skipped out of the guides and the print-head missed it. When it was finally in right and her job was running she stood back—Cob was sitting in her chair. She startled, which he observed, his eyes flickering like a streetlight through gale-blown branches. He glanced at the table—he'd been reading Walt's letter.

Moving fast she stuffed it into her jeans pocket, her stomach cramping, then her guts seemed to liquefy and she ran for the bathroom, arriving just in time, everything she'd eaten the last two days blasting out of her in a foul rush. When she was empty she wanted a shower—length after length of t.p. seemed to find more splatters. Feeling guilty leaving this mess, she wiped the toilet seat then flushed again—the janitor'd have to deal with the rest. She scrubbed her hands, the harsh soap and coarse paper towels setting her teeth on edge.

She wobbled slowly to the lab—the stack of greenbar was on top of her backpack, Cob sitting cowboy-style in one of the terminal chairs watching the doorway. When she came in he stepped over the chair back, to the table. Avoiding his eyes she stuffed things into her pack and went out; he moved alongside her up the stairs.

When she pushed on the left door to leave the building, he leaned the right far enough open to wedge his foot against it from the outside, looking at her.

"You have no right to read my mail," she said, eyes on her hand on the pushbar, her insides churning—might have another bout any minute.

"If it's private you shouldn't leave it out like that."

"I have to go." Then her gut which wanted nothing in it at all, having emptied its lower chambers, heaved, and she leaned forward to vomit. Cob jerked his foot back but not fast enough—she sprayed his knee and shoe.

"Shit!"

Her exit was unobstructed now but she sank to her knees, heaving again. Someone was coming, the stride rhythm changing as the person drew near.

"What—" A man's voice.

"She got sick," Cob said. "We need to call the janitor."

"Oh, ah, yes, I'll see if I can find him," hurrying off.

Cob knelt, hand on the middle of her back. "C'mon, I'll take you home."

"Leave me alone."

"You won't get there without some help. Can you stand up? Are you done?"

He lifted by her armpit but her knee buckled so he scooped her up, backpack and all, stepping through the vomit, down the outer stairs, over to the street where he hailed a taxi. Giving her address he climbed in holding her.

"Smells bad buddy," the cabbie complained.

"She's sick."

"Man I guess—I got to air out my car now."

He pulled up in front of her house, right behind Rusty. Cob paid him then struggled with her dead weight—why was lifting her out so much harder than getting in? The cabbie, pissed about the smell, didn't move to help—asshole. Cob wrapped his arms across her back and dragged her out, on the sidewalk hefted her again and walked to her porch, ignoring the open back door of the taxi and the angry protest of the driver who now had to get out anyway to shut it.

Lugging her upstairs, he got off her pack, parka and shoes, and towel on his shoulder carried her to the bathroom. She was in a state of shock, limp as her jeans as he undressed her. Naked too he held her back to the spray, swabbing her with shampoo—she'd really blown—then with a clean hand washed her face.

"Rinse your mouth and spit," cupping his palm for her to drink. "Blow your nose. Rinse again." Becoming conscious she was in the shower with him she shrank, arms tight to her chest, but he was businesslike, wrapping her in a towel and carrying her to her room, with his toes shifting blanket then sheet, laying her down.

"Take off the towel—it's wet."

She tugged it loose, moaning, "Don't touch me."

He lay behind her outside the blanket, chafing through the layers. "You're cold."

"Leave please." Broken by shivering, her voice came out in bleats.

"Once I know you're all right."

"I will be as soon as you go." Her voice grew clearer. "Your energy's hurting Walt. Get away from me."

"Maybe I'm stronger, this time. Maybe we have something to exchange too, in this life. Just because he's part of your karmic history doesn't mean I'm not."

"I never should've spoken to you."

"Never's a long time. We met ages before we got here," which had to be true. Compared to her, everyone else in his life were ciphers—she stood out like an old-growth Doug fir in a pine plantation. He moved to where he could see her face.

"I'm not one of your women."

He met her eyes, glad she'd brought it up. "I know—I've stopped seeing them."

"Why?"

"I was using 'em, getting my rocks off. I never felt what any of you did, but you were the only one who told me. Know how many orgasms I had that night?"

She shook her head: didn't care.

"Two. Pretty sizeable disconnect, huh? You kept coming, I figured that must be good." But that was all the apology he could stomach—she'd used him too. "Teach me—you're ahead of me, you know more."

"You're too selfish."

"I'll give you Rusty—Walt said Blue Book's zero, so pay me that."

"I don't want your car."

"Then why's he still here?"

Her loss for words reminded him what bad shape she was in. "Hey listen, my stuff's at the lab—I gotta get back. You be all right?"

"Yeah."

He kissed her cheek, dressed quickly and left.

WHILE SHE DID laundry she let her room air out, preferring the damp chill to some attempt to mask the stench, and by the time she got back it was tolerable. She reread Walt's letter—his flight was the 20th from San Jose. Her last final was early that morning—she should drive down and meet him at the airport. She was wondering how long it would take to get there when Cob tapped on her door.

"Feeling better?"

"Yeah. Guess I had too much coffee or something."

"Or something." He had a hard edge. "I came by to give Rusty some exercise."

She searched on her dresser, lobbed the keys, he caught them neatly. "No reason to keep it here." Oops—now she'd have to negotiate all over again—how else was she going to see Walt?

"Sure you don't need him? What about when you go to Santa Cruz?"

"I'll hitchhike."

He stepped in and pushed the door shut, leaning against it. "That wasn't bad coffee last night. What're you afraid of?"

"I don't want to talk to you."

"Be fair—give me another chance."

"You expect fairness from me while you undermine the ground I'm standing on?"

"Is Walt your ground?"

"Yes. And you're doing your damnedest to separate us."

"It's not me, our karma's doing it—Walt and I have some too. We need to open our eyes, don't you agree? I have some mushrooms—want to trip, once exams are over?"

"I'll think about it. Now please go."

He opened the door, tossing and catching his keys several times. "Want to study together for the final?"

No one knew the material as well as he did. "Yeah—I'll call."

Through her window she heard the starter skitter, the engine cough then chug. Cob showering her—*brr!* But he hadn't done anything. The extra undershirt that appeared in her wash today must be his. Wearing it was a tease—what flowed from her subconscious bore watching—she was sending mixed signals. Her heartbeat magnified in her groin—did her body still want him? She'd forgiven Walt for hurting her last year, they were closer now. But she trusted him—that was the difference. She remembered the open doors of the acid—maybe she should trip with Cob, find out who he was—or was she afraid of him? People connected through time aren't necessarily allies—cycles of harm repeat too.

She phoned Walt. "I had a bad time last night—wondered how you're doing."

"That's weird—me too. Somebody jumped me. The theater I was working's only a few blocks away so I was crutching home after my shift. Never saw the guy—came up behind me, hit me in the kidneys and stomach with a nightstick or something, grabbed my wallet and crutches, and took off."

"Your crutches?"

"To slow me down I guess. I had to crawl home—he hit me hard—couldn't even get outta bed till an hour ago, and now I gotta see the doc again—the cast's all torn up."

"How's your leg?"

"It really hurts."

"Walt, I wish—What time's your flight?"

"Lemme hobble to my room and check—hold on." Finally he picked up. "Eleven thirty," reciting the airline and flight number.

"I'll meet you at the airport—I want to kiss you."

"Goodbye you mean?" He sounded resigned, defeated even.

"No—I—"

"Me too. Gotta go." He hung up. She stared at the receiver in her hand, thinking she should call him back—but to say what? They needed proximity. All she could do from here was remind him of that. The image of him crawling home with that cast was so jarring, she felt his spirit had been mugged. He'd looked wounded before he left, damage she was party to. She decided to spend the break with Tom and Opal, creating a healing presence to bring him back—the link between her spirit and his was spinning out faint and fragile, spider silk across the miles.

DR. DOLPH GAVE back her paper, liberally marked in red. At first she was appalled, but reading his notes realized he just used a red pen—they weren't corrections. He praised her work and her attitude, complimented her insight and the quality of her writing, and on the last page offered to serve on her thesis committee. It was immensely gratifying, and when she saw Cob she showed him. Finished scanning, he grinned.

"You blew him away, girl." Then his eyes narrowed. "You weren't wearing your shirt open in class were you?"

"You don't think I earned this?"

"It's good, don't get me wrong. But it's not the best paper anybody ever wrote."

"Thanks for deflating me," snatching it from his hands.

"Well, somebody should," undeterred. "Flattery's poison—you of all people oughta know that." He leaned close. "You don't think that was flattery, all those months? Toughen up, why don't you."

He made sense, which infuriated her more. He gave her a knowing look, as though they both understood her anger was obligatory while underneath it she agreed with him. She felt she was dodging a bee determined to sting her, and no matter how she ducked and swatted, it evaded her defenses to torment her further.

"Ready to study for our final?" he asked.

"After dinner."

"Oh hey, isn't Walt leaving tomorrow?"

"Why do you care?"

"Because you want him, and I want you."

"Buzz off." She couldn't ask now to borrow Rusty, but how else was she getting to the airport? She'd exhausted every possibility including the bus—it didn't get there till noon thirty—he'd be gone. The exam period was 7:30 to 10:30—she'd never had a final last longer than two hours, but she'd have to be ready to move fast. In some vehicle—

IN THE STUDENT union at seven she and Cob took over a table, moving ashtrays and buying coffee, sharing some cornbread he'd brought, then spreading out their notes. Studying, they lost track of time—the woman inverting chairs onto tables interrupted.

"Hate to break up your party, but we're closing in five."

"Well, we hit most of it," Cob said, stretching.

"I feel shaky on the last part—mind if we go over it?"

"Where? It'll take an hour at least, and everything on campus is closed."

Argo was jammed, noisy and very smoky—they didn't even go in.

"My kitchen table then," she decided.

But Steve was about to take off for two weeks and a party was in progress. A case of beer stood on the kitchen floor, eight guys drinking long-necks and passing a pair of joints to the thump of the Stones' "Beast of Burden." Cob stayed on the porch, Laura walked in, took one look and whiff, and walked right back out.

"Forget that."

"That's why I like living alone—if there's a party, it's mine. Come on over."

She didn't want to but she had to review this stuff, and even in her room they'd be loud. So she matched her shorter legs to the pace of Cob's, and soon they were climbing the stairs to his apartment. He cleared his card table and they resumed studying.

"Must be late," she said finally, closing her folder of notes.

"It's—" he peered at his clock, on a box upended beside his bed, "Two fifteen. Bet they're partying hard now at your house."

"Shoot, I forgot," her hand frozen in the act of lifting her parka off the chair back.

"Stay here," he said off-handedly.

"Just how gullible do you think I am?"

"How big a jerk do you think I am? Gimme a little credit, willya? Maybe I'm more decent than that."

She looked out the window—it was raining, as if to seal her in. "You won't do anything?"

"I promise," hand on his heart, looking at her solemnly.

"OK," she said finally. "I'm gonna sleep in undies—will you wear some too please?"

"Sure, I don't care—just don't ask me to sleep on the floor," he grinned.

She gave him an icy look.

"If I wasn't a good student would you even speak to me?"

"Probably not."

"Thanks for clearing up that little mystery," and setting his alarm, went to bed.

A STREETLIGHT CAST outlines of the subdivided panes across the ceiling, semi-transparent shadows of drips rolling away from the window. Her undershirt and panties allowed too much contact with Cob's sheets, and this pillow was steeped in his scent, ragging her mind with the memory of subjugation while her body hummed faintly with desire. Which was deluded? Which understood?

She dreamed—Walt was a fish, one of those that came ashore to be the first land-dwelling animals. He pulled his body awkwardly, dragging himself over a huge piece of glass that gashed his abdomen. His fins became hands investigating his wound, he looked at her baffled, eyes dimming as blood pulsed from the laceration. She woke abruptly—the heartbeat was her own, thudding hard. Cob was asleep with his back to her, hair spread on the folded sweatshirt he was using as a pillow. She'd forgotten to ask about Rusty—maybe she wouldn't go. But she'd told Walt—

The evening's caffeine conspired with nervousness about the exam to keep her awake; turning onto her back and pushing the pillow away so she could lie flat, she watched shadows rippling across the ceiling—was the box filling deeper with rain in front of Walt's house? She smiled—until that moment, the song lyric had been meaningless—now that box was a cosmic promise.

The clock buzzed much too soon—she groped to shut it off, wanting more oblivion, but Cob was moving. When she opened her eyes he was crossing to the bathroom, hard-on pushing out his boxers. He'd behaved himself as promised—maybe tripping together was a good idea—the less conscious she was of her motives, the more harm rebounded on Walt.

Pulling on her jeans she ran cold water and splashed her face, hating the shock. She looked in the mirror as she dried off—Cob stood two feet behind her brushing his hair, eyes alternately watching his face, hers, her body. He gathered his hair back, let it loose and parted it, brushed it back one last time and banded it, then offered the brush; she accepted it avoiding his fingers—the air zinged with electricity—contact would raise such a huge spark they'd find themselves in bed before their heads could say no. While he set up a filter cone, measuring in coffee, she saw the bulge in his jeans.

"Put your shirt on please."

If he'd been insensitive she was more than matching him. "Sorry." She buttoned.

"Unless you want me, don't push it." He put cornbread in the toaster oven and poured boiling water. "There's half-and-half I swiped from a café—grab me one?"

She got out two—more than a dozen were heaped in a bowl.

"Why'd you take so many? If you abuse their generosity, pretty soon they'll withdraw it."

"Then I'll get my supply someplace else."

"You're contributing to the erosion of public trust," she fumed.

"What makes you so virtuous? Didn't you shoplift as a kid?"

"No, I never took anything without paying for it. Now I see it as the price of my integrity—would I sell out for a candy bar?"

"Hm—never thought of it that way. Well," he smirked, "feel free not to use it." She'd emptied one into her coffee. "You're not tainted by stolen goods?"

"It'd be even worse if it spoiled before you used it all."

"True." He looked smug. "I've always found the need for conformity stifling. You don't have to scam free stuff or approve of that, to tolerate that I do. Or do you?"

"If those close to you won't say you're doing something wrong, who will?"

"Ah, the cop answer."

"I think of it as the 'I don't need cops' answer," she said. "If people behaved with integrity, we wouldn't need laws and cops, would we?"

"The anarchist pipe dream," he said derisively.

"In small-scale communities that can work. Not Berkeley though."

"No, much as I dislike them I wouldn't live here if there were neither laws nor cops. Drink up, we gotta go." He pulled out the warm cornbread and they stood to eat.

Glancing around the room, she remembered. "Cob, can I borrow Rusty this morning?"

"We have an exam this morning."

"I need him right afterwards."

"To see Walt?"

"At the airport."

"Ah. Sure, help yourself. Coming back?"

"I have my recitation exams to grade."

"So do I—want to do that together?"

"Maybe."

He poked among the rubber bands hanging on a hook by the sink, hmmed, dug in his pocket, hmmed, then picked through the heap of clothes outside the bathroom, tossing garments. When one jingled, he pulled keys from a pocket, lobbed, and she caught them.

"What's the second key for? You never said."

"The trunk. But don't open it."

"Why—is that where you keep the bodies?"

He laughed. "It's tricky to latch—every time I pop it I think I'll never get it shut again, or if it does lock, maybe it'll stay that way."

"So what's in there?"

"The spare and the jack. Let's go—we should get him out of that spot—you can park closer to campus."

Once Rusty was choked down, she followed Cob's guidance out to the alley. Getting in he reached over the seat.

"Use this," handing her a black meditation pillow. She pulled out her backpack she'd sat on and put the *zafu* in place—it stayed put better than her chair cushion, sinking neatly into the sag. She didn't ask how he'd obtained it. They got to the classroom with another straggler five minutes late—the prof passing out blue books gave them the eye.

"I want nothing on your desk but your writing instruments and the blue book and exam. Leave backpacks and jackets by the door," he addressed his new arrivals, then walked around placing a set of stapled pages face down on each student's desk. At the front he nodded. "Begin."

She flipped through—six pages—three of multiple choice, matching and short answer, two of essay questions, an extra credit question. She did the quick stuff first, glad she'd studied with Cob. Thirty minutes so far—she turned to the essays. The instructions said to answer all six— three in one paragraph each, three at length. The short ones took her thirty-five minutes.

Her thoughts drifted out—traffic shouldn't be too bad on a Wednesday morning. Looking at the clock, she saw the prof watching her. He smiled as though she had plenty of time—she hoped she could do these questions justice before her urgency to meet Walt chased her out the door. Someone dropped a pen, a fly repeatedly bumped a window, every impact a louder buzz; she wasted five minutes on distractions then plunged into the first long essay—twenty minutes. The next was harder, she was tireder—thirty-five. The clock said 9:40. She tackled the last one, wrung out, her clarity fading. At last she'd said all she could remember—she had to go. She handed in her exam and blue book, the prof observed she hadn't put her name on either—would she care to claim them? Scribbling *Laura Reiner* she ran to the back of the room, yanked on her parka, grabbed her pack.

She sprinted to the car heedless of the pelting rain and read her map while Rusty warmed up. This morning the bedraggled hitchhikers at the on-ramp were headed north and east so she kept going, grateful for seatbelt and cushion, singing "Uncle John's Band" as she drove, taking 17 as I-80 veered east—chilled her to think of Walt's accident on another stretch of this same highway. He and Cob had been opposing forces then, but Cob's energy was cooperating now—*if* she got to the airport in time, she told herself, suddenly riven by doubt. She decided if the plane had left, she'd have nothing more to do with Cob—he was undermining Walt because she let him—that wasn't right. If that love came to an end, it had to die on its own merits not because she, or through her Cob, stabbed it in the back.

The cold damp whining in around the door made her shiver and bounce on the seat. She sang songs from the tape Walt had sent her, mind fully bent on him now. Morning was slipping away, she pressed the gas harder. Cob had said fifty max but that would take too long. The speedometer needle quivered close to sixty, the front end shimmying on the wet road. As she passed Milpitas she saw a sign for the airport—eight miles. Time closed around her like a fist—maybe the rain would delay his flight. Driving up to the two-story box that looked like a bus station, she left the engine running and rushed in, saw the line of people moving to the open door, the plane beyond the glass. She ran, yelling.

Walt turned, his face brightening—she'd been right to come. She slowed her impact as much as she could but with arms clamped around him and crutches dropping away, she had to turn him two complete circles to stay upright. He hugged her hard, people standing back amused as they kissed. She opened her parka and the buttons on her shirt, half-sobbing he ran his hands over her undershirt, she felt his hard-on against her but there was nowhere, no time. She pushed her hips into him, kissing around his neck and ear while he buried his face against her collarbone.

"Sir, it's time to board." The flight attendant sympathetically offered his crutches. Laura wiped his tears then her own, coming with him to the door, squeezing his arm; the flight attendant stepped out opening an umbrella, she had to let go. He crutched through puddles, slowly up the steps, turned at the top and waved, his flashbulb smile leaving a blind spot on her retinas. She waved back, then he went in. Crying hard now she stumbled back to the car. An airport cop was looking over Rusty— abandoned? When she got in he shrugged and moved away. As she finally composed herself she heard a roar and glimpsed the belly of the plane overhead, torn clouds drawn into its passage obscuring its ascent.

CHAPTER 8

Once Upon a Time

ob's multiple choice answers on her recitation exam were all correct, he drew plant cells in precise detail, his essay was a single paragraph dense with facts—she'd expected something longer but he hadn't omitted anything so she gave it full credit. Turning over the page she saw he'd written more.

> Once upon a time two men loved a woman and spent lifetimes obstructing and betraying each other, twisting the love she tried to give each in turn. One society talked openly about her dalliances, wagering which she'd favor in a given cycle of her inner tide. But nothing protected her from the wrath of the lover whose seed didn't root, and again the blood of jealousy was on their hands. Most recently their paths through the thicket of time were clear to read, showing them their history.

> Raised in a subculture that valued peace, this pair first avoided each other, then sought to explore their connection without violence. A psychedelic key opened the cage that trapped their spirits together in destructive repetition, and when they left that prison the immensity greeting them blew away their armor of favor, their weapons of fear. The sex energy they'd used to batter each other so long carried them into new territory, beyond the

*duality of "choose me not him." That fragment of universe healed, they
could move on.*

And they all lived happily ever after. The End.

*Buckminster Fuller has demonstrated that the triangle is the strongest shape,
and with the addition of connecting wires will hold up under conditions no
other structure can withstand.*

Below that he'd drawn a triangle, and beside that another whose three
sides each extended beyond the corner on one end, with thin lines linking
those termini to form a larger triangle. She smiled and gave him an A,
which was, she reflected, a triangle of sorts.

"Hey Cob, I'm grading exams. Do yours yet?"

"Just thinking about it—come on over."

THE CRACKLING ENERGY that had filled his apartment yesterday was gone,
as though rain had calmed the air. She worked at his card table while he
sat in his armchair; when he was done he brought his exams over. Hers
took longer to grade so she handed off the multiple choice sections to him
while she reviewed drawings and read essays. She assigned points then
totaled scores, he calculated the mean and median and did the curve—his
students' grades fell into a narrower range.

"It's easier to cram and slam than absorb ideas and think about
them," she said. "I wonder how much of this material your class will
know next week."

"As much as they're interested in. I look at it this way," stretching till
his fingers brushed the ceiling, "I haven't deprived anyone of financial aid."

"Have I?"

"Maybe," he joked; standing, she swatted his shoulder with her pile
of tests. The tease left his eyes. "May I please kiss you?" While her mind
was warning this was the first fluff of an avalanche, her mouth was asking
please could he? She had to reconcile them before impulse took charge.

"Not yet." Along with his disappointment she saw deep suspicion—
was she jerking him around? He wasn't playing... "Let me explain."

"I'm all ears," folding his arms across his chest, looking at her like a parent whose delinquent child is about to offer a carefully marshaled set of facts with only passing resemblance to the truth.

"I need perspective," she said slowly, "and it wouldn't hurt you either."

"And?" tilting his head to the other side.

"Let's drop the exams at the department office and stop at my house for a few things. Then let's come back here and have some mushrooms."

BETH WAS OUT, Petra and Steve had left town, Jack was in the kitchen making macaroni and cheese from a box.

"Some guy called for you," he reported, "Rej or Gary or something."

"Ray?"

"That's the one," talking as though Cob not only wasn't standing beside her but had never existed. "Going out?"

"Sure am."

He held the pot's mouth against the edge of the sink, noodles slithering out with the current of starchy water. A dome of steam billowed and vanished. "Back when?"

"Later, Mommy."

He made a face and righted the pot, shaking it to settle the macaroni. "In case somebody else calls."

"Then you can say I'll be back later."

He dumped in the orange cheese powder and stirred. "Y'know, a woman as attractive as you can do better. I mean, Walt's all right, but that other guy…"

"Fortunately that's not your problem," she breezed, putting some rice in a plastic tub, setting that in her pack with a ripe avocado and a lemon.

"Provisions, huh?" but she was done responding. She and Cob went upstairs where she packed her diaphragm kit, a clean undershirt, her corduroy skirt and a change of undies. As an afterthought she put in a second pair, turning to Cob just in time to catch his smile.

"If I'd known you were moving in—"

"Just being prepared."

"What about your pillow?"

"I'll use yours," she said mischievously. "Oh, got a cassette player?"

"Sure."

She put in Walt's tape and *Highway 61 Revisited*, then closed her door and headed down. Jack lounged in the kitchen doorway pan in hand watching them, his mouth contorted with a bitterness macaroni and cheese could not produce. She shot him a "don't say anything to me, buddy" look and grabbed her umbrella. Cob close as a shadow waited till they were down the block to spit out breath in an angry rush.

"I just want to stuff that guy's words down his throat one at a time till he pukes."

"We're here to evolve," she said airily. "I personally suspect Jack has a karmic function in your life you choose to ignore."

"And what would that be?"

"Not my karma—you'll have to figure it out."

His growl told her how likely that was; she just laughed.

AT THE CO-OP he paid for everything, over her protests. "It's cool—I have a job during the break—bet you don't."

"Besides TA-ing?"

"I was a janitor as an undergrad, so whenever I'm free the guys at Physical Plant give me work."

"Like what?"

"Stripping and sealing floors, cleaning dining hall kitchens—stuff like that."

"How much do they pay you?"

"Six an hour, and if I go longer than eight hours or more than five days, time and a half."

"Not bad at all. I wondered how you could afford an apartment."

"You probably think I'm getting handouts from home."

"Aren't you?"

"Nope. Once I graduated, my dad shut the wallet—he sells Chrysler products and thinks as the family son I should too. Picture me on the lot, all decked out in white bucks and red double-knit pants, peddling shiny gas-guzzlers with a big grin on my fat face."

"And less hair."

"None—then Dad wouldn't feel so naked."

"See your parents much?"

"Since they didn't come for graduation I went in May. They had a party and welcomed me back, then I got the hell out as fast as Rusty could take me."

"Before that?"

He shook his head. "That life's a large hungry zero—I stay away from the edge."

Though it was only midafternoon, the clouds were so dark streetlights were on. She set her pack on his table and while he put away groceries, took her diaphragm kit into the bathroom. She'd opened the plastic case and got out the tube of gel when she looked at what she was doing—she'd brought this to "be prepared," but she sorely resented the planning a diaphragm entailed. The Pill had freed her from any sense of obligation or compulsion—she was always ready for sex, which translated to engaging in it only when circumstances felt right. Having to insert the device in advance, hemmed her in and taunted her—he'd assume she was ready because in this narrow sense she would be—which meant she was making the decision now, for what happened the rest of today. Then if she didn't want him, would that make her a prick-tease for leading him on?

But what if she didn't wear it, and with the mushrooms clouding her logic, decided it was "unnatural" and had sex without it? She was due to ovulate any day now, and she'd experienced more intense desire at maximum fertility. Pregnancy was worse than hurt feelings, she concluded, unscrewing the cap from the spermicide. When she emerged to wash her hands he was making two piles of dried mushrooms on a plate. At five apiece he rolled the Baggie shut on the remnants, licked the long edge to seal it shut, and stashed the extra in his freezer.

"Madame?" He offered the plate.

"Together."

He winced, and she wondered why she'd come—being unwilling to enter a vulnerable frame of mind except with him matching her step by step, proved more vividly than any statement that she didn't trust him at all. Head drugs could be a source of creativity, flow, spontaneity, but she and Cob were off on the wrong foot: wary, suspicious even. As though on a dare, each picked up a mushroom, movements mirrored as they raised the desiccated fungi to their mouths, paused, then chewed in unison. They ate with that same watchfulness till the plate was empty.

"Allow me to adjust the ambiance." He switched the floor lamp on and the bare overhead bulb off, popped open his cassette deck then considering her tapes, started Walt's. The opening line of "I Want You/She's So Heavy" was jarring, as though she'd summoned her lover to join them. He punched Stop, ejected it and put in her Dylan tape.

What made her imagine Walt's blue letter to her belonged here? One action after another seemed calculated to hurt Cob—but did her self-disgust give him the advantage? As far as she could tell, whatever guilt he let slip was more a consequence of getting caught, than true shame.

Something about him brought out her perversity—that night he helped with her paper, her resentful accusation of rape backed her into an ethical corner where all she could do was recant. Under his fury was hurt: she'd reduced the quintessentially personal experience of sex to rhetoric—and him to a stereotype. By dehumanizing his role she'd erased her own responsibility, but how could she abdicate and still hold him to a high standard?

Here she was, doing the same thing again by bringing Walt's mournful headspace into Cob's territory. If she was so intent on reminding this man that she loved someone else, why hadn't she demonstrated more loyalty? Why'd she let Cob draw her in with his bullshit lines and all that foreplay, all the while keeping her heart solidly barricaded? Cob put up a front of being tough—did that make it all right to project her needs and desires onto him without acknowledging his?

She was her own worst adversary—whenever her thoughtless reactions managed to land a glancing blow, he just rolled with it, coming back with that same hungry look in his eyes. He offered no real penitence for his own selfishness, but he sure made her feel bad for acting the same way. *You can't win against an opponent who fights by different rules*, she thought. *Is it victory, when you prevail by compromising your integrity?* She put Walt's tape in her backpack and zipped the pocket shut as if sending him home. The rasp of the zipper and the texture of the sturdy nylon were amplified to her senses—she was coming on to the mushrooms. Her breathing slowed and deepened, her lungs asking for more oxygen, her blood hurrying to distribute it through her body. A fluttering in her chest made her think of a moth caught in a spiderweb—this day was turning dark.

Cob sat in his big armchair; she stood just beyond his reach if he were to extend a leg to touch her. Heat bounced into her head from his gaze—anger? Desire? Something else? While Dylan sang "Like a Rolling Stone" she abruptly sensed Death in the room with them, in the gloom clouding the corners, in the dark of his eyes. Dying subsumed all fears, didn't it? When you faced that, didn't the rest dissolve? Or turn into tombstone blues maybe—a melancholy so monumental even death couldn't touch it.

"What do you want?" he asked, barely a voice.

"To know you." They spoke slowly, many possible meanings of each phrase unfolding before the next was uttered.

"How?"

"Do you care?" she said.

"Yes." One large hand made a fist while his other lay open. He could throttle her, easily, and now she felt Death hovering: between the lines of the song, between his body and hers, between their dishonesty and the truth scattered through it.

"You can't look at me yet," she said.

"Want me to close my eyes?" he mocked, a wave of hatred flowing off him—she knew so little about him really. In their studies he was incisive and intelligent, but the lamplight casting a heavy shadow off his brow gave him the mien of a brute. She should leave, but instead merely observed that he was Death's willing tool.

"I'm trying not to hurt you anymore." She switched off the lamp.

"Giving me another chance?" he sneered, streetlight catching his forehead, cheekbone, jaw—leaving the hollows between black.

"Giving *us* a chance. You had one, I had one—or rather, you had two, I had twenty-two. But we—we as one?" shaking her head, "had none."

"Ask me if I want that."

"Do you want to fly with me?"

His words, turned against him. Watching his jaw knot she recalled her clearest impression of death: when she was thirteen her grandfather died working cattle on his small ranch in western Colorado. They weren't sure which killed him, the heart attack or the fall from his horse, but that didn't much matter. He was sixty-six, vigorous—Grandma was devastated, so was Mom, but to Laura it seemed he'd made the exit he wanted, doing what he loved—made her contemplate her own end, the where and how of it. Never gave much thought to "when" other than expecting to live a long time—but this could be her last moment. She was far from done, most of life unlived yet, but the lightning assessment forced by the prospect of death showed her that she'd met challenges, taken risks, had fun, loved and been loved—she'd hoped to add more to that, but in essence she was satisfied—she hadn't waited till some ideal set of conditions was met, to be alive.

"Shall we be one?" she offered, serenity making her buoyant, magnanimous.

"That's imaginary."

"In this room we can't see the redwood groves of Humboldt County—are they imaginary?"

"That's a weak analogy." His argumentative reflex made her smile, sure of her ground now.

"But being one," she said, "that's strong. Don't tell me you haven't been there."

"Like I said—"

"Find out." She extended a hand, and undoing his fist to touch her fingers he stood, his shadow covering her. She stepped back toward the bed, drawing him by fingertip contact as though he was Walt's car on the winch, the tow truck extracting it from snow burial on Donner Pass. When she bumped against the bed she unbuttoned her jeans with her other hand and sloughed them off, nodding at him; he shed his too, one-handed. Undies were next, and with those on the floor, fingertips still touching, she set her knees on the mattress and shuffled backwards from the edge, Cob following while Dylan sang "It Takes a Lot to Laugh, It Takes a Train to Cry." She reached for his dick but his hand intercepted hers and again she felt Death, close now, impatient—what was he waiting for?

IT WAS THE strangest thing—he'd imagined the mushrooms would open them to each other—that was the point—but instead a chill clamping onto his brain was urging him to choke the life from her. Sure, she'd hurt him, used him, treated him as though his feelings were disposable—but kill her? He wouldn't even kill plants, which most people assumed lacked sentience—and yet he was available, host to this urge—Death had claimed his muscles and bones for its own purpose, and once that was fulfilled, would presumably depart—leaving him to manage the horror. What a prospect.

Why wasn't she afraid? He was poised, ready to move at her first quiver of fear—until then he was a mere statue of a threat.

With psychedelics dismantling his defenses brick by brick, he felt acutely how he'd hurt her by staying aloof emotionally during sex. But she didn't understand—

"I—can't please you," he stumbled. "All I can do is dry a pile of tinder and set a match to it." He couldn't even remember the last time he'd cried, but tears were coursing down his cheeks.

"I can't teach if you're afraid to learn." Before their final, the spark had been strong, loving would've been thoughtless, but now he cowered. Her voice was gentle. "You can kiss me." Not "you may"—permission—but "you can"—freed from paralysis.

The kiss was an upheaval of his senses—in her mouth he tasted everything he was not—though she'd lost the fruitarian sweetness he'd cultivated in her, the tang of wheat and onions didn't repel him now—had narcissism driven him to change women's diets so their kisses would be extensions of his own? For the first time he understood how his lies had undermined not just her regard but his own perceptions.

She worked open the buttons of her shirt and his, then before he could prevent her, placed her palm over his heart, triggering a spasm of pain as though she'd stabbed him; he clenched her waist through her undershirt, she kissed tears off his face while shedding her flannel shirt, helping him out of his then pushing so he collapsed backwards on the blanket. She straddled him taking just his head inside, he gripped her pelvis, she took him in a little more then lifted again to hold only his head. He shoved his groin at her in an effort so naïve he was transported back to his most painful high school experience. She pressed him to the mattress. He keened as she played him, the tension in his thumbs bruising her.

"Now join me." She came down on him fast, clear to his root, and he gasped and pulled her against him, rolled her under and began to thrust, but she put her hand on his sternum. "Wait." He froze with a strangled noise. As she rubbed her palm over his galloping heart his fear subsided and with it, the need to conquer and be done. Flinging her leg across the backs of his thighs she flipped him, then crouching with knees spread, pivoted her hips, releasing and taking him slowly while he clawed at her almost in panic—then the barrier was suddenly gone and the waves of her arrival met his, surging back and forth. He roared and cried, hugging her hard; she kissed him again and his own mouth was pungent, as though his palate was sweating. Between gulps of air like a swimmer racing, he kissed back wildly; she let him roll her and he was with her now, her every thrill and breath his own. When he slipped out he lay gasping, prostrated by her generosity and his sense of shame.

She brought up the covers and in the growing warmth as he mumbled incoherently, Death made its exit.

"I know nothing," he said faintly, lying on his back holding her. "I'm sorry." But paranoia goosed him—she'd triumphed, now she'd walk away. "You have Walt—what do you need me for?"

"I don't 'have' Walt, I love him. When I got to the airport he was in line to board and we only had about two minutes, but that was enough to put things right. But it wasn't the kiss, it was the seventy-five-mile drive in the rain, the perfect timing that got me there just before he left. As soon as I left I ran out of gas—that's how close it was."

"So the cosmos smiles on your union."

"It didn't before, when he wrecked his car trying to come see me. You have to believe what you wrote on that exam, Cob."

"That was a fairy tale." Now that she'd exposed his appalling weakness, he didn't feel so wise.

They lay listening to Dylan's lilting guitar on "Desolation Row," eyes communing through that long beautiful song, his hand covering her ribs, outspread fingers reminding him of the damage he could've done. He rested his cheek against her palm—release had emptied his entire skin of structure: he'd become a water balloon like the ones he used to fill from the backyard hose, small enough not to burst immediately—even falling on the grass wouldn't break them. He'd roll one from hand to hand, enjoying that he could hold something almost entirely liquid, enclose it with his palms and let it slip out past his fingers. He felt that malleable now, but more amazing than his physical overthrow was emotion turned inside-out, preconception vaporized—she hadn't just blindsided him, she'd come at him from a different dimension—how was he supposed to counter that?

"I'll be your perfect lover," he said. "Teach me. Forget I ever hurt you. Be my—"

"You'll learn better if you don't think you own me."

"I know I don't. I love you—do you even care?"

HE WAS STILL feral, dangerous, but her body and mind were resolving their disconnect in his favor. If she stayed, she'd be alert to the harm they both so easily dealt out. Weighing the extent of her guilt versus his was a heartless exercise—time to let all that go, to start afresh. "Teasing becomes abuse," she said. "We have to stop that."

"Don't wear those undershirts anymore. They make me crazy."

She touched the left-veering bridge of his nose which must've been his finest feature when it was intact—under his skin she could feel the narrow seam where the bone had knit. "Tell me why you were crying."

"When I was sixteen I was with a girl, she was hot for me but I came almost the second I touched her—on her clothes. She was grossed out and told her friends, they told their friends and by the end of the day every girl in school was calling me Dunn Quick—"

"So you've been having revenge ever since."

"I found a way to make women need me so bad, it didn't matter what I could do—worked too, till I met you."

"Anything less than complete honesty will trap us worse."

He laughed cynically. "Speaking of honesty, does Walt know you're here?"

"This moment specifically? No. But that I will be? Yes."

"And doesn't mind?"

"He understands. This life's an opportunity—another one—to get it right."

"I'm too late—you two already have everything sewed up—whatever you do with me, you'll go back to him."

"Whatever I feel for him, I've come back to you. Doesn't that count?"

"Only one of us can claim you," he reminded her.

"So is this another cycle of jealousy and vengeance?"

"Good chance."

"Then I should leave now," she said.

"That's right." Their eyes met.

"But this is where I want to be," she murmured into his chest, the squeeze of his arms answering. Walt was wide open, now Cob was risking his fortressed heart—could she accept them both and keep her balance? The failure of any leg of a triangle collapsed it from two dimensions to one. "I think there's enough love for us all."

CHAPTER 9

Projection

"Playing DJ?" he asked, looking up from the fridge.

"Think I'll make some tapes," waving a record jacket his direction.

The phone rang—Cob's supervisor asked could he start in the morning? He agreed to be there at eight, then knelt behind her where she sat on the floor. Knees apart he hugged her spine to him, arching over her head to kiss upside down on her nose.

"When I come home from work tomorrow will you be here?"

"I'll tape some stuff—when I'm done I'll go pack. Yeah, one more night I guess."

He rested his arms across her neck and shoulders, cheek against her hair—he'd never been possessive, had nothing but contempt for those who were, but here he was, badly in love, acting just like the rest of them. Once the heart was in charge, a person would do any damn fool thing—like drive seventy-five miles in the rain in an old clunker low on gas, to kiss a guy for a minute. Or give another chance to a power-tripper who'd hurt her? Well, there was plenty of foolishness to go around—how about Walt breaking his leg coming to see her on a night when he must've known he should stay home? Or doing nothing to stop Laura from being here? That definitely qualified as foolish.

She shifted the album cover—there in her lap was his dog-eared *The Hite Report*. Now that he'd completely dropped his guard, she was spying on him—that was so weird—"Ever read it?" sitting beside her.

"No" she said. "But it appears you have."

"Some of these women are sure they can have endless orgasms, bing bing bing."

"And how does that make them feel?"

"Fantastic, I assumed—sounds great, doesn't it? Men are so bounded—this book convinced me women are unlimited sexually."

"So you studied this, and used what you learned for domination."

"I didn't think of it that way."

"But you used it," she pressed.

"To overcome my—" He began to shake. "Sex and power have a lot of overlap, but heart is one place power never takes you." She turned to hug him while he cried; when he was done he wiped his face then blew his nose.

"Bet you haven't been blubbered over like this."

"ACTUALLY I HAVE," thinking of Walt. Sometimes she wished he'd stayed in Colorado—by uprooting and setting up sixty miles away—a separation emphasized by the Bay Area being on the northern half of her California map and Santa Cruz on the southern—he'd come partway, neither with her nor severed, but opposite to everything here—coursework, Cob, her housemates, Berkeley itself. She felt smarter and more alert than she'd ever been, but wound tighter too—seeing Walt was a vacation for her nerves. But now that she had a month to decompress, when she could really enjoy being with him, he was gone. Cob's new devotion felt heavy, airless, selfish. She thumped his shoulder. "Let's go out."

"There's a Peter Sellers movie at the rep house—my treat."

"First I need a shower."

"Down the hall."

The long tub would need serious scrubbing before she'd bathe in it, but plastic curtains hung into it from an elliptical rod suspended by wires from the ceiling; the big showerhead on its tall freestanding pipe resembled a giant sunflower leaning down—even Cob could stand under it without bending. He soaped his loofah and scrubbed her in loving detail, then she scrubbed him—he had soft black hair in a line from crotch to breastbone and a little fur across his chest—wet, it looked like the letter T. He squatted in the tub so she could wash his fine abundant hair—took two passes to get it clean, then a lot of rinsing. When he washed hers she leaned against him while his long fingers worked her scalp. Once he'd rinsed her she puddled shampoo in her hand and swabbed his dick, then shut off the water while they fooled around. The bath was a dangerous place, slippery with shampoo, the wall too far away for leverage. He pushed the curtains apart and sat on the rim of the tub where she straddled his lap, but as their hard breathing and skin slapping together got noisy, someone banged on the door.

"Hey man I need a shower—go fuck somewhere else!"

"Five minutes," Cob yelled back. He didn't want to stop but she climbed off and restarted the water. "You're so considerate," he said deprecatingly.

"Pretend you're the person out in the hall." They dried quickly then she put on his robe, he wrapped his towel around his waist. On their way back to the apartment the guy checked her out, pulling Cob aside and after a brief exchange laughing crudely.

"Comparing notes?" she said, closing the apartment door. That guy was a creep—why even talk to him?

"He was pointing out I don't bring women home. But here you are."

"He must think that means something."

"It does." As she started to put on her bra he shook his head. "Wear your undershirt tonight."

"You asked me not to."

"I know. But—" eyes at half-mast. She let the straps slide off and pulled on her clean undershirt, watching him watch her. Buttoning her flannel shirt she frowned—he hadn't moved.

"Going like that? You'll get cold."

He shook himself awake and got dressed, glancing out the window. "Umbrella weather. I get really tired of rain sometimes—in five winters here I've never seen it snow."

"I'm not as in love with snow as I was before the plows buried us— fine with me if it's somewhere else."

Cob bought the tickets then they went to a tavern across from the theater so they'd see when the line started. Ordering glasses of wine they considered the appetizer menu—nothing he'd eat. He made a face when she ordered garlic bread.

"You have too many rules," she laughed. "Loosen up."

"I've been fruitarian three and a half years—some people have to force themselves but it suits me." He took a small bag of almonds from his pocket and dipped out a handful to heap on a napkin between their glasses. The waitress put a red plastic mesh basket in front of them, and Laura tore off a piece of bread dripping with butter. She pressed a napkin to it, soaking up the excess before taking a bite.

"Wish you wouldn't eat that." Her kiss was going to gag him.

"But I like this."

She was done obeying. Last summer he'd told her to purify her temple so he could worship there—a pearl of lies around a grain of truth—now he was on his knees no matter what she ate, what she looked like, anything. Only moments of revelation in biology had ever reordered his perceptions so thoroughly. When he was in control she'd seemed like every other girl he'd taken on—he still didn't understand how he'd been so wrong. But he was. They finished their wine while she ate about half the garlic bread, then they went across the street.

"Working Saturday?" she asked as the early show audience streamed out.

"Every day except Christmas and New Year's. Thinking of staying?"

"No, Saturday's a good day to go."

He'd been lucky to interest her this long. She was probably thinking about Walt the whole time. He must be a better lover—wasn't that what stoners were good for? Doubts pierced him like skewers, punching through his vitals. She reached up, cool fingers on his neck bending him to her kiss, and chided, "When you can't see the whole picture, leave the blank spots empty."

"How do you know so much?"

"Maybe I've been hurt more than you." As his face pinched she said, "Walt's hurt me too. Stop feeling sorry for yourself."

In the auditorium she headed for the last row.

"Why sit clear back here? You can hardly see."

"I don't want anyone behind me."

"Let's move to the middle," he suggested. "There's still decent seats, and I'll sit behind you. Then I can lean over your shoulder and put my hands on you."

She grinned and kissed him. "Yeah." She'd never seen a couple sit that way but she liked fooling around in the semi-dark, sounds and images surrounding them. Walt cared about movies too much—this'd be fun.

The Party was a plotless comedy—Peter Sellers, a movie extra who blew up a fort before the actors and cameras were in place, through a mixup got an invitation to the producer's party. Waterways throughout the mogul's hip modern house set up Sellers's clumsiness to cause an escalating series of problems. His Indian accent and obsequiousness were pitch-perfect, but by the time the host's hippie daughter and her wacked-out friends showed up with a small wildly painted elephant to frolic in a house now full of soapsuds, the movie had lost all sense of proportion. The producer's eventual discovery of his klutz guest's identity was anti-climactic, which was fine with Laura. Cob distracted her more and more till they weren't even pretending to watch, his hands all over inside her shirt, his mouth on her neck. Back home an usher would've told them to cut it out, but this was Berkeley—as long as they didn't disturb their neighbors nobody'd stop them. When the lights came up they stood, embracing across the seat back, kissing. Again she had misgivings—all this was likely to blow up in their faces—but she owed it to him and Walt both, to neutralize their jealous history, if that was possible.

On a different route home they passed the Keystone—she'd only gone once, last summer. But: Saturday night—Commander Cody and his Lost Planet Airmen. She grabbed his arm. "Cob, let's go!"

"Thought you were leaving Saturday."

"Oh I love Commander Cody—we have to go—it'll be my Christmas present."

"Really? Thanks." They checked the time—two shows, 8 and 10.

"Let's go to the late show—mind losing a little sleep?"

"I've lost my peace of mind—why would sleep matter?"

SHE MADE TWO tapes, one rock'n'roll—Little Feat, Commander Cody, New Riders of the Purple Sage, Jefferson Starship—and the other more thoughtful—Laura Nyro, Bob Dylan, a couple Leonard Cohen songs, Joan Armatrading. Midafternoon she was done, and as she wrapped them in a bandana so they had a chance of surviving the US Mail, she thought of Cob's *sinsemilla* and took it out of the freezer. She got a laugh as she helped herself—Cob had no qualms about stealing, and Walt thought anybody's stash was fair game—she was creating their first bond. Carefully bundling the fat bud inside several rolling papers labeled LATER so he wouldn't open it at his parents,' she jotted a note.

> Walt Sweetheart—
>
> Here's your Christmas present—tunes for a long drive. I'm going to Santa Cruz Sunday—right now I'm at Cob's. We did some mushrooms. You two should talk—the way your energy attacks each other hurts me too. Think about it.
>
> Walt when will I see you? We don't have to wait till your cast is off...
>
> Another kiss like the one at the airport—mwaa! Laura

From the post office she went to her house but it was four thirty—she had to get back to Cob's with his key. Jack looked her over.

"Staying with him?"

"For the moment. Anyone call?"

He shook his head. "Laura, Cob destroys women."

"You're always bad-mouthing him—if you have a reason let's hear it." She dropped her pack and sat on a kitchen chair facing him.

"Three years now I've watched him in action. He picks up women—like he did you—and in a matter of months they're gorgeous junkies following him around like he's the Giver of the Fix—he's another Rasputin."

"You're wrong Jack. But you said—"

"I knew this freshman from Oregon—you wouldn't believe how beautiful she turned out to be. Before she killed herself."

"And you think that's because of Cob?"

"It was. Emily and I were friends, and she used to talk about him—not much, like it was all secret—but I got the picture. She was crazy for him, but she couldn't handle that he had other women. He didn't care, so she turned it on herself."

"Well Jack, thanks for your concern, but things have changed since Thanksgiving. That won't happen again." She narrowed her eyes at him. "Do I look like a junkie?"

"You did."

"If I start looking that way again, be sure to tell me."

WHEN SHE OPENED the door to Cob's knock, he grappled her to him—his day had been weird—maybe it was the afterburn of the psilocybin, but his former ease with the mostly Mexican custodial workforce had evaporated. He used to imagine they could understand his fractured Spanish—today he recognized their smiles and nods as the reflexes of underlings, and sensed the gulf between his world and theirs. Despite working side by side scraping the urethane off the edges of a gym floor where the sander wouldn't reach, he had higher-paid more interesting options in his future; they were parked in this job. Around other students he flaunted being fruitarian, but at lunch he could feel his co-workers observing every mouthful, comparing his hard dry nuts and figs with their burritos and tamales, thinking he was strange. When being in college implied living in a comfort bubble, he'd set himself apart by keeping his fellow students' toilets clean and sieving butts from the big sand-filled ashtrays outside lecture halls. But this underclass didn't consider him one of them.

"Let's do the rest of those mushrooms," he told Laura, letting her back out of his embrace. "I only got halfway—everything's coming apart."

"Tripping won't solve your problems, it'll just make them obvious—"

"What if I eat some, and you just oversee? You're my teacher—don't abandon me when I really need you." He watched her weigh that—she must be thinking this was an opportunity to get even.

But she said, "I'll stay."

He got out the Baggie—seven caps left.

"Give me one," she said.

He chewed up the rest and they split an apple to clear the taste; at the window she looked out into the darkness. The rain had let up and finally the clouds were breaking apart. When she turned, he was right there, urgent with questions he couldn't articulate.

"What did you feel yesterday?" she asked.

"Death. Didn't you?"

She nodded. "Right here with us."

"Why didn't you leave? I thought you'd be afraid, but you never—"

"I accepted it. Once you're willing to die, fear has no power."

His face crumpled. "It's gonna be so bad when you leave."

"This room's a box—feel the anxieties trapped in here? Let's walk."

It was Friday night; though students were sparse, townspeople were out in crowds. She set their course past bars and cafés bright with chatter and bustle, out of the business district, climbing toward the ridge, quieter, only an occasional car passing. The air was clean and chilly, their breath puffs of steam. They paused to look at the city grid of lights below them, the dark water, the Bay Bridge lit by parallel red and white rivers, and across, San Francisco. Lights described its terrain, a single rosy crescent of cloud hovering like a partial halo.

"Do you love your mom?" she asked.

That caught him by surprise—he only thought of his parents in terms of how alienated they were—that woman who wanted certain things from him and refused to know the rest—did he love her? What did that mean? Finally he said, "That connection's weak. I look at how narrow they are—her and Dad both—and I feel like an orphan. The family I belong with is here—fruitarians I can share a holiday meal with and not feel like a freak, some other biology students, you. That's about it."

"No friends in Nebraska?"

"When I went back in May, the guys at my parents' party wanted to compare cars and go shooting and get drunk—nothing there for me."

A glow surrounded her hair, an aura that wasn't streetlights. Her face was changing as though different people were passing through her, each manifesting briefly; he watched fascinated while they grew uglier, distorting into demons, monsters. Fear stole the heat from his body, he recoiled as their grotesqueness increased. On the verge of screaming, he caught her eyes again—still hers, no death-mask, just her calm gaze. The faces superimposed on hers were kindly now, and he was startled to realize that all he'd seen—was still seeing—were projections from his own mind. The comfort of wishful thinking gone, frigid clarity flooded him. He clasped her hands, the circle of their contact channeling energy from Earth to sky, their bodies elongating as it drew them upward like a strong wind. When he thought that flow would buffet his mind loose, he let go. The rush ceased.

She headed downhill, he followed dumbly. When they reached his apartment she took out the key—she had a key to his place but he didn't—she was controlling him—

"I feel odd having your key." She put it on the table. Even as paranoia crept in, the threat he'd tensed to fight off, dissolved—still projecting. He drooped, humbled again. She lit a candle and they sat facing on the floor, the window behind her.

"I couldn't understand anything until now," he said.

"Let's make a pact."

She extended her right hand, fingers pointing at the ceiling, the sky beyond it. He met it with his left, her palm in his.

"Let's break the cycle this time," she said. "We'll include Walt when he's back—we should make peace."

"Let's make peace." He bowed to her. "I love you." To which she said nothing, but put her hand over his heart, a sensation that hurt like feet thawing.

Later he dreamed he was walking on the beach with her; Walt was in the water and she swam out, they played beyond the surf zone while he stood on the sand calling. They body-surfed in together, and as the wave receded he saw they were joined sexually; he turned to go. But they came up fast behind him, one on each side, and pulled him into the water. A wave smashed down, his face hit the bottom, he thought he should just let the ocean finish him off, but as though he weighed nothing they led him through the next crest, guiding him out. Now he understood to pierce the rising wave so it broke behind him, and the swell lifted him, his legs pedaling. The surge passed, he was floating.

They held hands on the surface, the flow between his heart and theirs forming an inscribed triangle. He felt Walt's love for Laura and hers for both of them, then, tentatively, a bond with Walt. Back on the sand that certainty blurred—he was an outsider, their promises made to each other not him. She wrapped her legs around Walt and they rose into the air, leaving him alone, cold. While he sat in the sand stricken, arms gathered up and rocked him, a voice cooing and singing—his mother. He felt huge and awkward in her embrace but she didn't seem to notice, petting his hair; he put his arms around her remembering that original love.

In the dimness Laura's eyes were on him, perceiving his dream, her finger on his chest like an arrow going through him. He moved so their hearts were aligned, heat and energy lacing them together—this was the missing element, in whose presence everything fit, worked, made sense. As love swept through, the accretion of pain eroded from around his heart, dissolving into the energy stream, broken smaller and smaller, becoming the salt of spent tears.

CHAPTER 10

Across the Miles

L aura Toots—

I ran into a guy I knew at CU and I'm crashing at his house in College Park, going places in my '65 Dodge Dart—what an ugly crate. If Rusty's charm level is zero, this car's well into negative numbers. But I can drive! It's an automatic, and with my cast across the seat I can use my left foot for the gas and brake. Small, but a victory.

Your kiss at the airport was the best thing that's happened to me since we moved to California—thank you thank you thank you (you may imagine my gratitude filling a ream of paper). I'd given up, knew you weren't coming, knew there were reasons, but—Then, my name in your voice, your sweet body in my hands—(thank you)

Didn't have time to tell you—that mugging messed up my leg—I'm back to zero, condemned to crutches till mid-February. I asked the doc could he make this cast shorter, he said he'd rather wrap it clear to my balls. Well I tried...

Hope you're with Tom and Opal—miss you bad but it's better not to be near you till I'm healed. Are you and Cob figuring it out? Love's not a cage, at least ours isn't.

Wishing to be your undershirt, Walt

AS IT NEARED midnight, the noise emphasized Walt's isolation. He wasn't close to anyone here—Brian was a cruiser, doing what felt good and avoiding whatever didn't, and as for his brother Grant, talking to him was work—there was so much he didn't know, yet he resented having anything explained. In the pantry off the kitchen Walt closed the bifold door and scrunched back where sacks of beans and rice and canned goods somewhat muffled the party, and dialed his house in Santa Cruz. Tom answered.

"Oh hey Walt, I was hoping that was you. Opal and Laura and I dropped acid 'bout an hour ago. Whoa buddy, you didn't tell me—"

"Lotta changes, yeah," he said flatly—was Tom drooling over Laura now? That was ugly squared: the prospect of his best friend hustling his girlfriend was multiplied by how that would hurt the woman Tom had supposedly gone out there to visit. If he was being a jerk and falling for Laura for her looks, where did that leave Opal, waiting years to be with him, keeping her heart clear for his love? But Walt had no standing to say that—Tom might feel the same way about him.

"You're our number one topic," Tom went on. "If you trip I bet we could hook up—want to?"

"Yeah, I'll see what I can find. Put Opal on."

"Hi Walt," her melodious voice. "We'd love it if you could home in on us."

Then he had to ask, "Everything cool with Tom?"

"Of course," then in a voice rough with emotion, "God I've missed him."

Hope you don't miss each other completely, he thought, but he said, "Lucky lady. Put Laura on now."

"Hi babe, how come you're so far away? I was gonna come kiss you—"

When she said that, he was back at the airport and she was slamming into him with the full force of desire. She wouldn't do anything with Tom... He laughed, his heart rising choked him. "Toots—I wish—"

"Maybe we can just have five minutes every couple weeks, till your cast is off."

All he could do was kiss the phone. He heard shouting and horns. "It's midnight here. Happy new year my love." She said something he couldn't hear through Patti Smith singing "Gloria" loud enough to blow the speakers. "Look for me in the ether." He came out into the crashing din, found Brian pogo-ing with a girl. Once the song had ended Walt tapped him with his crutch.

"Psychedelics?"

Brian waded back into the party; Walt stood by a window where no one would knock him off-balance. As *Horses* blasted, a guy came over whose pupils obliterated his irises; hair matted, beard long and tangled, he looked like he'd been living in a culvert.

"Head drugs?" he shouted.

Walt nodded.

"Quiet?" he hollered.

On their way upstairs the noise relented slightly—with Walt's door closed they sighed with relief.

The guy took a pouch from inside his jeans, removing a pill bottle. "How much you want?"

"To get to California."

"One hit should work." Walt accepted one of the turquoise cylinders—like beads without holes. "What can I offer you?"

"Could use a few bucks."

He thumbed through his wallet. "Five OK?"

"Five'd be great man."

Paying him, Walt lifted the water glass he kept on the windowsill. "Cheers." He swallowed the tiny pill. "And thanks."

WHEN HE CAME on to it he tried to visualize Laura but her face kept sliding off and changing so he focused on her kiss at the airport. As he extended she was reaching too; he pictured his living room, the three of them sitting on the threadbare rug with herb tea in front of them and a candle burning. He heard music—not the cacophony downstairs but Joni Mitchell singing "A Strange Boy," and then as though they'd walked in the door of his head they were in him, speaking and listening; he could feel the room in Santa Cruz, they could hear the party.

Opal was a being made of light, he felt her eyes looking into his, assuring him love and freedom were interknit between them. Tom was the guy he'd learned the projectionist business from, the only friend he'd told what happened between him and Laura—both her grad-school surprise and the way their relationship heated up in response. Tom and Opal were like a pair of almonds in a single shell, formed against each other, distinct but with one origin, one substance—and both loved him. And Laura was completely inside him, one with his body and mind, her face fitting his skin—if he looked in a mirror he'd see her features instead of his own.

He took them all on the pain tour of his leg, and in concert their energy bound up the psychic wounds that had bled away his strength since that night when Cob's dominance had shoved him off the highway. A crowd of mistakes like ravenous baby birds clamored for him to regurgitate hurt and anger, but as he and Laura shared that thought, they knew the futility of appeasing them.

"It's OK to be with Cob," he promised. "I know I haven't lost you."

"We'll understand more, and love better," she pledged.

Then they danced, Walt's body propped on a bed in Maryland while his spirit wove figures with these three he loved. They didn't leave so much as fade, and when they were gone he re-awoke to where he was, at peace—as long as Laura kept her head clear she didn't need his protection. And if she couldn't, there was nothing he could do anyway.

PART TWO

"Angels Can Fly 'Cause They Take Themselves Lightly"

CHAPTER 11

Stream

rriving in Berkeley late Friday afternoon, she planned to go home first to unload her stuff, but as though piloting itself, Rusty took her to Cob's. She knocked on #7. He opened the door partway, blinking, shuffling, looking past her.

"All right if I come in?"

"Oh, um, yeah." As she stepped in she saw the young woman sitting up in his bed, a sheet pulled to her breasts.

"Hi," she beamed, "I'm Stream. You must be Laura—Cob told me about you."

"We met at Diane's Christmas party," he said, pushing the door shut, eyes darting everywhere except to meet Laura's. "She's—ah—been here since."

"Oh." She'd dreaded he'd be an emotional wreck, clinging and needy, but… Stream's auburn hair was as dense as Walt's and some of the same colors, her wide smile crinkled the bridge of her nose, her small hands letting go the sheet revealed big breasts as tanned as her face and shoulders.

"I was stayin' at my dad's in Mexico but he kicked me out, and I was s'posed to stay with my mom but her boyfriend kept hassling me so I came to San Francisco and met a lady who knows Diane. We came to her party on Christmas, and soon's I met Cob we clicked. So now I'm here."

"For how long?" Not that it mattered one way or another.

"I dunno—long's it's OK." She looked at Laura with a shrewdness her air of naïveté belied. "Is it? I mean, Cob told me you were his lady, but he said you have this other guy too, so…?"

"That's up to Cob—I don't live here."

"I mean, he said he'd see you when you got back."

Laura'd just left Walt. Her month in Santa Cruz overlapped by maybe an hour with his arrival from traveling cross-country, but in that short interval he'd plunged into depression. Disinclined to dwell on what that gloom might mean, she'd driven back here thinking about Cob, welcoming the prospect of his affection. She scolded herself—that's what fantasies did—set you up and let you down. "So, um, Stream, what're you up to?"

"Hangin' out. Berkeley seems rough though—there's some weird people around."

"Not everybody likes it. I'm a grad student here."

"Oh wow, you must be smart," glowing with admiration. "I tried psychology but we hadda learn all this anatomy and brain science—it was so boring. I thought we were gonna study dreams, stuff like that."

"I think eventually you do, but you need to understand the physiology first."

"Not me. I seen plenty of shrinks, and none of 'em ever got inside my head far enough to believe what I told 'em—that's why I wanted to be one myself—I wouldn't act like that. When people tell me why they do stuff, I take their word for it, not 'she's this type so when she says this she really means that.' None of 'em had a clue." Getting up she pulled on a t-shirt, flowered undies and a long skirt made from an Indian-print bedspread, then on her knees began to grope around under the bed. "Cob, seen my shoes? Thought I kicked 'em under here, but—"

Her question summoned him from the kingdom of lost thoughts. "By the chair." She crossed the room quickly and stepped into a pair of broken-down penny loafers, saw it wasn't raining out, grabbed his jean jacket and her purse, saying, "See ya later," and breezed by Laura. It was a measure of Cob's transformation that she had wide hips and a rounded belly she made no attempt to suck in—last fall he wouldn't have given her a second thought. He went to the window.

"Shit," he muttered, glancing back Laura's direction, looking like he'd been caught emptying the till and was about to get fired or worse. "Uh…"

"Hi Cob," Laura said neutrally.

"I'm sor—"

"No, it's OK. I hoped you weren't pining for me."

He dropped into his armchair. "I have been, kind of."

"I'd think you were too busy for that, between work and Stream."

"No, there's always time for misery—I fit it in somehow," wryly, meeting her eyes finally. She started toward him then stopped—wasn't letting him off that easy.

"Tell me about her."

"Well, at the party we got really stoned and camped out in Diane's room, and when it was time to leave we were still exploring, so she came with."

He wasn't trolling for sympathy—should she walk out now?

"She's the most unattached person I've ever met—owns almost nothing, just borrows what she needs then gives it back or passes it on. Street people have stuff, nomads have stuff—not Stream. She has what she's wearing, but even that—somebody gave her that skirt." His voice thickened. "She's studied tantric sex—I've learned a lot. I was hoping to share that with you."

Laura sank onto the hard chair at his card table. It wasn't that she cared if he saw other women, this was just such a complete surprise. He was too far away, over by the window—she couldn't cross all that space. They looked at each other, the room seeming to stretch, carrying them further apart. Noticing in the silence the hum of his fridge, she wondered if he ever cleaned the door seal—a repairman once told her a torn seal would double your electric bill. The phone rang, he came to the crate by the fridge to answer it.

"Oh, hi…. Yeah, a little space'd be good… No, it's too—don't go… Yeah… Thanks." He hung up. "She won't be back till tomorrow when I get off work. It's funny—after you were here I got another key made, but I never gave it to her."

"She didn't need it?"

He shrugged. "If she was going out she'd just wait till afternoon—wasn't a problem. But I had an extra the whole time." He shook his head, looking at her. "It's yours." He separated the key from his ring and put it on the table in front of her, giving her a quizzical look. She touched it with one fingertip, he knelt and put his cheek against her knees. Without asking her permission, her fingers snagged the band off his ponytail then wove into his hair, massaging his scalp. One of his hands traveled up her thigh, the other down her calf to her ankle. She bent to kiss his upturned ear, his cheek, he met her mouth then they stood as one, as though she'd just now arrived and Stream had never been here.

"Will you use a rubber?"

"Don't you have your diaphragm?"

"She probably lays every guy she meets—I doubt they're all clean." She hated to sound catty but that had to be true.

"I don't have any."

"Then do us a favor and go get some."

He grabbed his wallet off the fridge, kissed her quickly and dashed out. As the door rattled against the frame and the thump of his shoes left the stairs, she looked around—why was she staying in another couple's bedroom? She flipped through his tapes, put on Miles Davis's *In a Silent Way* then watched the flow of cars in the clear darkening evening—students were back. She'd imagined she'd be spending the weekend with Cob, but now it was looking like time for reading, laundry, a long walk. She might be damming up Stream's interlude but that didn't mean she was going to have one. They hadn't talked about which classes they were signed up for—she'd benefited studying with him, but expecting this term to be like fall was just another fantasy.

He came in breathless, grinning wide, and turned off the overhead light, hustling her to the bed with such earnestness she had to smile. He undressed fast, then hands on the top button of her jeans, stopped.

"May I?"

"Yes." He resumed getting her clothes off then dancing her in a tight circle by the bed, arching his neck, breath on her shoulder, his new awareness tuning his stimulation to hers.

This delayed welcome was everything Walt's return hadn't been— their "triangle" was really just a line with Laura in the middle, pulled from one man to the other.

"It's GOOD I met up with Stream," he said, aglow with enough happiness for both of them. "I was so lonesome."

"How long will she be around?" shifting to press her spine against him, fitting the bend of her legs to his.

"I don't know—she's just here," stroking her hip, "and one day she'll be gone. I won't have to say anything."

"But what if—" She had no right. She tried to see it differently. "It was considerate of her to give us space."

"She's an outstanding human being. I told her how I feel about you."

"Which is—"

"I love you," his breath in her hair. "You saved my heart."

"I just showed you where it is."

"How's Walt?" amorously mauling the back of her neck.

"Bummed. He's stuck in that cast another month—if he doesn't cheer up then, I'm not sure what to do."

"How's his car? Is it as good as Rusty?"

She laughed. "On New Year's he and some friends got high and gave it a wild paint job. He put in a tape deck and decent speakers, so it's nowhere near as bad as it must've been when his mom signed it over."

"My heart didn't exactly skip a beat when I saw my car the first time. My dad's a practical joker. On my sixteenth birthday Rusty was parked in front of our house in the morning. Dad made a big deal giving me the keys—'your first car son.' I was thinking the whole time 'he's hiding some other car, and once he gets the right level of misery out of me he'll let me find it.' I mean, he's a car dealer, right? I had my eye on this blue '66

Mustang on his lot, thought for sure he was saving it for me. But Rusty was it—I didn't believe it for a week. It's his favorite joke—he loves to tell his friends how I kept looking for the 'real one,' then laughs at what a sucker I was."

"I see where you get your sharp edge."

"It's second nature to carve up assholes—like Jack."

"Speaking of, he told me he hates you because you made a girl commit suicide."

He was momentarily silent. "Who?" his voice remote, not offering a name. Waiting for her to say it.

"He said she was from Oregon—Emily."

"Emily," he said flatly. "She threw herself at me, wouldn't take no, then when I said no anyhow, she went off the deep end. But I have to say in my defense that she was from a little town and the whole trip of trying to fit in on such a huge campus was very hard. She got mugged the first month she was here—I think her whole Berkeley experience was like that."

"Including you?"

After a pause, "Yeah."

"Could you have prevented that?"

"Sure. I coulda married her—that's what she wanted."

"Was she pregnant?"

"No, she just wanted to own me—to her that meant marriage. When I wasn't interested she flipped out, drank a tumbler of vodka with a bottle of sleeping pills. By the time her roommate wondered why she wouldn't get up, she was dead."

"Jack knew her—he said you turned her into this gorgeous—"

"Look, Jack thinks I'm some evil magician. I brought her beauty to the surface—that's all I've ever done, with any woman," and folding her into the closing arc of his arms, "With you. It was already there."

It seemed early but he was bustling around. "Going somewhere?"

"Work. Today and tomorrow are pure gravy—time and a half. Can't pass up seventy bucks a day. I pay the landlord for the whole term when I get my check—I don't have to think about it for months, and he appreciates me."

"I've never even met my landlord—Beth's on the lease, and everybody pays her. So is he rolling back your rent?"

"I doubt it—he already gives me a deal. Yours go down?"

"Not yet, but Beth thinks maybe in February."

He kissed her tenderly. "Will you be here when I get home today?"

"No. Isn't Stream coming back?"

"Probably." He had a possessive little grin. "I just like the thought that you'd lie around all day thinking about me, and when I got back you'd be all hot."

"No Cob." Stream probably did, but what else did that wisp have going on?

"TA-ing again?" he asked.

"Two sections."

"The department gave you mine," he nodded approval. "Good for you."

"Then what're you doing?"

"After you complained about that dolt in the stat lab they gave me his job." He shot her a bright smile and grabbing his parka went out. "See ya Toots."

She flinched—only Walt ever called her that. Putting on Cob's bathrobe she took her new key and his toiletries, and padded to the shower, planning her day while she scrubbed herself. On her way back to the apartment she encountered the guy from #8, who stopped to look her over.

"What happened to that other chick?" he said.

"She'll be back."

"Cozy," his leer taking in the curve of her hips, gauging her breasts beneath folds of terrycloth.

She went past him and let herself into Cob's apartment, thinking she'd rather have housemates who shared the whole place—she sure didn't like being in public between showering and getting dressed. She dawdled over tea, finally put on her parka and pack—but when she opened the door there sat Stream, looking ragged.

"C'n I come in? Cob here?"

"He's at work." Laura stepped aside.

Stream came in and dropped her purse. "That was so bad."

"Are you OK?" Already adding water to the kettle, "Want some tea? Rose-hip?"

"Thanks." The girl stood blinking, tears magnifying her light-brown eyes. "That guy was so mean—why'd he wanna hurt me?"

"What guy? Tell me what happened." Laura put an arm around her, guiding her to the armchair where she folded up.

"After I left here I was gonna get a room at a hotel, there was this guy in the lobby, a business suit. He bought me a glass of wine, started comin' on to me, we went to his room. He was in town for some conference—prob'ly married. We did some sex, that was good, we fell asleep. I like sleeping with guys—they're so warm. But then he woke up and freaked out, like he forgot I was there only there I was. He yelled at me, I put on my clothes—it was two in the morning—I mean *jeez*—and he pushed me out the door. I called that I needed my purse, then he opened the door really fast and yanked me back in and started slapping me around, telling me to shut up and calling me names—he was nuts! Then he turned on the light in the bathroom and he had a drug kit on the counter—I didn't see that before. He got out the syringe then I completely freaked, grabbed my purse and ran out. There was one light on in the lobby, the guy at the desk was asleep so I scrunched down in a chair and spent the night there. I got so cold."

"After you have some tea you should get in bed."

"What about you?"

"I'm just leaving."

"I gotta find a better setup—I was freezing in that chair, and all I could think about was Cob, but he was with you. I've slept a lotta places, but it kinda caught me by surprise." She snuffled. "Dad says I have no anchor."

"Why'd he kick you out?"

"He told me to stay away from the servants, but the guy who took care of the cars…" She closed her eyes, head tilted to one side, mouth partway open as if tasting his kiss. "When Dad found out, he fired him and told me to leave. I begged him to keep Rodrigo on—I felt so awful costing him his job—but he wouldn't. Dad said he'd give me six months to get my head straight, then commit me if I didn't."

"What for? You're not—"

"One of the Shrink Parade told him I was schizophrenic, that's why I couldn't hold a job or behave myself. That's complete bullshit—the guy laid me twice then got some guilt trip about it and made up all this shit he told my dad. He said drugs had made me crazy—I dropped acid a lot, but it didn't mess me up. Didn't make me see things Dad's way—maybe that's what was wrong with it."

The kettle whistled. Laura poured tea and brought her the mug. "Take care, OK?" kissing her forehead.

LAURA WAS BRINGING things in at home when the rain arrived, and finished at a run—the bottom fell from the cloud and her last box got wet. Wiping the covers of her books she thought about Cob—even knowing the circumstances, it pinched her to think of him with Stream—their pleasure, and now the distress he could soothe away…

CHAPTER 12

New Wave

Grant, free paper of music news in hand, raced home through the downpour excited. "Hey Walt, there's this New Wave band called Dead Kennedys—clear out on the edge. I gotta see 'em—wanna come?"

"I'm working tonight. Where they playing?"

"Place called Mabuhay Gardens in Frisco."

"Don't call it 'Frisco'—that's a tourist thing. Call it SF if it's too much work to say 'San Francisco.'"

"Yeah yeah. Can I borrow the car?"

"That's pretty far—isn't there anybody playing here in town?"

"Not that I wanna hear—I just gotta go—they have this lead singer named Jello Biafra—I heard he's really great."

"I'll give you Laura's phone number in Berkeley—I don't want you driving back here at night with it raining like this."

"You sound like Mom—I'm not a kid y'know." As Walt glowered he backed off. "Aright aright, gimme her number." Then he laughed lewdly. "She's pretty hot—you're not worried we might do something?"

"Shove it Grant. To her you're my little brother."

"She doesn't even know me."

"Sure she does—she lived with me in Boulder, remember?"

But that was impossible—that woman had been a real hardass—when he visited that summer, while Walt was at work she decided to set him straight about all the hassles he got into with authority, and gave him endless shit about being lazy and irresponsible, causing every problem he complained about. They had a horrendous argument and by the time Walt got home they were ready to go at each other like cats. No way was she this sexy woman. "Nah, that was somebody else."

Walt looked gut-punched. "She's changed, but that's her."

Still, he handed over his keys, so Grant left. Heading up the coast he got what Walt meant about driving—he could barely see the road. When he got to Pacifica he called Laura.

"Maybe I'll go too—come here first." She gave him directions, he got lost three times trying to find the place—it was ridiculous how many roads there were. Around seven he finally knocked on her front door. A guy opened it and looked at him.

"Um hi, I'm here to see Laura."

"In the kitchen." He followed him in, there she was. He studied her—yeah, same person he'd met a couple years ago, but she looked so different, she almost wasn't—the Laura he remembered from Boulder had an ordinary build, OK face but nothing special—this woman radiated sex—she was beautiful.

"Hi Grant. Want something to eat?"

"What is there?"

"I'm having rice with vegetables."

He made a face. "I guess."

"What do you usually eat?"

"Hamburgers, pizza. Stuff like that."

"This is better for you."

"You and Walt—man, I feel like I'm gettin' the lecture, like you're all tryin' to reform me or something."

"There's worse things," she teased, and his chest tightened.

"Feed me then." He gave her a come-on look and sat down.

The guy who'd let him in was standing there watching. "Want a beer?"

"Yeah, hey thanks." He wasn't old enough—maybe the guy couldn't tell.

"So how do you know Laura?" Handing him a bottle he sat. "I'm Jack."

"Hey Jack, thanks for the beer. I'm Walt's brother—maybe you know 'im?"

"We've met. Live around here?"

"No, I'm visiting from Maryland. I have to fly back tomorrow but I came up to see a show—I'm into New Wave music."

"Punk you mean?"

"Yeah—band called Dead Kennedys playin' in—" he caught himself— "SF."

"I've heard of them—they're supposed to be good. Going by yourself?"

"Well, Laura said she'd come."

"I will too, if there's room—got a car?"

"Uh, sure, yeah." He was drinking the guy's beer, but Jack kind of crowded what he'd thought was going to be an evening with Laura. Still, if he was staying here tonight, maybe something would happen later…

He looked at his bowl—rice—bleah. There were a couple bottles on the table—one was soy sauce, he picked up the other—Szechuan hot sauce. "Is this really hot?"

"Sure is," Laura said, so to prove he wasn't a wuss he poured it on liberally. The bite went in all right but then his eyes flooded with tears, his tongue was on fire, he could hardly breathe. He choked the mouthful out into his bowl, embarrassed, scorched, and swigged at his beer, hearing them snort and snicker. Well, why should anything be that hot? His goddamn palms were sweating. And how was he supposed to put out this fire? The beer did nothing.

"Drinking just bloats you—bread's better." Laura handed him a roll he tore into, taking the scorch from a million degrees to a few thousand. "Want to start over?"

"Yeah," he wheezed, so she dumped and rinsed the bowl, refilled and gave it back. He ate the stuff plain—not that his tastebuds worked anymore. His lips still burned after he'd finished. He was just a kid to her now.

He let Laura drive into San Francisco—she knew her way around some. They located the club on Broadway—where they parked they could see the blinking red nipples of Carol Doda's silicon-packed tits beckoning from the Condor strip club's tall neon sign nearby. Mabuhay Gardens' doors were just opening and a line of punks stood waiting in the rain. Laura and Jack had umbrellas, but most of the punks didn't seem to care how wet they got. A few had safety pins run through their ear lobes, hair in spikes. More had slogans painted on their jackets and pants: NO RESERVATIONS, NUKE ME NOW, ZOMBIE NATION. One girl wore a studded dog-collar, a tight black leather jacket, a short skirt of black and white horizontally striped canvas like a shop awning, and torn black fishnet stockings and combat boots. Her skinny boyfriend had a choke-chain collar, leather wristbands, tight jeans with holes ripped in them. Another girl's nest of black hair matted to her scalp as it got wetter. Laura, Grant and Jack looked like the audience at a circus.

Inside, tables were arranged against a tropical décor, behind the stage a red brick wall. By day the place was a Filipino restaurant, by night a low-rent club. Everyone crowded around tables, a waitress taking orders. Most of the audience, under drinking age, got sodas or water to relieve the effects of the salty popcorn. Grant decided when he got back to Maryland he'd get into the punk scene—he was ready to go up against the status quo. Walt—and Laura and Jack—seemed perfectly happy clinging to the remnants of the anti-Vietnam movement, but that war was over, the '60s were long gone—the '70s were almost gone—and the world was going to hell, fanatics leading the way—those old men in Iran, Pol Pot, cults like Jonestown that devoured people's willpower—'60s dreamers just seemed like another cult, worshiping the past so the present would leave them alone.

The emcee came out wearing a penis-nose and moustache, hurling insults at the audience including some choice words for the opening act, then out came the warm-up band, fast and loud like a group he'd heard at

U of Maryland. Pretty soon he concluded they had two tunes they knew how to play, with interchangeable lyrics he could sometimes distinguish through the distortions of the sound system. They ran through about fifteen songs in forty minutes, then after a break when everyone who could prove they were twenty-one drank bottled beer, Dead Kennedys came out. Jello Biafra, solider than most punks, short black hair bristling out around his head like he'd been electroshocked, welcomed his audience to the real world where freedom was a commodity the poor couldn't afford and the rich had corrupted into license to do anything they wanted. The Supreme Court said money was speech: if you opened your mouth without it they'd lock you up.

Launching into "Kill the Poor" he spat out every syllable in that hard-driving voice, and despite the speakers' limitations Grant hardly missed a word—he wasn't just snarling like the guy in the opening act. As the crowd in front danced, Biafra suddenly dived into them, they caught him and pushed him back on stage while he kept singing, lurching from side to side stiff as the microphone stand he gripped, a Frankenstein's monster thrashing his way through the darkness of chaotic times. Forgetting Laura and Jack, Grant jostled into the crowd, jumping to the beat, exhilarated, and when Biafra crowd-surfed again he helped pass him along. Before the band took a break they did "California Über Alles" with everyone screaming, Biafra's raw voice above the racket belting out the words, full of righteous scorn and deprecation.

As they nursed sodas through the break Grant kept pogo-ing, he was so excited—this was the start of something new. This seethed, alive, the future, and he was part of it. A guy at the back was peddling copies of *Search and Destroy* magazine—he bought one so he could find out when the DK's album was coming out.

"It's not melodic," Laura complained. "The bands I like have musical skill—these guys play like they just picked up guitars yesterday."

"But they have so much energy," Grant exulted. "Walt dragged me to a Grateful Dead show and those guys really were dead. Jerry Garcia looks like Santa Claus—talk about fantasyland."

"But they're harmonic," Laura said. "This is just banging."

WHEN THEY CAME out, ears ringing, Grant was leaping around like an excited dog, splashing through puddles, and the whole drive back he raved about the bands' attitudes, their stripped-down sound—these guys didn't want to be famous for their own benefit, they were out to shake things up. Back at the house Jack wanted to hang out but Laura went upstairs so Grant followed. In her room she pulled out her foam pad and sleeping bag, dropping them on the floor. Her lack of hesitation galled him—he didn't really register as male, just a kid brother—some species of nuisance. She told him if he showered he should use her towel and soap, not other people's. That seemed like a hint so he took a shower even though he didn't want one. When he got back to the room she was doing yoga stretches. He watched, wishing she'd take him seriously—even through her t-shirt he could tell how gorgeous her body was. When she finished she turned off the light and lay down; he unzipped the sleeping bag and peeled off his clothes before getting in. Lying there he listened to her breathe, his blood still zinging from the show. Maybe she thought he was a virgin?

Grant's current girlfriend was a freshman at Maryland—Steph was pre-med and smart—she'd probably get through all those hard classes with a GPA good enough for medical school, but she never went out on weeknights, wouldn't let him stay over, didn't seem to like the people he hung out with—this punk show had set him on fire, and it was pretty obvious Steph wasn't gonna be part of his new life. Laura was only four feet away—how great it would be to lie beside her, pull off her t-shirt… He only kept it going with Steph for relief—she wasn't anything special— well, everybody was, Walt would say, but to him she was just—there. Just there. By Friday night every week he'd be jumping out of his skin, and there she was, and for the price of a pizza and beer, maybe a movie, he could get laid. He was tense most of the time—felt so good to get unstrung a little. If she thought it meant more than that he felt sorry for her, but she didn't seem too attached—she invited her roommate home for Thanksgiving, not him.

Why was he even in school? The only class he liked was Sociology—he got C's and D's in math, English, biology, Spanish—college was like high school except the profs didn't care if you came to class, so fairly often he didn't—who ever decided eight in the morning was a good time to learn, anyway? Half the time he couldn't drag himself out of bed till nine thirty or later. Dad was royally pissed when he saw his grades but when Grant talked about dropping out, he got even madder. There was no pleasing him.

"He wants my nose to the grindstone till I'm too tired to care," he thought, "then he'll plug me into real estate. Father and son in business—that's his thing." Walt was smart, moving so far away. But Dad couldn't make him stay in school—he was over eighteen now. He'd just have to face that he couldn't control him. Maybe Dad thought if he dropped out he'd move back in with them? He'd live in a refrigerator carton on a street corner first. The best thing about college was getting out of that house. Their lives were over—he couldn't talk politics without pissing off Dad, they had these ruts they went around in—their biggest thrill was Walt showing up for Christmas—they gave him that car, money for the trip out here. Maybe it was his broken leg—Mom didn't usually fuss like that, and after one comment Dad said nothing more about his hair.

Looking shaggy didn't shock people anymore—a guy could wear tie-dyes and go to a rock concert Saturday night with his long hair flowing loose, then Monday put it in a ponytail for his straight job, and hardly anybody'd care. But Grant was gonna get a bizarre haircut, and compromise would be impossible, whether he was at the grocery store or in class, or having dinner with his parents—he'd be a punk all the time, stared at and despised, but he'd have his tribe...

In the morning he asked Laura if she had a razor.

"I think Jack does—why?"

"I want a mohawk."

She snickered. "Really?"

"Yeah." He gave her a tough-guy look—who was she, making fun of him?

"What time are you—"

His eyes popped wide. "Oh shit, I have to get back!" scrambling for the door. "My flight's at one."

"Easy, Bud—you have stuff at Walt's?"

Agitated he turned while he thought. "My duffel's in the trunk."

"I can drive you to the airport then take his car back to him—got your ticket?"

He checked his wallet. "Yeah," then slumped, relieved. "That'd be great."

"Have some breakfast before you wake up Jack."

Frying an egg he broke the yolk then overcooked it and ate the rubbery thing anyway, then tapped on Jack's door. Nothing. He rapped with his knuckles. Nothing. Banging with his fist, he heard a groan.

"Hey Jack, it's Grant. Gimme a haircut?"

"I can't cut hair," he mumbled.

"Laura said you got a razor."

The door opened, Jack squinted at him, face swollen from sleep and beer. "So?"

"I want a mohawk."

Jack kind of laughed, a pained shudder. "Wanna be a punk huh?"

"Yeah."

"Then it doesn't have to be beautiful right?"

He was on the brink now—"Right."

"Five minutes."

Laura found a sheet and clothes-pin, moved a chair away from the table in the kitchen and put the trashcan near it. Jack shuffled in shirtless, barefoot, with messed-up hair, and gave an evil grin—again Grant dreaded what was coming. But the worse it looked, the more it would commit him.

"Do it."

Jack plugged in his razor—a trimmer really—and started on one side, around his ear, working in arcs higher. When he got near the middle he moved to the other side, then fluffed what was left—a band of six-inch-long wavy brown hair that flopped over, maybe four inches wide in the back, narrowing to an inch on top and a little wider in front. He used a kitchen knife to hack some length off what remained, took off more in back with the razor, brushed at the loose hair then stepped away. Laura shook the sheet outside and swept up while Grant went to the bathroom to check out his new look.

He was a fright—ears sticking out, patches of stubble dotting his bluish-white scalp—his tanned face seemed dyed, the mohawk chewed-on—looked like he'd lost a fight with a lawnmower. He slapped his face, bared his teeth at his reflection, and coming out met Jack returning to bed.

"Hey thanks man."

"Don't mention it," closing his door hard.

Grant felt bold and extremely stupid. "Hey Laura, c'n I use your phone? I should tell Walt what's up."

"Wait an hour—he works late Saturday nights."

Restless, he said, "Wanna go out?"

"Sure, I'll take you to Argo."

Hardly anybody was in the place. Laura commented that the regulars weren't working this morning—some legendary crew, the way she described them. The woman running the espresso machine was old and fat and looked like she wished she was still in bed, the cashier was a guy his own age with a dark scruff of beard and heavy black-framed Elvis Costello glasses. Grant expected stares but Sunday morning in Berkeley, people looked blank—maybe he seemed like everybody else—damaged.

"Too bad Walt won't get to see your new hairdo," Laura said as they sat near the big window with their tiny cups.

"Got a camera?"

"Yeah—I'll get a picture of you next to his car."

Walt had said he couldn't stand having another white car so Grant helped him and this guy Brian paint it. Grant did an undersea scene on the driver's side—a yellow octopus against green and black kelp over a deep blue background. On the opposite side Brian painted a jungle scene complete with monkeys and parrots, and on the hood Walt did a pair of dragons. Brian made a very realistic buffalo on the trunk then

Grant and Walt together painted bright red lips around the grill. It was fun but the total effect was a hippie-mobile—if he was painting it now Grant would do more slogans like the ones at the Dead Kennedys' show, maybe a mushroom cloud instead of an octopus. Laura seemed at ease, but he felt strange: his head was cold, hair leaning over tickled his bare scalp. Espresso was bitter and dense as coal slurry.

"Last night when I heard that band," he said, "I realized how screwed up everything is. I wanna make a statement about it, something I can't back away from."

"That haircut should work—it'll take a while to grow out."

"Man, I can't wait to get their album." Thumping his feet, having a hard time sitting still, he sang the chorus to "California Über Alles" under his breath, then wondered why he was being polite and sang it again at the top of his lungs. People looked up—he saw some contempt, some irritation, but mostly the jaded glances of people for whom the world's capacity to amaze was exhausted. But the cashier grinned at him; grinning back he suddenly felt right. Grant was ready to claim this new sound, this new wave, and ride it into the future while his brother's generation spun slowly in their backwater, relics of the stoned age.

CHAPTER 13
Pinned

The hour Laura'd spent with him before going back to Berkeley had been unsatisfactory in every possible way—before he even went into his house, there was Rusty hulking at the curb like a surly bear; Walt wished he'd bought the damn thing and junked it someplace just so he'd never have to see it again. He recalled his first wrestling match, when he was in seventh grade—Neil was short but solid muscle, and he'd taken Walt down and pinned him so fast he felt like a rag-doll—they weighed eighty pounds apiece but Neil's was concentrated, Walt's all over the place. When he started to get up, the kid planted his hands on his chest and pushed him down again to demonstrate how totally in control he was; the rest of the day Walt could feel that mat under his shoulders, his helplessness. Later he'd learned some moves that worked for his stretched-out skinny frame, even winning a few matches, but Neil pinned him immediately, every time—the sight of him drained the strength from Walt's muscles.

His body remembered that when he and Grant drove up the street—over the phone and in letters he and Laura were humming, in accord, but the sight of Rusty put his back to the mat, defeating him. He was tired, stiff and strung out from days of driving, and grungy but unable to clean himself properly. Laura wanted to roll him but even if he'd had the energy that would've been too weird around Grant, all eyes and ears like an underage voyeur. And he felt like a visitor in his own house—she was playing Ray's records, putting books she'd bought on a shelf—he hardly knew what he was doing there. When she saw his misery she'd packed up quickly, promising to see him soon.

So now he sat in his living room throwing a superball at the wall opposite, trying to catch it when it came back, spending a lot of time dragging himself around retrieving it. Opal had given it to him after the accident, telling him that when circumstance knocked him flying, he should bounce. Her uncomplicated affection was the only part of his life that felt positive at the moment—having left Grant at the airport, Laura was driving over the mountains on 17, a road he planned to avoid now and forever; Onion lay dead, in a junkyard or crushed for scrap; the only other piece of the accident was this poor leg. Back in December, the nurse who'd cut away the damaged cast did a perfunctory wipe-down then without pause started applying the new one—later he realized he should've insisted on a real shower before they wrapped him up again—deprived of light and air, that skin was a breeding ground, foul-smelling and itchy.

His leg didn't ache much but he was still a cripple—what he wanted now was to walk, without crutches and effort and planning, just walk till he felt tired, along the ocean then home. He'd expected to see Grant before he flew back east, but now he'd see Laura instead… He threw the ball harder so it ricocheted off the ceiling, the wall behind him, the floor, the opposite wall then back toward him. This time he caught it, then turned and threw it toward the farther wall separating this long room from the kitchen. He had stories Ray'd like to hear, and wondered when he'd be back. He didn't miss Kathy's complaints about dope-smoking—which she addressed in an undertone to the stove or bathtub or a book in her hand, as though that object was supposed to chastise him and Ray in her stead—but the house was too empty. He should feel like a king in his castle, but kings don't live alone.

When Laura knocked then came in, he set aside *Jitterbug Perfume* and hoisted himself onto his crutches. Her kiss was friendly, his blunted by depression.

"Shouldn't have told you I'd be coming," she said. "Would've been better to surprise you."

"Anyway—you're here."

"Should I take you grocery shopping?"

"Yeah, good idea." Carrying things was tricky.

While he drove she sat in the back, hands on his shoulders. "Any good movies in town?" she asked.

"*Women in Love* is back. I've seen that three times."

"Let's go."

"Nah."

"C'mon, we'll make out. Bring your toothbrush, we'll leave from there."

"I'm coming back tonight," he said.

"No you're not, you're spending the night with me."

The projectionist had Walt's name on his permanent guest list so the manager let them in free. They sat in the back corner, Laura on his good side while he parked his cast on an armrest in the row ahead. Partway into the movie she squatted on her seat and leaned sideways across him. He kissed her neck and ran his hands around on her breasts, ribs, down to her waist—might as well be fooling around in a car—if he wanted to watch the movie, too bad. In Maryland he'd had some time to think, and at one point pretty much decided not to come back—instinct was telling him this relationship wasn't balanced and never would be. But then tripping on New Year's she'd been focused and clear—wouldn't have been right to just walk away after that. Jealousy, greed and ambition were getting plenty of airtime—shouldn't love?

The movie let out before nine. "I'll drive," she said. "Does the heater work?"

"It's pretty good."

"I want it hot enough I can drive in my undershirt."

"You're makin' me crazy."

Hands on his hips, she pulled his groin to her. "Don't you like to be turned on?"

He focused on her throat. "Not if I can't do anything."

"But you can." She kissed him, and maneuvering to catch his gaze said, "Walt, I've missed you so much." Well, if she really wanted to see how empty their future looked to him... He met her eyes, revealing his sense of futility and the compromise that bankrupted him, and her unwillingness to give up anything—him, Cob, Berkeley. But maybe desire kept her from recognizing the truth—she gave his butt a squeeze and helped him into the back seat, started the engine, popped in the cassette he'd made her—"I Want You." Listening to music so heartfelt when he'd taped it struck him now as empty ritual—say the magic words and the feeling comes back. Did that ever work?

Once they were out of town she put on the heat then maneuvered out of her flannel shirt. He took off his too, warm air circulating against his bare skin. Before Half Moon Bay she pulled into a beach lot, parked facing the ocean, and cut the engine. With the headlights off, high fog became starless night; white patches of broken surf shifting in the dark sounded like "I wish, I wish, whoosh—see?" She leaned over the seat back to feel his biceps.

"You're stronger."

"All that crutching around."

She stretched till she could kiss him, then with her neck bent back, let her head descend till she reached his heart chakra, kissing around it.

"Cop coming," he said, and she slid back to the driver's seat and restarted the car, pulling out as the trooper drove alongside. He gestured to speak, she rolled down her window—his eyes expanded as he checked her out.

"Just going home officer," she smiled. "Classes start tomorrow."

"At the University?" he growled.

"That's right. See ya." She waved and rolled up her window and drove away, not too fast, putting the fan on high—the salt breeze that had billowed in was cold.

It was late when she parked behind Rusty. Walt stiffened. "Is Cob here?"

"No, just the car. Some hippie-chick's staying with him."

He would've left but she was assisting him to her room where she helped him undress then ordered him to sit on the arm of her chair and lean back, his cast on her upended laundry box. With a squirt of lotion in her palm she massaged him erect.

"I can't—"

"Let me." She eased over him, teasing his head, one foot on the seat cushion, her other on the floor. With lotion on her fingertips she drew on his torso, tracing a dragonfly whose body was his breastbone, stripes on his wings; his hands answered on her skin while her labia squeezed him. He began to feel hot everywhere except the lotion's tracks, she sat on him abruptly as though she'd just noticed he was there, moving faster and harder. His chest tightened, muscles created by his infirmity—she appreciated them with her warm hands. When he came he hugged her close, amazed his leg hadn't interfered—for a moment he felt free of it. He smiled, and kissing felt the arc of her mouth smiling back.

"What's your schedule?" Nine, she was still warm against him.

"A ten o'clock and a one o'clock Monday Wednesday Friday, then I teach Intro Bio recitations on Tuesdays, at one and two thirty. My lab class Tuesdays and Thursdays runs nine to noon."

"Cob in any of 'em?"

"I don't know yet," and with a trace of impatience, "You're not jealous are you?"

"When he sees you and I don't, how could I not feel like a sideshow?"

"You're wrong—you're the main attraction."

"No, school is, or you'd be with me."

"That's true. But it's you Walt. Don't doubt that."

"So why do you keep seeing him?"

"We have something to work out—you too. He knows I love you." He watched her dress, then she went to the bathroom and he slumped back onto the pillow, marveling—he'd sworn not to visit till his cast was off, but here he was. He'd decided not to attempt sex with her, but she'd taken him anyway and it didn't even hurt. So why could she do what she chose and get what she wanted while he struggled his way to failure? Was her karma so much stronger? She claimed to love him... No, that was depression talking—she did. That kiss at the airport, after he knew she wasn't coming...

She returned, collecting clipboard, pad and folders, making sure she had pens, then sat beside him, cheek to his shoulder. "Will you be here when I get back from class? For one more?" asking but no longer demanding.

"OK," thinking he'd never be free but captivity wasn't all bad.

STUDENTS MILLED IN the hall till the prof came to unlock the door just before ten. She felt a twinge of disappointment—Cob must not be in this class—he was always on time out of respect for the teacher. But fifteen minutes into the course overview he showed up, taking a vacant seat across from her.

"Sorry, had an emergency. I won't be late again."

As the prof resumed talking, she and Cob looked at each other, and she wondered what was happening with Stream. After class he collected the handouts, apologizing again, then caught up with her in the hall.

"What—" they said simultaneously. "No, you—" They stopped again, laughing; he gestured her to speak.

"Why were you late?"

"Stream freaked out this morning—had a nightmare. I told her to just stay put but she wouldn't let go of me. She was so light, and now all this fear's dragging her down—I don't know what to do."

"Will she stay?"

"It's not good to travel when you're afraid—people prey on you."

"Yeah," she agreed. "Just be with her I guess."

"I was gonna ask if you—"

"Walt's here—"

His face hardened. "Then why stand around talking to me? Isn't he waiting? Go."

WALT KNEW SHE'D been around Cob—his vibe made her skittish, as though she felt guilty—whatever they had going was stronger than she'd admit. He wished he'd left with the glow of union to sustain him.

"Hey, thanks for staying—now my bed'll smell like you."

"Yeah, good." He forced a smile.

"Let's have breakfast."

"I'm not hungry."

"You have to eat something, Mr. Hollow Eyes." His mom had told him he looked like a vagabond, and she wasn't just referring to the length of his hair.

Laura put on *Terrapin Station* and made a real breakfast—relaxing in her kitchen he watched her grate then wring out potatoes to fry, start a pot of coffee, make toast and finally flip eggs to a perfect over-medium finish and whisk it all to the table on warm plates like a pro. Her performance reminded him of their ease with each other back in Boulder, before California ever reached over the horizon to claim her. Between memory and breakfast he could've basked the rest of the morning, but just as that thought crossed his mind the record began to skip. By the time she'd set the needle on another song he was up on his crutches, so she carried a last half-cup of coffee apiece out to his car. He sat in the driver's seat, scooting over so she could get one hip on, and with an arm around each other they sipped then put aside mugs for a kiss—all he had to do was decide this was over, and it was new once more. But as soon as he committed to another run of the Walt and Laura Show, there was Cob, or Rusty—or Berkeley. Things about this city he liked—some very creative people, good music, interesting books and newspapers—couldn't counter the egos, self-righteousness, the hardness that equated sympathy with weakness. And Laura was thriving here. As soon as he got out of range of her desire he was going to regret letting her prevail, but in her orbit he could only cooperate. Was that love, or something less noble?

He let this momentary joy fill him, knowing their next high might be a long time coming. "Bye Toots." She got out, he started the engine and pulled around Rusty, down the street, turned at the corner, gone.

CHAPTER 14

Love's Body

The bookstore was a madhouse—tomorrow. Laura picked up a film schedule and a list of events for the semester. The student union cafeteria was wall-to-wall bodies—not today. She went to the Bio building to see the prof she was TA-ing for; he'd just arrived, sorting through the heap on his desk.

"I have the syllabus here somewhere. We had a faculty meeting over the break—recitations have been inconsistent, so we're requiring all TAs to cover the same material at the same pace."

Students had rated her Excellent—why was she getting stuck with more rules?

"I read over your master's proposal—it's fairly ambitious, but I think we can get a thesis out of it. Have any other professors in mind for your committee?"

"Dr. Dolph."

"Oh yes, he mentioned your research paper. You'll learn a lot, but he's very demanding—no BS."

"I'm not here to BS."

"Good. See if you can round up a third adviser and we'll set a time to meet—you should design your project so you can get started."

She went down to the stat lab wondering what Cob's hours would be and there he was, loading greenbar in the printer. He scanned her face, she looked away—why'd he have to see everything? It would only hurt him...

"Walt leave?"

She nodded, studying one of the terminals. "How's Stream?"

"I haven't been back. Laura, you'd be more help to her now—d'you mind?"

"What am I walking into? Did you promise her something?"

"No, just talk to her—listen to her. She's so—exposed."

"Yeah, she is. All right." He was a puzzle—deliberately provoked women's emotions then didn't know what to do with them. She walked to his building, up the stairs. Though she had a key now, she tapped on the door.

A muffled, "Who's there?" came from inside.

"It's Laura. Cob said you need to talk to someone."

Stream opened the door, her face haggard, hair in tangles, rolling her eyes like a spooked horse. She tugged Laura to the bed. "You'll think I'm crazy."

"Cob said you dreamed someone attacked you."

"He strangled me—that guy from the hotel. He laughed, then he fucked me while I was dying. It was so horrible—so real."

"Sounds like you need to get out of here."

"I'm afraid to leave this room. I can get a plane ticket but—"

"I could drive you to the airport this afternoon—would that help?"

"Oh, would you please? I'd appreciate that so much. I'll buy you gas—money's not a problem for me."

"Where you going?"

"Santa Barbara. If that's cool I'll stay there, if I have to leave I'll go to my mom's in Malibu."

"Wow, she must have money."

"Yeah. A very screwed-up life and a ton of money. Or I have some friends in Venice—if her boyfriend won't leave me alone I'll go there."

"Sounds like you have some options."

She drooped. "Not really. I'm treading water, and my options are getting soggy."

"Well, what're you doing to change that?" Laura didn't mean to sound harsh but shouldn't Stream be looking out for herself?

"What c'n I do?"

"Plant yourself somewhere—get a job and a room, cool the sex for a while—then see where you are."

"Oh god, a job? I never did that—I got money. What kinda job?"

"Where they expect you to show up and be awake—a grocery store? Maybe you don't need the income but I think you need to work, sweetie."

"Usually I don't feel so—marginal. I think it's this town—I really don't like it."

This girl was a five-year-old—instead of scolding any more Laura hugged her. "I'll be back around two—will you be ready?"

Stream nodded, pitiable. "You're glad I'm leaving Cob, huh?"

"No—that's OK. Take care."

AFTER HER ONE o'clock she wanted to prepare for her recitations but first, Stream. Halfway to Cob's apartment she remembered Rusty was at home. Well, Stream didn't have luggage—they could walk over—might do her some good to be out if she wasn't by herself. She rapped. No answer. Using her key she went in. The first thing she saw was Cob's kitchen knife on the card table, jelly on its serrated edge, a trail of darker red on the surface of the table. She looked past it—Stream sat cross-legged on the floor in front of the armchair, back resting against it, mouth open. The blood from her wrists was all over her skirt and the floor. Laura ran over, skin clammy with panic—*surely not*—touching Stream's hand—*cold*. But her own hands got pretty cold sometimes. First aid from a long time ago came back—she moved her fingers trying to find the carotid artery at the neck.

Couldn't feel a pulse. She grabbed the metal lid Cob used as a tray, holding the shiny side to Stream's mouth and nose, looking for clouding. Nothing. But she didn't look—*dead*. Did she? She'd never seen a dead person except in a casket—what did one look like? Had Stream bled that much? How much could you lose before—

She ran from the room, back to campus, pack slapping her back at every stride, to the stat lab to find Cob. He was talking to a prof when she burst in, eyes wild, voice cracking and shrill. "Cob, you have to come, now! Come now!"

"Excuse me, professor," standing up. "What's the matter?"

"Stream—it's—she's—come now!" she shrieked, racing out. He ran after, his longer legs quickly overtaking hers.

"What? Is she all right?"

"No, I think she's—I don't know—what does a—I don't know!" But they weren't the first to arrive—Laura'd left the door open and someone had called the police. The fire department was there, two squad cars were parked and a third was pulling up.

COB PUSHED HIS way in, past milling firemen shaking their heads, to the cops who stopped him coming any closer—*oh no*—Stream. *No no, she's too alive to*—

"Don't touch anything in this room," a cop bellowed while another slapped cuffs on him. Laura was three steps behind, and as soon as she crossed the threshold they had her manacled too. Cob's neighbor from #8 stood to one side in the hall, watching.

"This is my apartment—why am I in handcuffs?" Cob demanded loudly, hoping his voice would carry to the street—wished Laura'd stayed outside.

"We have to dust for fingerprints," the first cop informed them.

"You'll find plenty of mine," Cob said, still breathing hard from his run.

"Who are you?" the guy barked at Laura.

"I discovered her—" gesturing with her head since her hands were bound behind her.

"We need to talk to a lawyer," Cob said. "Don't say anything else Laura."

"All right smart guy, let's go," and the next pair arriving had to step aside—a cop pushed Cob, another gripped Laura's elbow twisting it forward—she was half-jumping to avoid strain on her shoulder.

All this was too sudden and irrational, Cob thought. What could've happened in two hours? Or had Stream already chosen suicide this morning? Sure she'd been upset, but she was too full of life to do anything so—

The head cop instructed the new arrivals to radio a photographer and a fingerprint man. Cob and Laura were hustled to a cruiser and shoved in the back, caged. It smelled bad, fear and urine mingled in the seat cushion. Maybe the cops thought they'd talk but they rode in shocked silence.

LAURA WAS BROUGHT alone to a square gray room with chairs on either side of a small table, and they unlocked her handcuffs—she rubbed her wrists where bruises would be showing up tomorrow. A man in suit pants and a white shirt and maroon tie came in, sat behind the table as if it was a desk, set out a portable tape deck and gesturing her to sit opposite, punched Record/Play. At his prompting she described her morning— omitting Walt—ending with her confusion over being arrested.

"Why didn't you call the police, or an ambulance?"

"She was Cob's friend—my first thought was he should know."

His gaze swept upward in disgust; he probed further, she told him about Stream leaving Friday, coming back Saturday morning. The investigator was very interested in her unhappy night at the hotel then pried into Cob's relationships—with Stream, with her.

She decided she'd said enough. "You're just being nosy."

"We decide what's relevant—what do you think happened to her?"

"I think she killed herself. The guy she was with Friday night really unhinged her—she was tuned in to the energy around her, and hostility pulled her spirit down."

"So she was—unstable?"

"Things were falling apart for her."

He quizzed her about keys—whether Stream had one, why she did. "So this 'Cob' has two girlfriends."

"Not that it's your business," she glared.

He punched off the tape recorder. "Come with me."

Cob was seated on a bench in the hall, still in cuffs—she stopped in front of him.

"No, come on," the investigator said brusquely as she touched Cob's cheek and their eyes met, his gaze cool and still.

"I'm waiting for my lawyer," he said in an undertone as the investigator pulled her away. Up front a uniformed cop handed over her pack.

"How do I get home? This isn't—"

"We're not a taxi service."

SHE WALKED BRISKLY past reeking blood-eyed derelicts, past liquor stores with bars on the windows, across a main artery into a part of the city hospitable by comparison, the panhandlers here young, not burned out yet. The guy who favored the alley by the army surplus store was a welcome sight with his soft voice and dog eyes—she gave him the contents of her jeans pocket—a couple dollars of change and her penknife. Wouldn't Stream have ended up like him, drifting with the flotsam? Walt liked to talk about Flow, how things worked out fine in the absence of ambition and planning—he was so wrong. That girl was tomorrow's wino, junkie, lost soul—she'd been nonplussed when Laura suggested finding a job.

She drew a hot bath to soak, the image persisting of Stream leaning against the chair with her mouth open like she was napping not dead: no fear or distress. Laura'd heard you had to keep your wrists in warm water to prevent clotting, but maybe because she'd used such a crude knife she'd made bigger cuts? How could she do that then relax? Did Stream believe death was the end of pain? Was she crazy, or "unstable"—what a handy word—or was her spirit being stalked? She was too innocent for this town, that was for sure.

Laura showing up had started Stream's downward slide—didn't that make her partly responsible? Was this some karmic punishment for an attraction that ravaged others, or were she and Cob bystanders? Was there such a thing? How could you do anything in this world without affecting other people?

Back in her room, she wondered whether his apartment was still full of cops, and if it was, where he'd stay tonight—in jail? If she called the station they'd tell her nothing. She looked at the syllabus for the recitations she'd have to teach tomorrow but the words were just marks on a page. She put Joan Armatrading in her cassette player and sang along on "Willow" till tears froze her vocal cords.

COB'S LAWYER—A GUY from campus Legal Aid barely older than himself—asked them to take the cuffs off so they finally did. His left hand was numb—assholes. They sat in a small room and Cob told them what he knew about Stream. The investigator fixated on Laura having a key while Stream didn't—Cob's distinction seemed lost on him.

"Stream didn't need a key—got that? While I was at work she was there."

"Does your apartment have a bathroom?"

"A toilet. The shower's down the hall."

"How could she use the shower without locking herself out?"

"She could set the latch—it has a button you can move down to keep it unlocked, or up so it locks when the door closes. The knob keeps the door shut either way."

"But if she left the apartment unlocked, someone else could go in."

"So?"

"How well do you know the other tenants?"

"I recognize all of 'em, and know their names from the mailboxes. The guy in #8—Len—I see in the hall—his apartment's across from mine."

"Are you on friendly terms with him?"

"I'd say neutral."

"Would he have heard if Stream left your apartment to take a shower?"

"Yeah—he'd hear the water running. And my door, probably."

"So if she had no way to get back in besides leaving your door unlocked, he could've come in while she was in the shower."

"I guess." Did he really think Len—

"Has he ever spoken to you about any of your—visitors?"

"Yeah—he's kinda crude. Laura and I were going back from the shower once, and he was looking her over. Another time he said Stream was sexy."

"Did he talk to her?"

"Not around me."

"So, if he had relations with her, you wouldn't know."

"Whoa, that's a leap—sure I would."

"How?"

"I—" He didn't want to go into his dietary thing. "I'm very sensitive to taste." The investigator, completely blank, waved him to continue. "If I already know how she tastes, when I kiss a woman I can tell if she's been kissing someone else."

"What if he didn't kiss her?"

"His smell'd be on her skin—I think you need to talk to Len."

"We are," the investigator said. "Tell me, how did you feel toward Stream?"

"I loved her."

"But you never gave her a key."

"Some people don't need keys."

"Maybe she did. Maybe the fact that you never gave her one has something to do with the fact that she's dead." Eyes narrowing at Cob.

"Or else it doesn't," bouncing the accusation right back. He could feel how much this detective wanted to blame him for her death—wasn't going to let that thought stick for a second. The guy stepped back, eyes still slitted at him. When Cob asked if the cops were still at his apartment, the investigator said he ought to stay somewhere else tonight.

They released him in the evening. Down the block at a pay phone he called Laura's house. Jack answered, that sneer in his voice.

"What can I do for you?"

"May I speak to Laura?" Cob said evenly.

"I'll see."

He stood with the cold receiver pressed to his ear, looking around. A breeze had kicked up trash circulating in a column about six feet across, climbing to fifteen feet. Newspaper, burger wrappers, leaves and grit, paper cups, Styrofoam. A paper bag bellied open, spinning in the dark. Finally, Laura's voice. "Cob?"

"They said not to go home till tomorrow."

"Stay here."

"Thanks. I'll be over in half an hour if I don't get mugged—this isn't a great neighborhood."

"I noticed. They can drag you in, but when they're done it's your problem."

Walking he thought about Stream, how easily she'd absorbed into his life, sharing his food, adjusting to his work hours. Her favorite joke—*Why can angels fly? 'Cause they take themselves lightly.* Until that guy mistreated her the night Laura showed up, she'd been unblemished by worry or pain—in her clear eyes he could see into her soul.

"Where are you now?" reaching upward, the hair stirring on the back of his hand, imagining her breath. In sight of Laura's house and the light on in her room, he couldn't keep going, sank to his knees on the sidewalk, tears drowning vision, and hugged his torso while he shook. Though conscious of someone approaching he couldn't move or control himself. Worn cheap athletic shoes stopped in front of him.

"Cob?" Jack, in disbelief.

Was the guy really gonna watch him breaking down?

"Hey, what is it man?" His voice softer this time.

He didn't want Jack's sympathy and couldn't withstand his scorn, not right now. A palm on his shoulder—Jack was actually touching him, squatting in front of him. Cob didn't move but his eyes began to clear. A hand came to his cheek, smearing away tears—why'd the guy have a hard-on?

"It's OK man," Jack said gently, wiping his other cheek. Laura said they had karma to sort out—did he have to fuck him now?

He found his voice. "I need to go in." He slowly stood, knees wobbly from the concrete. Jack turned to hide his arousal and walked swiftly back to the house, his outline black in the oval of yellow light before the door swung shut. Cob followed slowly and came straight upstairs. Laura sat cross-legged on her bed, her tense mask dropping at the sight of him. They hugged hard.

"Berkeley was the wrong place for her," he said.

"It's because I came over—when she left her safe haven this town took her apart."

"It's not your fault," he soothed. "She stayed too long—I should've encouraged her to move on."

"She asked if I was glad she was leaving. I told her no, I didn't mind— but maybe she thought I did."

They pushed their guilt in a circle till it exhausted them—reminded Cob of the trash-twister by the pay phone—they could go around all they wanted, they weren't getting anywhere, and couldn't do anything for her. Finally they went to bed, and in their drifting semiconsciousness Stream visited, her spirit filling the space between them.

"Don't be sorry for me—I'm free now. But never turn your backs on love. There's so much pain in the world—only love can heal it, but it needs bodies—you have to be love's body." In the near-dark they could see the shine of each other's eyes.

"We have to be love's body," Laura murmured: they'd shared Stream's message.

"Excuse me, someone needs me," he said. "I may be a while—don't worry." Jeans and bottle of lotion in hand, he went downstairs quietly, to the back bedroom where Jack lay facing the wall. Cob set the lotion next to the alarm clock, stroked his hair—Jack stirred but sank again—heavy sleeper. Cob reached beneath the blankets, running his hand down Jack's bare chest—he mumbled and moved, grabbing Cob's arm.

"Wha—"

"Shh. Do you want me?"

He woke more, realized it was Cob, grunted.

"I can love you, or I can go. Tell me." His voice, quiet but firm, cut through the pillows of sleep.

Jack clung to his hand, guiding it down to his dick.

"Can I come in?" Cob asked.

He nodded forward and back on the sheet.

"Tell me when to stop, OK?"

"OK," tense all over now.

"No, easy. Relax so I don't hurt you." But even his slippery middle finger was causing pain, he could feel Jack wincing, pinching, saying nothing. So he withdrew it and hugged him instead, even kissed him though he tasted unbelievably foul, jerked him off then lay petting him while he sank back into slumber. Cob got up. The house was quiet—no need for his jeans. He tiptoed upstairs, washed his hands then returned to Laura who woke as he lay down.

"Where were you?"

"Downstairs performing an errand of mercy."

"Didn't know you went both ways."

"I don't. That was for Stream—she told me to."

"Did you—"

"Now he knows what he wants. That was my function."

"Maybe he'll stop bad-mouthing you."

"Doesn't matter." He began to kiss her, seeking Stream, and they sat up, her legs around his hips, loving. They slept again, later in the night Stream urged them back into union. Each time her embrace was further inside them until in the clear dawn they loved heart to heart, thinking this joy might shatter them. Their eyes met and they could see her in each other, and kiss her in each other, and their fingers of her stroked each other's skin of her.

CHAPTER 15

Polarized

After lab class Laura and Cob went to his apartment. They gazed on the disaster, taken aback—the room was so much worse than yesterday, as though a pack of twelve-year-old boys had staged a free-for-all. The cops had thrown things off shelves, strewn papers, spilled food, pulled blankets and sheets from the bed; the mattress hung skewed on the frame, the pillow flung in a corner. In front of the armchair blood had dried in pools, drips continuing across the floor.

"My space has been raped."

"I have to teach this afternoon—"

"This isn't your mess. I'll take care of it."

Laura stopped at the door. "Cob, if it's too depressing, come over. I can help you tonight, or tomorrow after class."

After she'd gone he stood looking down the hall, reluctant to start.

The door to #8 opened and Len wandered across, eyes trained on Cob's shoulder. "Hey man, wha'd the cops do to ya?"

"Asked me a bunch of questions. They talk to you?"

"Yeah—last night they beat on my door and took me in. You say somethin'?"

What a coward Len was, unable to look him in the eye even to accuse him. Cob said, "They asked if I thought you hurt her, I said no."

"That's so weird—she invited me over." He was in the apartment now, surveying the chaos. "Next thing I know your other chick comes back, and she's dead. I didn't do nothin'." Or give anything either, it would appear.

"She killed herself. But did you love her, or just fuck her?"

Len grunted dismissively. "I didn't even know her."

"I didn't know a lot about her, but at least I cared."

The guy nudged a book with his toe. "Yeah, well, too bad." He left, Cob glaring after him. What a slimeball. Sweet Stream, too good for this world. He shut his door and started picking up. Groping behind his shelf he felt his pipe still there in its pouch—at least they hadn't handled that—cops violated whatever they touched. They'd dumped his tapes and about a dozen were out of their cases, mostly unlabeled—he'd have to figure out which was which. Turning on his amp he put in the first; recognizing Peter Tosh's *Equal Rights*, he decided reggae was good to work by. He thought of his stash in the tiny frost-caked freezer—of course the film-can was gone, but below it in the fridge was the fruit salad she'd made.

He sat on the hard chair to finish it, remembering the sticky spot on her elbow where the juice had dripped down as she was cutting pineapple—she missed it washing up, he only noticed when his hand cupped her there while they bounced on his bed laughing—even after he licked it clean he could still smell it, sweet, acidic and fresh. He poked through the sodden remains of oranges, grapes and darkened banana slices—did she ever say goodbye, or was her freedom partly in her refusal to acknowledge the beginnings and ends of—not "relationships"—confluences? Connections? Was she some cosmic visitation, conducting energy from a higher plane? Had he been merely a salmon swimming upstream to his origin, through her liquid affection?

Why didn't she take her body someplace else instead of leaving it here torn and dull-eyed for him to find? Was she punishing him? Or Laura? She could've disappeared—why not swim out in the ocean—the Great Mama she called it—till she tired, and drown? Sawing life from soul with the same knife she used to cut up fruit, what did she intend him to think and feel? She'd remarked on how happy it made her that he shared—was death the only thing she had left to bestow exclusively on him, since she gave her sex so freely? Was her appalling self-destruction an act of intimacy he was too limited to comprehend? He tilted the big bowl—when he'd drunk the last of the juice he felt he'd begun purging her from his surroundings—he'd wash this bowl, its empty cleanness would challenge him to recall what she'd put in it—she was vivid to him now, but for how long?

He pulled the stained bedspread off the armchair, starting a pile to wash, then noticed ants clustered around the blood spots on the floor like cattle at watering holes. Ordinarily he'd be philosophical about that—they were Nature's recycling squad—but that blood was Stream's. They had no right. Cob, who took pains never to kill anything, began stamping and rubbing his shoes back and forth to crush them. By the time he stopped, appalled at himself, the bodies were black crumbs on and around the stains. She wouldn't have minded being an insect feast—why'd he do that? Was dying the only way to avoid the brutality of instinct?

"Sorry, ants." He swept them up but, about to dump the dustpan, saw the used condom in his trash, right on top. *Oh.* Stream hadn't gone anyplace between Laura's visit before class and when she came back and found her, but someone had been here. Had to be Len. *The guy didn't cut her wrists, so from a legal standpoint it doesn't really matter, but if he has to face some kind of accusation, maybe he'll realize—* He'd hate the cops coming back, but Stream was leaning on his mind to speak up so he phoned the police station, got passed around, then told the investigator what he'd found.

"I'll radio a squad car to pick it up. Don't put anything else in there."

He set the five-gallon bucket near the door and got out a grocery sack to dump the dead ants into. Len's treatment of a fellow human was a worse harm than stomping fifty or a hundred insects, but rationalizing made Cob's act uglier somehow—how long would these ants have lived otherwise, what might they have accomplished that they couldn't now?

Like Stream. Why'd she check out on such a downer? *She gave up.* Suddenly it was clear: she'd fallen in love, but between his studies and his relationship with Laura—his intellectual equal—they had no future. Things had been fine while he was doing janitorial work but once he resumed classes, she knew she didn't fit—but by then she'd lost the freedom of spirit that protected her from circumstance. When she had to leave, there was only one place to go.

She loved him and he loved her back—how did that make him guilty? Why did love smudge her free heart with despair? What else could he have done? What if he'd given her that key—wouldn't that just have intensified their claim on each other, suggesting some promise? He'd lied to other women but never to her, and convinced himself his new honesty cleansed him. The more distinct the outlines of this tragedy, the less sense it made.

Rap! Rap! Rap! derailed his thoughts. He opened to a pair of cops.

"Lessee—we gotta pick up—what? A bag a trash?" A crackle from his two-way, a loud garbled sentence—he OK'd that. To Cob it seemed they spoke another language, not a word intelligible. "This?" reaching for the new sack.

"No, that one." He pointed at the condom nested in an avocado rind.

"Oh, right. One a yours?" he leered.

"No." Cob looked at him coldly as the cop picked up the trash, container and all. "Would you leave my bucket?"

"We don't tamper with evidence."

"It's not tampering to lift the bag out."

"Yeah it is." So they took it. At his window he watched them emerge and cross the street, talking, laughing; one set the bucket in the back seat then they slammed doors and drove away. He started the next tape—Steely Dan—and squared the mattress on the frame—wouldn't use these sheets again till they'd been washed, but he didn't know if he was up for the laundromat. Maybe he'd crash at Laura's, deal with this tomorrow. At a sharp knock he opened his door—there stood Len gripping a can of Schlitz, face twitching—and still not meeting him eye to eye.

"Hey man, why'd the cops come back? You rat on me?"

"If you didn't do anything, you got nothing to wor—"

"You gittin' even, that it? Shit man, chick like that, she'd fuck any-body—don't act like you had a monopoly."

"Could've showed a little heart you asshole." Cob's fist came up—in high school his arrogance goaded those corn-fed bullies to pummel him till their guilt made them stop, and he'd put up no resistance: he was brilliant and they were idiots—he'd be ascending in the world while they rotted in dead-end jobs—they were just erasing any regrets he might have about leaving. Sometimes he could still see the lime-green sear flashing into red as the bridge of his nose broke under the impact of Kent Townes's heavy silver ring. Both of them felt the bone move, and Kent shaking the sting off his hand hustled away with his buddies while Cob leaned into his open locker, blood starting to drip through his nostrils, eyes closed—wasn't sure if he'd be able to see anything but that fiery surge of pain when he opened them. Tears were a purely physical reaction, the proximity of his eyes to the injury—he had no feeling to waste on Townes and his clowns.

After the swelling receded and it was clear the bone would heal crooked, Mom wanted him to see a surgeon. For once he and Dad were on the same side of an argument—Dad said he'd caused the altercation by being so full of himself, so he'd have to pick up the tab. Townes had done his worst with that punch, but Cob flaunted the injury, liking the respect—the awe—it brought him. Mom winced every time she looked at him, and overrode Dad's objections when he applied to faraway schools: Berkeley, Wisconsin, Stanford. How could Cob hate those bullies when they'd red-carpeted his exit?

But this jerk was due for a faceful of knuckles. Len dodged, Cob came after him, Len dropping his beer knotted both fists, Cob with the advantage of longer arms popped him on the cheek, Len head-butted him hard, they went down grappling, flailing, cursing each other, rolling. Cob got him underneath, a knee on one wrist, holding the other down with his hand, looking at him steely-eyed.

"Say 'I'm sorry Stream—if I can't love a woman I'll leave her alone.'"

"Fuck you."

Cob slapped his face hard. "Say it, damn you—apologize to her."

"You're crazy you mutha!"

Cob slapped him again. "Soon's you say it I'm done here. C'mon—I'll smack you all day if you don't." When he struck him again, Len heaved, bringing his leg up. Cob reached back and got a pincer-grip just above his knee, making him kick.

"I'll gitcha for assault ya bastard!"

"Be my guest," shifting to smack his other cheek, then said casually, "I should break your nose." Len was so petrified he probably couldn't even feel the slaps anymore—hadn't he ever been beat up? The physical part wasn't so bad. The first time Townes's clowns caught him he was frantic, terrified, and after they'd run off, instead of going home right away he climbed a tree and sat awhile, looking down at the street and out where the water tower and grain elevator pierced the flat horizon. His lip stopped bleeding, his arms didn't hurt, and he realized all he could remember was being afraid. So when they cornered him a couple months later he made a calculated decision to suppress his fear and pay attention—not only was he startled at how quickly he recovered, they were bothered that he didn't react. After that they only attacked him when he taunted them with his successes: once when he was named the school's first-ever National Merit Semifinalist—that was when Townes broke his nose—and the last time, when he told them he'd been accepted to Berkeley and they could go fuck themselves. This jerk under him needed some practice being on the receiving end.

"Screw you," Len panted.

"All you gotta say is—repeat after me—'I'm sorry Stream—if I can't love a woman I'll leave her alone.' Please say it."

Len's resistance was sinking fast, and "please" did him in. "Sorry Stream," he mumbled, "if I don't love a woman I won't fuck her. That good enough?"

"Long as you mean it." Cob stood, offering him a hand up. Len, the shapes of Cob's fingers scarlet on his cheeks, bared his teeth and ignoring the extended hand, pushed himself to his feet, leaned over to pick up his beer can lying on its side, the hole providentially upward, and ducked into his apartment. Palms tingling, Cob went back to #7 where he sank onto his heap of laundry, shaking.

When Laura got home Cob was slumped on her front steps in the chill. She sat beside him, he put an arm around her saying, "I see you had a fun day too."

"I'll never teach a recitation unprepared again—an hour and a quarter's too long to fake it. How's your apartment?"

"I brought my laundry. Didn't scrub the floor yet."

"Maybe you should get someone else to do that." She looked around at the fading afternoon—a beautiful day, for some people.

"This feels like a huge karmic backlash—men taking not sharing, draining her spirit—I did that to women—why'd she have to pay for it?"

"Learn from her generosity—you can work through it."

"Had a fight with the guy across the hall." After explaining why he'd called the cops he concluded, "I never narc-ed on anybody but she told me to. So now I have an enemy."

"That's a drag."

"Listen, you have to be careful—Len would hurt you before he'd come back at me. You have Mace or anything?"

"I could get some I guess," she said reluctantly. She hated the very notion of fear governing her choices—she'd never indulged that.

He couldn't talk about it anymore. "Look over the assignment from yesterday?"

"Didn't have a minute."

"Come to the laundromat and we'll study."

The place was deserted—everyone was starting the semester with clean clothes. He loaded three washers and they spread notes and handouts on the table, talked and wrote, he rotated stuff to dryers and loaded in dimes, they discussed the lab class. She copied his work schedule in the front of her calendar—every afternoon.

"Twenty hours a week? Seems like a lot."

"All I have to do is make sure the terminals are working and the printer's loaded—most of the time I can study."

"Except when you're helping people who can't figure out what they're doing."

"Well, yeah. If it's too much I'll drop an afternoon or two."

"And give 'em back to that space cadet?"

He grinned. "Can't have it both ways, can you?"

"Forget it—I'm just being selfish."

"It's OK," he said gently. "I like that you want to see me." Kindness was a glimpse of Stream through the murk of her departure—in her church-less way she'd been thoroughly religious, with Love being the sum total of her dogma. He emptied the dryers, they folded sheets and blankets. The bloodstains had washed out of the Indian-print bedspread but the colors had run, streaking black and red across the sun-gold paisley—now it looked like flowing water surrounding some obstacles, rippling over others.

They marveled—surely this was Stream, her name and her spirit. "What'll you do with this?" she asked. "You can't just drape it on a chair anymore."

He lifted one corner high, she held another to display the whole thing. He shook his head. "If I hang it up it'll depress me."

"What if it was in the light, so it could fade? She liked sun—a curtain?"

"Don't need one—on the second floor nobody can see in."

She suggested the end of her front porch, a shield against the busy street down the block, so back at her house they rolled one edge of the fabric and tacked through the layers every few inches to anchor it to the porch ceiling, then stepped away to look—a comfort zone, streetlight filtering through without exposing them. They sat on the mouldering couch in its shelter, kissing in the semi-dark, thinking about her.

SHE WAS CHOPPING vegetables when Jack burst in waving the newspaper.

"What the hell," he raved, then stopped short, noticing Cob. "What're you doing here?"

"Laura offered—"

Jack slapped the paper on the table. "Read that."

They bent over the article—"Woman Found Dead in Student Apartment"—a single paragraph based on a police report, withholding her identity "pending notification of relatives," but Allen Dunn and Laura Reiner had been interviewed.

"Your name Allen?" Jack demanded.

"I don't go by that, but it is."

"What happened?"

"Someone was staying with me. She—killed herself—yesterday."

"At your apartment."

"Yeah."

"A suicide—" He looked at Cob, fear rounding his eyes. "Laura, how can you let him near you? He's like a poisonous snake, don't you see? It's happened again."

"Cob didn't—"

"That's just crazy," Jack said, shaking his head in frightened disbelief.

Cob had withdrawn deep into himself, eyes burning the floor, arms crossed and hands tucked into his armpits as though he was cold. There was enough truth in Jack's accusation to overload and sink whatever vessel he'd used to flee this calamity. Cob brooded while Laura read the article again, then raked back his chair, went up the stairs two at a time, back down in a moment with his stuff; without a word he pushed his way out, thudding on the front steps, gone. As though he'd called she came to the door fishing out Rusty's keys, tossed them to him where he piled laundry on the seat. He got in, the starter squealed, the engine stuttered before catching. She sat out on the porch, very cold now, listening to the idle smooth out then speed up. She and Cob had been in some bubble since yesterday surrounded by Stream's love, and now it had burst, exposing them to a toxic atmosphere and polarizing them so they couldn't help each other.

He choked the engine down, put the car in gear and drove away; she thought she could hear Rusty all the way back to his place. Where she wouldn't go. She felt as though Cob had died too, but had no tears now, only this emptiness with sharp edges like a shattered lightbulb. Stream's bedspread moved in the breeze—he'd meant her no harm, but was he nevertheless a man gripping a live wire, fatal to anyone who touched him? Jack declaring a pattern of suicide aligned the facts on such a compelling meridian, she saw herself as the next casualty. If it was Len who destroyed her, it would still be Cob's doing. She'd have to sever their connection. That detective had got all worked up over Cob not giving Stream a key, implying access equaled safety—what did he know? For her, now, access was death.

CHAPTER 16

Assault

C ob made up his bed, smoothing every wrinkle from the pad then the bottom sheet, threw on the top sheet and blankets then put his pillow into the clean case, sorry because now it didn't smell like anyone, just laundry. He needed soap and water for the bloodstains but the cops had his five-gallon bucket—never see that again. Nothing he used for food… The plastic trashcan in the shower'd work. On his way back with it half full he heard #8's door open and kept walking, aware something was coming when Len attacked him. Because he warded off the blow, the baseball bat smashed into his right forearm not his skull, the impact knocking him onto his back, a mass of water separating in flight as the trashcan left his grip. Len came to strike again, so intent he failed to see Cob's hard kick to his groin that folded him to a helpless curl on the floor. Cob staggered up, back and shoulder wet, right arm limp, grabbing the bat in his left hand. Len moaned, knees to his chest.

"Gimme a good reason not to kill you," Cob panted, bat raised.

Len looked up groaning, face cramped with fear. "I—no don't—"

"That ain't it," cocking his arm.

"I—I'll move out man—I'll split. You'll never see me again." When Cob's face tightened, he moaned, "Please."

"Aren't you a student?"

"No man—I work at Jack in the Box."

"What if the cops wanna talk to you?"

Len's voice cracked in a wail. "Pleeease—"

Cob laughed suddenly. "There's blood on my floor. Feel like scrubbing?"

"No man," horrified, "I can't—"

"Yeah you can. There's the bucket—" nodding at it. "Fill it in the bathtub. Move!" Len scrambled on hands and knees, put it under the spigot in the tub and turned on the tap. "*Hot* water," Cob barked, his sense of power stronger than the pain in his right arm. Len adjusted the water then crouching while Cob menaced, carried the trashcan to #7. Cob pointed with his foot at the cleaning stuff, Len splashed in some liquid soap and stirred it around with the scrub brush.

"What about a rag?" he half-squeaked.

"Use your t-shirt."

Pasty skin exposed, Len bent to the first bloodstain, lifting the dripping brush from the suds, moving it on the wood, the bristles painting a furrowed arc of dark red. "Oh man I'm gonna be sick."

"Go right ahead—you can clean that up too." Dominance—the same high he'd got with all those women. He still liked it. Len vomited but a glance at Cob's hard face told him to keep working. He mopped with his t-shirt, rinsed it in the bucket, scrubbed, when the red began to climb the bristles he stopped to wipe again but his stomach revolted—he threw up again, into the bucket this time.

"Dump that in the toilet and get clean water," Cob commanded, and Len moved sluggishly—fear had eviscerated him, all he could do was obey.

Half an hour later Cob finally let him stop. "Rinse out the trashcan and put it back in the shower, toss that rag in the dumpster, then I never want to see you again—that clear?"

"Y-y-yeah," and he lurched to the stairs. Cob watched him go and scurry back, slamming his door—standing in the hall he could hear him sobbing.

Fuck the guy. Stepping into his apartment he brushed the door-frame with his right arm, the pain like hot orange fireworks—he'd been so intent he'd blocked it out. He pulled his jacket carefully over his shoulder and grabbed his wallet. It was a mile to the hospital but he couldn't drive so he walked.

By NOW IT was nearly ten; activity had slowed in the emergency room—a woman with something in her eye screamed as they wheeled her to the back. Cob checked in with the triage nurse, easing his jacket off—his arm was swollen, red and blue around the break. She took his name and address, asked more questions then told him to have a seat. His right fingers were tingling then going numb like the bulbs on the three-foot plastic Christmas tree in the waiting room. He sat watching them wink on and off, synchronizing their rhythm with his pain, till the TV news came on with a short piece about the young woman found dead in a Berkeley apartment. The broadcast image was the floor in front of his armchair, the bedspread trailing into the blood. No pictures of Stream yet, or her name, whatever it was. The reporter said it appeared to be a suicide.

He realized they'd been calling him, and followed the aide through the swinging doors to wait in an alcove separated by curtains from everyone else's misery: the rattling wheeze of bronchitis; the gasping sobs of the woman with the eye problem; the moans of a large person in agony—like a cow lowing. Fifteen minutes later the aide came back.

"X-rays. This way." Cob plodded after him, the throb huge, and the aide arranged his arm on the table, draped a lead apron over him, zapped, he cried out as the guy turned his hand over to zap another. Left in his cubicle once more, he was reduced to cold and pain, but lit by a small glow of satisfaction at forcing Len to scrub the floor.

The doctor swept in with the aide on his heels.

"Well, what have we here?" he asked briskly, turning on the viewer and slapping the x-rays onto it. "Both bones broken, the radius in two places," touching the white lines with his pen. "We'll put in plates."

"What, now?"

"Going somewhere?" the doctor asked testily. "Certainly now."

"Can't you just put a cast on it?"

"Not if you want full use of this arm. You're right-handed aren't you?"

"Yeah." They were gonna cut him up—they'd already decided.

"You'll be able to use it sooner—you should be grateful," the doctor snapped, fed up with people who didn't appreciate what he did for them. "We'll do it under local anesthetic. Gavin, set up an OR."

"Yes doctor." The aide left, he turned to Cob.

"Now, if you're interested—" he beetled his brows, waiting for Cob's attention, "we'll insert a piece of titanium along the radius, and pin it here and here, and up here. We'll put a shorter piece along the ulna, pinning that here and here."

"Can those be taken out later?"

"No, your bones will grow onto them—they'll be your newest body parts."

"Wonderful," Cob muttered.

"Could be worse—a colleague of mine had to check out a suicide yesterday."

Cob clutched his knee with his left hand, eyesight blurring—why would Stream do that? The doctor said something else but roaring in his ears overwhelmed the words. Next thing he knew he was lying flat, blinking at incredibly bright lights. He couldn't feel his arm but he could sense tugs on it as they carved apart skin and muscle, down to the splintered bones. He tried to sit up but a strap across his chest prevented him raising more than his head.

A dull sensation he knew was pain, that his nerve endings were saving up for when the anesthetic wore off, told him they were attaching the plates to his pieces of bone. His mind floated—he was a paper being hole-punched before he was turned in, then they'd put him in a folder, in a pile with other papers in a prof's mailbox. He remembered the story he'd written on Laura's recitation exam—how foolish that seemed now, thinking they could escape the grindstones of karma. They were trapped in this configuration like every other recurrence of themselves, compelled to act out the next scene written for them—couldn't change a thing.

Laura was through with him—he might as well have killed Stream. And that other girl too—Emily. He'd forgotten that till Jack brought her back, using Laura as his messenger. Rage boiled up and he wished he'd fucked him last night, hard, hurt him bad. Then he remembered kissing him and nearly retched—how could a human being taste so filthy? But most of them did. Them. Ha. Not Cob. Not Mr. Clean, Mr. Pure of Body whose soul was fouler than the most putrid orifice of the most polluted one of them. He felt Stream's fingers—or were they Laura's?—prying at his clamped heart. Stream dried up at her source, Laura alienated—how could he love anyone now, and what idiot would dare love him?

THEY WANTED TO keep him overnight but he had no insurance and didn't care to burn up all his earnings. He was patched up—what was the difference, which bed he couldn't sleep in? At the ER they were used to people leaving after treatment so nobody made a concerted effort to keep him there, they just gave him a prescription for painkillers and the doctor's card with an appointment in a week to get the stitches out. He had a thick wrapping of gauze instead of a cast, a sling supporting his arm from pinky to elbow. It was 2:30 AM when he left the ultraviolet glare of the hospital for the sulfurous glow of streetlights, stopping by the all-night pharmacy where he slouched in a chair waiting for his prescription. He took a pill as soon as he'd paid for them—damn, this stuff cost more than dope—then headed home, his only thought that his bed was made so all he had to do was fall down on it.

But activity swarmed around his building—what now? An ambulance, three cop cars, a fire truck, a TV van, spotlights. A clot of people stood talking—a reporter and cameraman from a news station, cops, firemen. The ambulance put on flashing lights but no siren, driving away slowly.

He came up to the group. "Hey, what's goin' on?"

"Some guy fell out a window."

A finger of cold started at his tailbone and ran up his spine—if his hair wasn't tied back it'd be standing on end. "What guy?"

"Who are you?" The reporter pushed his mike at him, the camera zoomed in.

Cob swatted the mike away. "Can I talk to somebody who knows something?"

"We're looking for the resident of Apartment 7," a cop said. "The light's on but no one's there."

"That's me. What do you want?"

The cop grabbed Cob by his left arm, steering him toward a squad car. "I'm taking you in—we have questions."

"Ah man, can't it wait? I'm tired, I'm in pain—"

They pushed him into the back seat, he leaned away as they slammed the door—what did they care if it hit his arm? He watched the city going by, thinking if he walked home from the cop shop this late somebody'd finish him off.

When he woke his lawyer, the guy got all excited and promised to come down right away. The cops parked him on the bench where he'd been yesterday, as though time had doubled back on itself to dump him here. Someone sat beside him while he stared at the floor. He glanced sideways—that investigator.

"Want coffee, something to eat?"

Which reminded him the last thing he had was that fruit salad. Stream—"Water."

The investigator's leather-soled shoes clapped against the floor as he walked away—for the moment the only sound—and he returned with a Styrofoam cup and a doughnut. Cob accepted the cup—mineral-flavored tap water with undertones of lead and a chlorine bouquet, with a polystyrene finish—he should be a food critic. The guy held out the doughnut a moment longer then shrugged and took a bite himself, sitting back down, chummy as you please. Cob shifted to the far end of the bench, noting that the pattern of broken streaks on the floor tiles resembled algal growth in riverbeds where nitrate runoff polluted the water. He retreated into memory, sitting with Laura by the Feather River last summer, her eyes closed as she awaited his touch—was her love a closed chapter while he resumed his old persona? Was he a monster after all?

The lawyer showed up and they went to the little room. The pain was coming on now but they'd emptied his pockets at the front desk.

"Could I have another pain pill? I'm liable to start screaming."

"Be right back." The investigator left. The lawyer didn't say anything—he wasn't really awake, blinking, sipping his acrid coffee.

Cob took two pills then resigned himself to interrogation—calling the cops about his trash; his conversation and fight with Len; forcing him to apologize.

"I know he didn't cut her wrists, but he made her decide to."

"So you beat him up."

"It was the least I could do for her." He glared at the investigator. "What were you gonna do? He didn't break any laws, just her heart."

"Go on."

He skipped visiting Laura, told him about deciding to use the trashcan from the shower then described Len's assault, and gaining the advantage despite his broken arm. He admitted making Len clean up—they'd find blood around his cuticles—if he said everything now maybe they'd leave him alone.

"So do I get to know what happened?" he demanded when he'd finished.

"According to police, a ground-floor resident heard a crash outside, turned on his light and saw a body near his window—apparently he landed on some debris—"

"Yeah—people pile shit over there that won't fit in the dumpster."

"Evidently your neighbor from #8 went out his window, landed head-first and broke his neck—died instantly."

"'Went' out?"

"We don't know if he fell or was pushed. We were hoping you could tell us."

"He was crying in his room when I left."

"Where's the bat?"

"In my apartment someplace."

"But you didn't hit him with it?"

"It was so tempting. No. I threatened him—he was very afraid of me."

"Let's assume for a moment he jumped out his window—does that surprise you?"

"He said he'd move out—woulda been fine with me."

"That doesn't answer my question."

"Should he have killed himself? Probably. Why's it matter whether I'm surprised? If I kill myself later tonight would you be surprised? Who cares?"

"Are you contemplating suicide Mr. Dunn?" The investigator's tone was kinder.

"All I want is to lie down in my own bed, but I'm stuck here with my arm killing me, answering stupid questions like any of this shit matters."

His lawyer took the investigator aside for a quick conference, then put his hand on Cob's left shoulder.

"C'mon, I'll give you a lift."

HE STRUGGLED—GETTING INTO his apartment was a two-handed job. Turning the knob he put his thigh to the door so the latch wouldn't slip back closed while he worked the bolt—that was hard to retract because of his pressure on the door, but he finally popped it. Disabling the doorknob was his next challenge: his clumsy left hand wrecked several lengths of duct tape   as soon as he tore a piece from the roll it grabbed itself—finally he pulled out just enough to stick to the inside face of the door, then wrapped it across the knob latch and around to the outside. He crumpled the end tearing it off but it held—now he could get in one-handed. The apartment stank of vomit and soap and blood and Len's rank sweat—he opened the casement pane of his big window, welcoming the cold air, exhaust and all. The floor was still damp—he'd see if it looked clean in the morning.

Morning. His ten o'clock class—with Laura. Was there another section? He dropped his spring course schedule on his bed, flipping through. Nope. Well, it was unlikely she'd speak to him. Taking notes would be tough—he was thoroughly right-handed. He thought about taking a bye this semester, pleading personal difficulties, letting her get ahead of him in the program. But he'd only had two days of classes—early to be bailing.

Undressing was too much work so he took off his jacket and shoes and lay on the top sheet, pulling the blankets over him. He was wiped out but his brain wouldn't shut up—every question that wasn't "why" started with "if"—no one had the answers except God, if there was such a thing, and God wasn't saying. Despite the risk of bumping his arm he turned restlessly, finally realizing he was seeking her scent he'd washed out of his bedding—the hint clinging to his blanket was so faint as to be nothing but his longing. He was awake a long time, thoughts pooling and spilling, going through his head like water, like a stream…

CHAPTER 17

An Open Door

Laura steeled herself to go to class, wishing Cob would just vanish. She waited to go in till several people were already there, taking her seat between two of them in the horseshoe desk arrangement, and resting her pack on the floor got out her clipboard, pad and pen. She sat up and there he was across from her—he looked terrible—clothes rumpled, hair unkempt, bags under his red eyes. And his arm in a sling. He wouldn't look at her. All through class as she wrote and listened and asked questions she kept stealing glances at him but his face was set, expressionless between grimaces as he scrawled awkwardly on his pad. At the end of class she packed up—he was still sitting near the door, putting things away slowly. As she neared his desk his folder fell open, papers cascading to the floor. He went on one knee to pick them up, she squatted to gather those near her feet. As she handed them to him he raised his eyes to meet hers.

"What happened?" She wasn't going to speak, but that was before she saw him. Watching him fumble sheets into the folder and stuff it in his pack, she thought this must madden him—he always kept his notes and papers neat.

"Len jumped me. If I didn't have a broken arm I'd be dead."

"My god, what—"

"Can we talk someplace?" Standing he slung his pack on his left shoulder, waiting while the room emptied.

That would entangle her more than just asking a couple questions to satisfy her curiosity—should she? Overnight he'd become this utter stranger, with a stare that didn't acknowledge his surroundings—looking for Stream? Thinking of joining her?

"In here," she decided. "I don't think there's another class right away." She took a chair, he left an empty seat between them, resting his right arm carefully on a desk, his gaze frozen and remote as he spun out the story. When he told her about Len's broken neck she shook her head.

"Another one," she said softly, and that seemed to bring him back.

"Huh? Yeah—I should keep score. Think I could get in the Guinness Book?"

"Very funny."

"Ha. Ha."

She'd shifted her feet to stand when he spoke again.

"I shouldn't talk to you but I wonder—"

She wanted no more of his misery, but how was she supposed to refuse? "Wonder what?"

"Did the last two months even happen? Everything was different, my life was turned 180°. I had all this love—with you, with Stream—and now she's gone and it feels like you're next." He whispered, "What can I do?"

"Hang around people you want dead I guess," and grabbing her pack she fled.

HE STAYED IN the classroom through the next hour, staring at the one white smear on the black chalkboard, the writing still visible—after the crew washed them during the break, the first couple weeks nothing erased properly. It annoyed the profs, but Physical Plant liked to impose their order between terms, and he helped them do it. Most students despised janitorial work—if they were even aware of it—he was one of the few with a foot in both worlds.

But now he had one foot in life and the other in death, and couldn't move. When the investigator asked if he was contemplating suicide, he'd jarred something loose—Cob wasn't thinking about it so much as invaded by it, vermin taking up residence, gnawing at the strands of reason that held his act together. If he didn't find a way to clear this out he wouldn't last. He hardly had close friends anymore… Diane—they'd never had anything going sexually—maybe she was safe from his bad vibes. He found a pay phone. Of course she wasn't home—she worked days. He dropped the receiver into its cradle and headed for the stat lab.

LAURA ASKED SOMEONE in lab class to switch partners with her, ending up with a woman who was precise and fussy—good traits for this kind of work, she supposed, but humorless. Cob made no effort to speak to her. She checked in the department office to see if there was another section to transfer to, but in the graduate program everyone was thrown together. Well, Cob had a right to be here, but the very sight of him nauseated her. Memory kept boiling up like the overflow in front of Walt's house, the flood stranding her. Picturing that porch surrounded by water made her realize she should tell Walt what had happened; her letter started in the middle and splattered all directions like a dropped egg. Rereading she thought she'd never been so incoherent, but a phone call would turn into interrogation—she mailed it anyway.

A week later when she came home from class Friday afternoon, Walt's car was parked out front. She raced inside, upstairs, into her room where he sat reading. He pushed himself upright, standing a long time with his arms around her, and when her nervous jumps subsided he turned her face so they could kiss, her mouth welcoming until abruptly her edginess returned. He sat on the arm of the chair holding her hand.

"Hey Toots, you're all wound up—tell me how things stand."

"Every time I see Cob he looks worse, like he's dying in front of me, and I'm the only one who could help him, but—"

"All that death around him—I don't blame you."

"But just watching while he disintegrates—isn't that wrong?"

"I don't know what's right for you—seems like you're in pretty deep now." Then out of the blue, he said, "Want me to talk to him?"

"Can you? I mean, does that make any sense for you?" She'd given up thinking that could happen, and since Stream's death, had no reason to want it.

"We're not enemies—not yet anyhow. Maybe we can just see each other as broken."

HE CRUTCHED UPSTAIRS, forward to #7. Laura's house had a homey feel—music, something cooking, conversations. Living here you'd only see people if you made an effort. Knocking Shave-and-a-Haircut he waited for Six Bits, didn't get it, then rapped it himself. Rustling inside, a heavy tread, Cob opened the door a foot, face frozen into lines of repudiation.

"Whatta you want?" he rasped.

"I came to offer a little FAC libation and cheer, one cripple to another."

"Hm," pursing his lips, looking at Walt's cast. "Yeah, why not." He pulled the door wide, Walt crutched past him. "Don't have much furniture."

"Long's I can prop up my cast I'm OK—this kitchen chair'll be fine."

"I'll bring it over by the armchair—want some music?"

"Friday afternoon—let's have rock'n'roll. New Riders?"

"I'll put it on." Cob started *Panama Red*, switched the amp to Phono and music came out. He turned it up then dragged over a crate while Walt got the bottle of wine out of his backpack, using his Swiss Army knife corkscrew to open it.

"Carrying stuff's a pain isn't it?" Walt called over the music as Cob brought a pair of jelly glasses folded into his left hand.

"Not as bad as trying to write."

"I just want to take a walk." Walt poured wine and set the bottle on the shelf; they raised their glasses. "To whole bones," he toasted, Cob concurred, and while they drank the first glass they said nothing, nodding to the beat, relaxing, letting down their guard.

"Laura send you?" Cob asked eventually.

"I volunteered—we seem to've ticked off the universe—I'm trying to find the Flow again, get back to where things work. How about you? You looked better before Christmas." Cob had dark patches like bruises under his eyes, the leftward angle of his nose was more obvious, hair hung around his face in strings—without the breadth of his fine forehead to neutralize it that brow gave him a Neanderthal look—you'd cross the street to avoid this guy. Walt wondered idly how to brush and band a ponytail one-handed, whether that was harder than tying shoes.

"Yeah, I'm startin' to look like my car," Cob said.

"Seen mine?"

"No."

"Remind me—we have to go down before dark so you can admire it. We got stopped—" raising fingers to count, "let's see—Maryland, West Virginia, Ohio twice, Indiana twice, Illinois, Missouri twice, Kansas three times, Colorado, New Mexico, Arizona twice, and yes, even California. Seventeen times."

"Every state?" Cob grinned. "When I drove Rusty out they pulled me over in Wyoming and Utah but not Nevada. But in California they really checked him out."

"Probably thought you were an Okie late for the migration."

"I was, fleeing the barren Midwest." He snorted cynically. "How many fruitarians do you suppose live in Nebraska?"

"There's eccentrics everywhere—I bet there's a few."

Refilling their glasses Walt remembered his bag of tortilla chips; Cob's face lit seeing it. "I have two ripe avocados—let's make guac."

At the table Walt leaning on his crutches spooned avocado into a bowl, chopped tomato and bell pepper, plopped in yogurt, squeezed the lemon. Cob seasoned, then both sampled.

"No onions or garlic, sorry," Cob said, "but cumin and chili powder— I looove chili powder." He pressed out more lemon juice. They tasted again, nodding.

"And some cayenne for zing."

"Good." Cob dosed it then carried the bowl back and set it on the crate, Walt tore open the bag of chips and they dug in. "Wow, haven't just kicked back on Friday afternoon for a while—thanks for coming over. Laura tell you our horror stories?"

"Not the gory details but I got the gist."

"I feel like a leper—everybody's avoiding me."

"Everybody who? Laura you mean?"

"And Diane—remember the lady in San Francisco?"

"Where we met? Sure."

"I've been desperate to talk to someone but she brushed me off—said she's wrapped up in some boyfriend right now, but I think she sensed the chaos and didn't want me any closer."

"Well, here I am," Walt offered. "We have Laura in common, and some ancient history too it seems. Gimme a shot—I'll listen."

Cob sank back in his chair, looked upward and sighed. "I've been wondering how you can ever know another person. I thought I knew Laura, then last fall she blew me away—everything I believed just collapsed. I expected her to turn her back—hell, I would've—but instead she opened me up. Before she went to Santa Cruz she stayed here a few days—I never loved anybody like that, not just sex but her confidence, her understanding—her courage. We talked about working it out so this lifetime we wouldn't all destroy each other, we could break the cycle and be free.

"After she left I came home to such an empty place, I missed her so much, like I'd left the door to my heart open and it was freezing. Stream was a hit of the tropics—no greed, no guile, no hesitation, no fear—nothing in her mind but love. Then Berkeley mistreated her—" his face began to contort, "my neighbor screwed her, and she checked out—just like that." Tears were flowing now—Walt held his left hand while Cob laid his head back and wept freely. "She visited me and Laura the night she died—we were completely merged, all three of us, but the next day Jack—" his voice foundered, then, "Laura has to protect herself—I could destroy anybody." He cried harder. "I want out."

"Don't you want to clear up some karma first?"

"I just made it worse. The only door's the grave."

"Look again." Walt opened a cigarette tin to take out a joint. "My good friend laid this on me—all buds." By the time he and Grant were driving west, Tom was back in Boulder so they'd hung out with him and spent one night in his mousehole apartment, sleeping like cordwood in his twin bed because there was no floorspace big enough—Grant would've preferred the car which was actually roomier, but cops in Boulder would hassle you. They saw Ophuls's classic *The Earrings of Madame de...*, Grant sleeping through most of it—too slow and elegant for him. Tom said the characters reminded him of *Anna Karenina*—adultery was fine—even expected—among those aristocrats, but real love was bad manners—"put on some artifice," their fellows said, as though the pair waltzed naked among swallowtail coats and silk gowns, making everyone else uncomfortable.

Tom and Walt got high and talked about the nature of love, which of course circled around to women. In Santa Cruz, Tom had persuaded Laura to have sex with him—he claimed her unexpected beauty was to blame—but after one time she refused him—said she had too much going on, couldn't handle it. Then when he laid Opal, she was completely up-front about seeing Walt; Tom chafed at the imbalance.

"Opal's freer than most people," Walt explained. "I consider myself lucky to know her, and if you want to know the truth, unlucky I know Laura."

"But Laura's—"

"Not kind. Opal's affection is fresh air—Laura's a furnace—one of these days there won't be anything left of me." And blessed by the goddess marijuana, he and Tom got through that whole conversation still friends—and without talking about Cob, as though Walt was Laura's one and only. Getting high together seemed an obvious step toward sanity—if he and Tom could work it out, maybe he and Cob could too.

He offered the joint. "Laura sent me a very tasty bud for Christmas—"

"Hey, that was mine," Cob objected. "I noticed some was gone."

"She ripped you off?" She'd acted so superior when Walt helped himself to hers early in their cohabitation, forcing his confession and a promise to keep his mitts off, but then he couldn't score any and in another two weeks her paltry supply was gone. She brought a couple friends over on their way to a concert and discovered his perfidy—they marched out in a huff and he thought that was the end of the Walt and Laura Show, but when she got home much later she'd just shaken her head condescendingly. "You obviously have no self-control."

"Not about pot," he'd agreed, and that was that—she resigned herself to hiding her stash. He'd still find it sometimes but it was never there when he went back, even a day later. Laura the thief huh? He intended to get some mileage out of that.

"Well hey," Cob laughed, "at least somebody besides the cops got some—when they tore through this place they swiped my stash—can you believe that?"

"Sure—what were you gonna do? Ask for it back so they could bust you?"

"I had enough fun with them—they handcuffed me—Laura too—for walking into my own apartment." They smoked almost half the joint then Cob stubbed it out and put it back in the tin. "Hey, how come we never talked before?"

"We did—you tried to sell me your car. Which reminds me: come look at mine."

Outside Cob laughed, "Oh man, is this for real?" delighting in the colorful display. "Who painted these dragons on the hood?"

"I did—wanted to make 'em loving but I can't draw—they don't look right."

"No, they're beautiful. Wow, I'd get some paints and find a spot nobody decorated yet—if I could use my right hand."

"Hey," Walt protested, "how come I have this horrible cast but you don't?"

"Because they carved up my arm—when you're healed they'll take that thing off."

"Well, you can scratch when it itches."

"So it doesn't."

"Murphy's Law," Walt laughed.

"How much longer you dragging that around?"

"Three weeks minimum, then more x-rays—what about your arm?"

"Once the incisions are healed I can start using it, but I have to be careful. They cut through muscle—if I overdo it I'll be crippled for life."

"Bummer."

"Man I'm glad you're here. Want to go see Laura?" Cob suggested suddenly.

"What, together?"

"Right now—you said there are doors everywhere—we're opening one. Since we saved her half the joint, she should appreciate us."

"'Should,' right." They laughed again.

"Let's go," Cob urged, "leave the record playing, just drive over and kidnap her."

When they parked at her house he said, "Check out that curtain by the couch."

Walt crutched over for a close look—if Stream was anything like her name, this was her image.

"It's better from here," Laura said, beckoning from the doorway—the sunny glow lit the porch clear to the far railing.

He joined her. "Come with me Toots."

"Where?"

"Grab your pack and jacket—no telling how long we'll be gone."

"But where—"

"Hurry up."

But heading for the car, seeing Cob she stopped dead. "No."

"Yes Laura. C'mon."

"No."

"If you won't do it for him, do it for me, please?" It was so delicate—Cob was waiting for her rejection, for the last door to close. "It's Friday afternoon—don't make it so dire." He whistled *Panama Red*.

"You guys are stoned aren't you?" a grin hiding somewhere in her disapproval.

"Co-rec-to. Now get in." He crutched around to open the back door, she sat, flicking her eyes toward Cob then away. Walt drove, Commander Cody in the tape deck to maintain the mood over the terrible silence in the back seat. When he opened her door she gave him an empty look, as though he'd sent her to the gallows.

"Come on, we can't finish that joint out here." He headed for the stairs, Cob got out and with a last admiring pat on the fender came after him. As they went into the stairwell a patrol car drove up the street, and seeing Walt's car, stopped. Laura moved quickly, arriving in the apartment hard on their heels.

"There's a cop down there."

"They come around all the time," Cob said. "I'm their pickup-of-the-month—they're gonna name a doughnut after me."

"Well, don't you think we should wait to smoke till he leaves?" At the window she watched the black and white car sit a moment, then drive off. "He didn't get out."

"No, that's his superman identity," Cob said acidly. "He can make colored lights flash and different siren noises, threaten people with his bullhorn and spotlight, get on his radio and babble nonsense to overlords who babble back, drive fast and run red lights—when he gets out he's just a guy."

"OK, where's this joint? I either smoke, or I'm outta here."

She hit twice on the pass then Walt shotgunned her; she got glasses of water while Cob put on Commander Cody then began to sway.

"He played in town after finals, Walt," she said. "He's so great: 'Hot Rod Lincoln,' 'Two Triple Cheese, Side Order of Fries'—"

"Proof that in rock'n'roll it ain't the lyrics," Cob laughed, knees dipping to the beat. "What a show. This pregnant woman was dancing, I thought she was gonna have her baby on the spot—never saw anyone move like that."

"That kid'll be something, huh?" Walt mused.

"Yeah," Cob agreed, "born to boogie—that's what I want."

"You want kids?"

"Sure. Don't you?"

"When we get there."

"What about you Laura?" Cob asked, kicking his feet out to "Beat Me Daddy, Eight to the Bar" while Walt pivoted on his crutches—she was standing by the window clutching her glass.

SEEMED LIKE EVERY time her heart lifted, the comedown was harder—at this point she hoped maintaining her current level of wretchedness would keep the hurt from getting worse. "Ask me in five years," she said.

Cob whistled. "Long time."

"Not for something worth waiting for," Walt said.

"You're waiting for her aren't you?"

"As long as I have to."

"What do you say, Laura—does Walt win your hand?"

"Don't ask me this stuff—I'll leave."

"Don't leave," they chorused.

"Can't you feel Stream here?" she half-wailed. The girl's blood had soaked into this floor—how could they dance?

"She's happy now," Cob said. "The pain's starting to clear."

"I don't want to be in this room."

"Cob's bed is wider than yours," Walt said. She looked at him, incredulous. He grinned, and leaning on his crutches moved his forearms against each other remarkably like bodies loving. "Half a man's better than none, right?" turning around to "LA Lady." "And two halves are better still."

"I want no part of this," she announced, sitting in the armchair, drawing her knees up and tucking her head to her thighs, clamping her eyes shut.

Someone began to stroke her head and arms, too many places for one pair of hands. "We love you," Walt murmured, kissing where the hair ended on the back of her neck. "Don't shut the door Toots, please?"

Revisiting those months of anticipation, she let awareness pass to her skin where Walt's touch and Cob's cooperated to woo her. She let one leg then the other slide down but kept her eyes closed; their hands continued on her front now exposed. In honor of Walt's visit she'd traded bra and t-shirt for undershirt, and now the buttons of her flannel shirt were parting, the air cool when their hands opened it—she felt as much as heard their matched sigh, and sank back in the chair, her urge to fight gone. A mouth on each nipple—well that was novel. She put her hands into the long hair on two heads—Cob's flat and dense, Walt's rough and springy. Their kisses were everywhere—she couldn't keep track and finally stopped trying. Hands participated, she let them undo her jeans and tug them off.

The music changed to "Show Some Emotion," Cob kissed her mouth. Her last resistance pressed her lips together to keep him out but he kissed all over her face, humming to the music, then while his mouth wandered into her hair Walt's came to hers. She kissed him back, hands reaching to embrace him, but he guided one to Cob's shoulder. His lips moved on and Cob's returned. This time her heart wouldn't let her stop.

Cob lay his cheek to her belly; she watched between her eyelashes while she petted his head and Walt massaged his back and around onto his chest, revisiting his heart. When Walt stretched over him to kiss her mouth again, she began to giggle.

"What's so funny?" he mumbled through her lips.

"You—both of you." She belly-laughed and Cob raised his head, his eyes brilliant meeting hers.

"Don't make fun of us."

"I can't help it." Then she gave herself up to laughter, feeling Stream's glow in her heart as she accepted their affection.

IN THE MORNING she got up to pee and came back to look—head to foot, each with his injured right limb outward where it wouldn't get jostled, they were a face-card—King of Spades, with Cob's dark hair and their collective gloom. And she was the Queen—they'd taken her. She leaned over to kiss Walt—he cracked an eye and grinned, then she went around to Cob and did the same, his left hand at her neck till he finished. In undershirt and jeans she prowled the fridge—cold cornmeal mush, eggs, a can of jalapeños, red bell pepper, even some guac left. She heated his skillet while the teakettle creaked and hissed, then sautéed bell pepper, chopped in the pone, two jalapeños to finish, and heaping that on a plate with the guac on top, fried up half a dozen eggs she arranged around the mush while coffee dripped. When she brought the mugs and big plate with three forks to bed, the guys gripped left arms to help each other sit up, then leaned close to eat.

"So, how long's my reprieve?" Cob asked her.

"I'm not worried about your neighbor anymore."

"What about the next time Jack opens his mouth?"

"Betcha didn't know about him," she said mischievously. "Jack's in love."

"No. Who's the lucky—"

"His name's Larry, he's small, he's well-built—"

"Jack's gay?" Walt asked.

"I always thought he wished he was one of Cob's women, he was so jealous."

"Hey, I did all I'm doin' for that jerk," Cob said sharply.

"Anyway," Laura looked at him seriously, "If I shut you out it won't be for anything he says."

"Do you believe I caused all those suicides?"

"You have to be more careful how you treat people. But you didn't hurt Stream—you're the only one who didn't."

"She opened me so I could see you." He shook his head. "Thanks Walt, for shaking me loose—I was close to the bottom."

"You wouldn't do that."

"What do you mean? Everything's ready. Got my bennies, a bottle of Everclear—no defenestration for me thanks, no bloody mess."

"Glad I saved you the trouble."

"All right," Laura said. "We had a friendly night, and everybody's happy. What about the long haul?"

"One mile at a time please," Walt said.

"That's a cop-out."

"It's the only answer you'll get outta me."

"Let's go to Yosemite on spring break," Cob suggested.

"Yeah," Walt agreed. "By then I assume I'll have the use of both legs."

"Let's borrow a big tent, and a wide piece of foam," Laura said, eyes glinting.

"You're in charge of comfort," Cob said. "I'll do food. Walt, choose some hikes."

"Well folks," Walt stretched. "My first matinee's at one so it's road time. Laura, can I drop you at home, are you here awhile, what?"

"I'll stay—I bet Cob's notes are complete gibberish."

"Complete, no," he corrected, "but definitely gibberish."

"Happy studying. Walk me to the car Laura?"

Walt gathered his stuff, divided his last joint leaving half, then crutched to the bed. Cob shuffled on his knees to the edge and they embraced. "Take care of her OK?"

"On my honor," Cob said. "Don't be a stranger."

"I'll come up when I can." As they went out, Cob lay back with a sigh.

CHAPTER 18

Rehab

A fter a wonderful shower that brought his pale scrawny right leg back to a much-longed-for state of cleanliness, Walt wandered downtown just for the novelty of taking a walk, and spotted Opal flipping through used records. He stood behind her, when she paused at a Bob Marley album murmured in her ear, "Buy it." Noting his crutchless castless condition with a smile, she bumped her hip against his.

"If you'll come listen to it with me."

"Take me."

He thought he'd landed in heaven, everything yielding so sweetly—Opal, her feather bed, his knee, Bob Marley "Jammin.'" He told her about ending up in bed with Cob and Laura—now he thought that was nuts, but Opal credited the *sinsemilla*.

"It's a sacrament," she said, "because it dissolves our fixed worldview—we step out of our tight little knots of want and recognize larger patterns. If you hadn't got high with Cob, don't you think he'd have killed himself?"

"Yeah, but now he's with Laura—why'd I put 'em back together?"

"Think big," she laughed, slapping her substantial thigh. "I love Tom—someday maybe he'll even get his shit together and come join me—and you love Laura—and that's all good. There's room in this cosmos for every connection."

"But what's in store? He wants her as much as I do—for life. I just don't see how that's gonna work."

"Why not?"

"He's got too much testosterone. He's controlling it now, but the minute he lets up it'll run over me like a tank. His brain believes in evolution, but his body's possessive and selfish—hell, mine is too—I want him out of her life." He looked at her ruefully. "Karmafornia's gonna kill me—wish we'd never come out here."

"But that wasn't your choice."

"No, I just tagged along."

"Because you care about her—acting out of love can't be a mistake."

"I'm not so sure about that."

"Trouble is, love's in a minefield—jealousy, doubt, loneliness, need—hard not to trigger one, but love itself overwhelms all threats."

Opal was threading that labyrinth, but would Laura? He doubted he could—and Cob? The pot had amazed them with a harmonious vision, but if humans lived only at the heights of inspiration they'd be a highly evolved species by now—it was all those mundane moments, vastly outnumbering the brilliant few, that ran people's lives, forcing that higher nature down into the muck of continuum.

"What a tripper you are." Had to admire her faith.

"Instead of having a fixed attitude, wouldn't you rather flow?"

"Like Stream you mean?"

"Me too." She laughed light-heartedly, a sound as wonderful as water plinking off moss into rivulets high in the Rockies where he'd spent a June day a couple of years ago, the small bright notes as clear and sweet as the taste—that substance had cycled through evaporation, freezing into snow, hardening into ice after a load accumulated over it, then softening back into snow before thawing to water to grace his ears and throat—shaped by its surroundings into myriad forms, its essential structure was unchanged.

LAURA'S LIGHT WAS on by the time he got there. He poked his nose in the kitchen—Jack and another guy were cooking something and teasing each other the way people do with a new lover. He went upstairs, tapping his fingernails on Laura's door. As he stood waiting, thinking maybe she'd stepped out, fingers jabbed him in the ribs. He jumped. When he came down there she was behind him in her bathrobe, towel around her hair, grinning, eyes sharp.

"Risky, babe, very risky," he said, grabbing a lapel of her robe, flexing his other hand to tickle her, but she opened her door and pirouetting into her room pushed to shut it—he wedged his foot in the opening, barely saving his extended arm from a slamming, shoved the door open harder than he meant to, stumbled in, then as it rebounded off the wall he gave it a kick that banged it shut. That impact hung in the air, the brightness in her eyes dimming to unhappiness. Walt's foot hurt, his sides hurt—she'd jabbed him hard—pretty aggressive for play. He leaned against the door; turning to her mirror she dropped her bathrobe, unwinding the towel and picking up her brush. He slid to the floor to watch her breasts circling with the motion of her arms as she fixed her hair. Finished, she put her hand on his right knee, which had so recently celebrated being able to bend again.

"Sorry—but you were a perfect target standing there."

"It's OK—I'm too young for a heart attack." But she'd zapped his affection—if Opal had feather-bed nature, Laura was a mollusk-shell clamped tight over whatever softness she still possessed—Cob, or Berkeley itself—he wasn't sure which was to blame.

He wasn't touching her. "Would you rather go out? You can walk now, huh?"

"Yeah—let's walk."

They strolled in silence past stores closing, restaurants opening—the interface where day meets evening.

"I can take you to dinner," he offered. "My check finally came through for Onion—two fifty—we could go someplace nice."

"You shouldn't waste a chunk of money like that—use it constructively—take the summer and travel."

"Would you come with?"

"I'm ready for time off—we could go camping in Montana."

"Then let's buy something to cook."

They walked slowly, not to stress his leg. At the co-op they decided to make a fruit curry with pineapple, bell peppers, raisins and tomatoes. Cob could eat that but when Walt suggested inviting him she balked. "Look him up, but leave me out of it."

IN THE MORNING he hurried to Argo; Cob was already in line. They ordered and moved to pickup, Walt nabbing a table when a guy left, scouting another chair as Cob brought their espresso. The place was packed—high tide for coffee cravings.

"So how's she doing?" Walt asked once they were settled, leaning in to talk. This place must suit Cob's paranoia—no eavesdropping agent could hear a thing.

"Depressed, like when I shook off that downer it landed on her."

"Have you said anything?"

"She's still weird to me. Stream's death unleashed so much guilt and bad karma—"

"Oh, is there a difference?" Walt said wryly.

"Isn't guilt when you do something wrong this time, but karma's when you're dealing with shit from your history?"

"Maybe that's a false distinction—could all be guilt."

"There's so much," Cob said, "I don't see how I'll ever work it off."

They looked out the window as though Karma was on the hunt out there for people to visit, lives to rattle.

COB PUT HIS tongue into his espresso to savor the bitterness. Through his half-closed eyes Walt's hair looked like Stream's—the cosmos' sense of humor was as cruel as his dad's. "Her brother came to see me—I shut the door on the nosy press but I figured he deserved to know more so we killed a bottle of wine talking about her. He's a straight preppy type from LA, didn't understand her at all. I had the feeling he was looking for just enough information to dismiss her death—didn't really want to know her. Said he offered her space at his house—an empty room in a part of town miles from anywhere she'd hang out—I told him that probably sounded like prison to her, and after he came down off his huff he admitted that's what she said. It was people she wanted, not some sterile room behind a locked door. Y'know, most of us get the urge to chuck everything and be free, but it's really hard to let go of plans, to be willing not to know this morning where you'll sleep tonight. She trusted people to look after her."

"And one day they didn't."

"I think Berkeley killed her, or a head-on collision with me and Laura."

"Yeah," Walt said glumly. "Bad karma all right."

"How should I be working it off—doing something for you?" Cob looked at him shrewdly. "I know what you want—same thing I do—only that's not on the table."

"I know."

"Believe me, I've thought about life without Laura—might be my only sane move—but there's no way—when you fall in the ocean your choices are limited. She pushes me this way, that way, half-drowns me. The only freedom I have left is to check out, and I changed my mind—for now. Short of giving her up, how can I help you?"

WALT FOUND THE espresso a perfect accompaniment to Cob's give-no-quarter style—after telling him what he must be thinking—accurately—he was extending what he thought was sympathy. Well, there must be some way they could value each other. "What do you suggest for my leg? Even my butt's lopsided."

"Stand up." Cob circled Walt's right thigh with his hands—the first two joints of his fingers overlapped. On his left thigh, they just met. "What about swimming? If you kick twice as much with your right leg, you'll build it back up without the pounding you'd get walking."

"Good idea." Walt sat again. "Only, where am I gonna swim?"

"Use my ID at the student rec center. Back home, see if you can crash UCSC—bet they have a nice facility."

"That campus is pretty tight."

"The Y? Get a trial membership cheap, quit before it runs into money. Shouldn't take more than three or four weeks to get your leg back."

"Yeah, I could try that—the doc said not to walk too much yet."

"The insurance pick up any rehab?"

"No, I'm lucky they paid what they did—otherwise I'd be screwed." They listened to the racket for a moment. Walt liked this place—even Berkeley had something to redeem it. "Why don't you move? Laura said that apartment creeps her out."

"Stream's there, is the thing."

Walt squinted at him.

"I'm not morbid—it just feels like she's touched everything, and when I touch it, she's with me. But nobody knew her—Laura just shatters every time—"

"Thought you met her at Diane's."

"She didn't know her—friend of a friend."

"Diane might put you in touch though—have you tried?"

"Maybe she'll talk to you."

"I'll call her tonight," Walt said. "So, is our Yosemite trip still on?"

"Far as I know—just a month—be here before you know it."

"Good—Laura needs a change of scene." The coffee buzzed through Walt's nerves. "Think I should just go home?"

"No, you steady her—she'd probably do better seeing more of you and less of me. It's like we're comrades-in-arms—all that craziness made us close, but now when we look at each other we see damage."

"But you study together?"

"Yeah—biology's our life raft."

"Conscious effort," Walt said. "My housemate Ray says 'don't try to change the whole world, just fix what's in front of you.' He put the seatbelt in Rusty—wouldn't let Laura drive back without it."

Cob laughed shortly. "That's more than my dad cared."

"Or you?"

"Well yeah, guess I coulda done something." Cob stood. "Hey, drop off my ID at the stat lab after you swim, OK?" and offering a soul shake, he took off.

FEELING LOOSE, HIS leg tired in a good way, Walt found Laura in her room. That electric blue shirt she'd got for Christmas made her eyes dazzle—he stood on the landing just looking. She grinned and unbuttoned, he came in closing the door...

When they were in tune like this he could pretend for an hour life made sense, hide from the chaos. She lay half on him, running a hand across his pecs.

"Don't lose these—I like your new muscles."

"Guess I'm evolving." Their fingers idled on each other. "Isn't evolution karmic progress?"

"You've been talking to Cob."

"Yeah. He's trying."

"I look at him," she said, "and see a broken mirror—bad luck, splintered reflections. He misses her so much, he still might kill himself. If he does, know what that'll do to me? Do you have any idea?" Her fingers were claws in his shoulders, he felt her teeth against his chest—if she drew blood would he be closer to feeling what they did? Was this his role now—to receive her worries, prop her up? Did she continue to call him from some outdated sense of duty, as if obligation wasn't the kiss of death for love? Even Cob was oppressed by her persistent desire, but he like Walt was in thrall, and her sanity seemed to depend on keeping them on the string.

WALT GOT HIM three phone numbers. The first turned out to be Stream's father in Mexico, and Cob extricated himself quickly. The second was a woman in Santa Barbara who didn't know she'd been planning to visit.

"Yeah, she called Christmas Eve, but she was in SF."

"Anybody in Santa Barbara she was seeing—any guys?"

"Everybody she crossed paths with," she laughed. "But never very long."

The third number was a guy in Capitola who sounded drunk, who handed him off to another drunk, and Cob was about to hang up when someone else grabbed the phone.

"You calling about Stream?"

"Yeah."

"Oh man, I'd love to see her again. She stayed with me up in the hills—mighta been the best week of my life."

"Yeah? I want to talk to you. Ever come up to Berkeley?"

"No man—too many bad vibes."

"What if I came down? You around this weekend?"

The guy laughed. "You don't wanna come here."

"What about Santa Cruz? I have a friend who lives there."

"Yeah. Gimme the address." Cob gave Walt's, hoping he wouldn't mind, and they agreed to meet around noon Saturday.

THURSDAY—WALT WOULD BE gone. Cob went home first to drop off some things and get his pathetic notes. Standing by his door he felt Stream there, and pressed his hand to his heart where she still glowed. Because #8 was rented now he kept his leave-taking silent, saying goodbye to her in his head as sincerely as if she was sitting in his armchair watching him go, regret softened by the warmth of knowing he'd be back.

Jack came in while he and Laura were having dinner.

"Oh hey stranger—how's tricks?"

"Not feeling that tricky," Cob said.

"Tell him about Larry," Laura taunted.

"Who's Larry?" Cob asked.

"Is 'lover' the right word?" a mean glint in her eye.

"That's right," Jack said stiffly.

"Congratulations," Cob nodded as Jack got himself a beer. "Is it good?"

"Yeah," Jack said tightly. "Yeah it is." He twisted off the cap and snapped it at the trash, missing. "Cheers," and flashing a toothy grin any monkey would recognize as a threat gesture, left the kitchen.

Laura smirked at Cob, exactly like his dad needling while his victim writhed. He said, "No point hurting people if you don't have to."

"You don't think he deserves it, nasty as he's been?"

"Those are the people who need to change—why make it harder?"

They finished their corn mush in silence. Up in her room she spread out notes and dictated, Cob writing intently, hoping he wasn't straining muscles using his hand so much now. Since the doctor'd given him the go-ahead last week to resume fine-motor activity, Laura'd been reproducing lectures for him when they had time—he'd discovered in his struggle with his clumsy left hand that writing was how he committed information to memory—so much of it just wasn't there this term when he searched his brain. Done reviewing she sat behind him in her armchair, kneading his shoulders and the back of his neck. He leaned into her massage, feeling how rigid he held himself every day so grief didn't flatten him. Her thighs hugged his hips, breath warm on his neck as her hands visited his chest.

"Stay?" she murmured.

Last fall he'd controlled her with longing; her hunger persisted but now he was the slave—how could it work that way? "You love Walt—why do you want me?"

"There's a place in my heart that's empty without you."

So he let himself be taken. Mistake or no, he couldn't keep her out. He shut doors in his heart, she was right behind him conquering his latches and padlocks, passing through every closed chamber seeking him—however he held back she just helped herself to him. By morning he felt demolished; he was progressing toward a new identity and fighting it seemed pointless, his past contemptible, anticipating where these changes might take him, impossible.

CHAPTER 19

Butterfly

A chromed and gleaming Kawasaki 650 chugged slowly up the street. The rider reading house numbers pulled up in front and cut the engine, knocked down the kickstand and stepped off, taking the key from the ignition. Removing his helmet he shook out stiff collar-length red hair as Cob stood up from the couch out on Walt's small porch.

"David?" he called.

"Yeah. Cob?"

Down by the cycle they shook hands—Cob's fingers were longer, David had a harder grip.

"Thanks for coming."

"So where you wanna talk?" David asked.

"The beach?"

"Hey, I know a cool place—we can walk. Couple miles, but it's by the ocean."

"Let's go."

David unzipped his leather jacket, Cob let his jean jacket hang open. They checked each other out while they walked—David was lean but muscular with faintly freckled skin and watchful brown eyes under his red-orange thatch, almost Cob's height in his combat boots. In a wrestling match they'd have been paired.

They went around the point past Steamer Lane where the surf came in big, and on west, beach replaced by cliffs riddled with holes. The tide was up, seething against the rocks, and going further they reached a place where the incoming surge smashed against a vertical, shooting ten or even twenty feet into the air then splatting back onto a potholed rock shelf before colliding with the next wave. They watched awhile then continued, finally coming to a beach; out in the tidal zone, breakers had pounded an arch through a remnant of cliff.

"This way." Turning away from the ocean, David led into a eucalyptus grove well back from the water, the sand on the path giving way to dark earth, ending in an empty clearing with logs set in a circle like benches, arched over by small grayish trees. They sat, and Cob cooling off began to notice butterflies—monarchs, flitting from one long down-trailing branch to another. One flew higher, and following its motion he looked up, then he saw them—hundreds, no, thousands, of butterflies, clinging in neat columns to the drooping gray-green branches, their wings half-open.

"Whoa," he breathed.

"I brought Stream here—she was like a butterfly. They seem like these helpless little things but they migrate hundreds of miles—further than some birds."

Cob told him about meeting her, offering her space—then her suicide.

"Man, why?" David lamented.

"She was in the wrong place. How'd you know her?"

"In November before the rain I met her down on Pacific Avenue—we vibed on each other right off. After we came here, I took her back in the hills by Watsonville—I have a friend with a trailer, and he was gone for a week so we hung out there. God she was sweet. She mighta stayed but my housemates are bikers—they'd 'a been all over her, so I gave her a ride to Carmel and she hitched south."

"Where was she going?"

"Had a friend in Topanga—Crystal?—something like that. Said they were gonna get a place together."

"Know if they did?"

"No—she called right before Christmas from San Francisco— wanted me to come up. But I stay outta the city—I get in trouble too easy. This hair, y'know, it's a red flag. I get in fights."

"You like to fight?"

"Well, yeah." David grinned, "I like to kick ass. And there's so many people need their ass kicked. How 'bout you?" tapping his own nose.

"I used to get beat up. The only guy I fought, I damn near killed him."

"No man, that's just trouble. All they really need is to eat a little shit. I don't think I ever hurt anybody bad."

"Well I did." And told him about Len.

"He deserved it—I'd 'a killed him."

"Making him clean up the blood was pretty good."

"I can't believe she did that—she was so—"

"I know. Berkeley messed her up."

"How long was she there?"

"About a month."

"With you?"

"Yeah."

David raised his eyebrows. "From what she said, she wasn't with anybody very long—a week, maybe two. I think you set a record man."

"We—" Cob inhaled long and slow, David nodded.

As the grove warmed more butterflies woke, opening and closing wings, stepping off the branches to flutter around the small clearing, filling the air with the bright orange and black of their motion, and Cob began to hear the patter of their wings against the faint background of surf. Then he felt the first one—a butterfly landed on his hair, David's eyes telling him to sit still. How completely Stream belonged here—with every breath he felt more butterflies touching him. Out of the corners of his eyes he glimpsed them on his shoulders, the front of his jacket, bright against the old denim. He thought of Stream in this jacket, and all the clothes she'd worn of other people's that they were wearing now, her touch still in them somewhere. He looked back at David whose eyes were wide with awe.

The nerves on his scalp were prickling and tingling as more monarchs walked in his hair. He lifted his right arm; some alit on the back of his hand, climbing among the short hairs, resting on his knuckles, clinging to his wrist. Moving slowly he tugged the sleeve up to expose his scar, holding that skyward, and returning from his disturbance they landed all up and down his arm. He felt the deep ache where the doctor'd cut him and drilled and screwed, but the tiny grip of butterfly feet seemed to wick the pain to the surface, their wings fanning it off into the air. He closed his eyes, remembering how he'd claimed to be able to fly—a lie to seduce women. A surge of shame washed tears between his eyelids, rapid on his cheeks, falling off his jaws or sliding down his neck. When they ceased and he finally looked around, he was alone. The butterflies flew off him in ones and twos till they'd left him entirely. He stood, raising his hands.

"Thank you Stream. You can go now, if you want, if you have someplace else to be. But if you don't, stay with me—I'll never ask you to leave." Out on the beach he found David and sat by him, plunging his hands into the warm sand.

"She really loved you," David said.

"She loved every guy she laid—not enough loved her back, was all."

"Hey listen—that grove gave me an idea. I'm a welder. I have scrap metal and a torch back at my place—we should make a butterfly for her, and find someplace to put it where she'd be happy. I can see it in my head, real clear."

They walked back to Walt's, and Cob drove them to Capitola in Rusty, down a side street to an alley, parking in a backyard. David pulled out a ring of keys on a metal retractor and unlocked the padlock on the reinforced door of a freestanding garage.

"This equipment's expensive, and we got a lotta other stuff in here too." Three steps inside he pulled a chain for a bulb high overhead, walked to where a workbench crowded with motorcycle parts and tools and rags spanned the far wall, hit a switch there—two rows of fluorescent lights came on. To the right of the door several traffic signs were bolted onto the wall at the corner, edge to edge. Spots and streaks scorched the paint, some bubbled, in other places down to bare metal. "These keep me from burnin' the place down." In a series of five-gallon buckets, lengths of metal bristled, longer pieces stacked on cross-bars on a rack welded of rebar. Cob was impressed by how orderly it was, versus the mess on the workbench. A pair of tanks stood to one side, hoses connected to a torch head stuck in a bracket. David opened the valves on the tanks. "So, I was thinkin' of somethin' like this," and lighting the torch with a striker and adjusting the flame to a long yellow and orange jet, he blackened a butterfly outline into MERGING TRAFFIC.

"Yeah, that looks good. What materials do you have?"

"Help me choose—I want it balanced—y'know, same thing on both sides."

Cob lifted pieces out of one bucket. "What's easier to work with—round or flat?"

"Any of it—pick what seems right—I can put it together."

He found several lengths of signpost with holes every few inches down the middle, set those on the metal work table David walked out from the wall. Further down in the bucket were two stiff springs coiled into six-inch circles. David meanwhile was choosing sixteen-penny nails, then a garage-door spring.

"This'll be for the body," he decided. "The circle springs can be markings on the wings. I can do legs and antennas with the nails. There's not enough of this signpost to do all four wings though—see what else you can find—I could do the top pair in this maybe." On the rack Cob found flat metal with long oval holes.

David relit his torch and put on his helmet. "Don't watch while I'm welding," then dropped his visor. Cob went out and flopped across Rusty's back seat with his feet out the door, feeling he'd found kinship. He nodded off as the sun heated the car, and woke to a shout. Back in the garage David stepped aside to show him—the butterfly was two feet across and almost that tall, the wings at a 120° angle to each other. The circle spring was only attached at one point on each wing, appearing suspended in air. The proportions were good, the legs bent and antennae knobbed the way they ought to be.

"Wow, you're really good—it's beautiful."

"Thanks man. Think she'd like it?"

"I know she will. Where should we put it?"

"Up past Santa Cruz there's some good spots—I'll weld it to a rod so we can stick it in the ground. Should be a mallet on the workbench—find that while I finish here." Cob finally spotted it on the floor, its rubber faces deeply pitted; he picked up a heavy ball-peen hammer too and brought them over where David was shutting the valves on his tanks, letting the torch die. He hung up his helmet and shed his leather apron but kept on his thick gloves, carrying the piece outside.

"Heavy?"

"Eighty pounds maybe."

They carefully rested the butterfly along the back seat, cranking down the window so the foot of the rod could stick out. As Cob turned Rusty he heard the bass farts of big motorcycles.

"Keep goin'," David said. Six bikers wheeled down the alley into the yard single file, all looking at him; as Cob gave the car some gas to get over the last bump, David stuck his arm out yelling, "Later." On the main road he laughed. "You didn't wanna meet those guys didja?"

"Not particularly."

"They're mean drunks, and Saturdays they're usually drunk. They're cool with me 'cause I can fix things, sometimes I make parts for their bikes, but 'friend of a friend' don't mean shit to them. If you're around when they feel like kickin' ass, you're it."

"Thanks for getting us out."

"It's hard to find space for a welding setup like that without puttin' out the bucks—it's just not too good socially."

Beyond Davenport, David told him to take a road inland. A creek splashed on their left, then where another creek fed into it off a hillside in the timber, Cob parked. They walked to where the water swirled together, chose a place under open sky near the confluence, and carried the butterfly across the main creek, Cob with the mallet in his belt loop, David with the hammer. They pushed the rod into the earth just barely before it stopped, then David brought the mallet down hard. Another chunk flew off its damaged face but the rod didn't budge. Dropping the mallet he readied the hammer, smacking the top end of the rod. This time the metal sank half an inch into the ground while their ears rang. Each blow pushed it a little deeper until, eight or ten inches in, it hit something too solid and stopped.

It felt secure so they moved back up to the road to consider—the butterfly was descending toward a boulder in the feeder creek, wings outspread to land. An observant person would notice, but most would miss it. That was good—not everybody saw her.

"I have something to dedicate it." Cob filled his pipe from what Walt had left him—two hits apiece and it was gone. He tapped out the ashes against the butterfly's head. "You're free, Stream. We'll never stop loving you, but we won't tie you down."

"G'bye," David said. "I shoulda made you a home. Let this be home."

Back at Walt's house Cob invited David to stay for salsa and chips; with a six-pack and a bottle of wine they sat in the kitchen listening to *Brothers and Sisters* by the Allman Brothers. When the chip bag was down to crumbs, David stood up.

"You OK riding after all that beer?" Cob asked.

"Three's my limit—after four I stay put. Think I'll go home, maybe tinker around welding some scraps."

"You're talented—I really like what you made."

"Thanks man."

Beside the motorcycle they studied each other in the ultraviolet wash of the streetlight; Cob extended his hand, David shook it then they hugged. "Thank you," Cob breathed, as though not David's ears but only his heart should hear. David kicked the starter, pulled forward off the kickstand and did a U-turn, waving as he went down the block. Cob stood on the sidewalk till the cycle's rumble blended into the rush of traffic, then sat on the couch in the semi-dark singing "Sometimes I Feel Like a Motherless Child," wine and blues making his voice stronger and his notes truer than he could really sing.

A WEEK LATER he drove Laura and Walt to the site. The butterfly was elusive amid rocks and underbrush; they circled to see it from different vantages.

"What are you gonna do here all day and night?" Walt wondered.

"Commune with her." So they unloaded Cob's backpack, sleeping bag, pad and a sheet of heavy-gauge clear plastic he planned to use as a tarp. Once they'd left he crossed the creek to where he had a good view of the butterfly, did some yoga to calm his mind then sat, his heart drawing Stream to him. In the afternoon the sun came through, striking the sculpture. The light seemed to stir it like the monarchs in the grove—crossing back to admire it from the road he heard a motorcycle on the grade—David.

"Hey, didn' spect ya here," he boomed. He'd been drinking.

"Thought about her all week—I'm here for the night."

"Wheresher car?"

"A friend dropped me off—I was thinking about painting this."

"Wha' color?"

"Like a monarch?"

"Nah, tha'd look weird. Glosh black."

"Nobody'll see it. What if it was silver?"

"Gold. Lesh go get some shpray paint."

"You loaded?"

"Nah—jush four. I ride a lot—m' bike'sh parta me."

"My friend was in a car wreck and finally got the cast off, and I just got my arm back to where it feels useful. How 'bout we hang out awhile, then go?"

"Not too long—can't paint inna dark."

They sat on a big speckled rock overlooking where the creeks tumbled together, David doodling a lion's head on the cover of a blank matchbook.

"You're really an artist."

"Thash what m' mom says when oth'wise she'd tell me 'm a bum."

They talked and sat awhile, then David squinted at the sky. "Let's go get paint." He seemed steadier so Cob decided he could chance it.

"Got an extra helmet?"

He put it on; David started the bike, flipped down the foot-pegs and gestured him to climb on. "Ever ride a motorcycle?" he yelled over the rumble.

"No." A lot of boys in Pryor had dirt bikes, but when he was in maybe sixth grade he was down by the creek—it was a spring day and he'd been hanging out watching a box turtle and some newly hatched spring peepers—he'd always been into life, into biology—when those jerks came ripping through on their Yamahas. They churned up the bank and when they were gone the Earth looked like it was bleeding, and there was the turtle, its shell crushed. He hated the boys and their loud machines, hated where he was—that was when he knew he had to get out, go someplace where life got respect. But David's cycle was a road bike—different vehicle altogether.

"Put all your weight into your butt, and don't lean, just let it take you."

"Is it OK to hold onto you?"

"You'll want to." Once Cob's foot was on a peg David rolled it with a little gas, they lifted their ground feet and David throttled, clutched, toed it into second, accelerated, third, Cob focused on keeping his weight low, hands linked across David's chest, feeling his pecs tense as he shifted gears. David leaned back. "Relax man," he yelled, taking a curve. Cob let the tilt of the cycle lead his body into it, the road right there, the rush of wind, the heavy vibration in his thighs and butt, up through his trunk. No wonder people loved motorcycles—this wasn't anything like sitting in a box, going down the road. At Route 1 David slowed, saw it was clear, accelerated up to fifth. Cob thought of Stream riding, the fast flow of air, the road speeding beneath them, so close. He was sorry she'd been holed up in his room all that time—she must've liked this, flying along, ready for his heat when they stopped. David pulled in at a hardware store.

"How much you think we'll need?" Cob asked.

"One can—plenty left over to get high."

"You don't sniff paint do you?"

"I have—it's OK."

"No it's not—major destruction of brain cells, is what it is."

"Yeah, well, there's lotsa ways t' do that. I got a friend sniffs glue—nothin' left," tapping his temple. "Goes by instinct, but he's pretty sharp with it."

"Don't do it around me."

"Hey, I haven't for a couple years—don't freak out."

Cob bought the paint.

"I'm hungry," David said. "Want a burger?"

"No—I don't eat those."

"Oh, are you vegetarian?" Only an afterburn of scorn—Cob liked that about California—rednecks here were used to all kinds of people—the ones in Nebraska would pound his ass—everything unfamiliar was lumped into one category: "not like us," which meant "destroy it."

"Sort of—I have what I want."

DAVID SHOOK THE can vigorously then passed it to Cob while he unwrapped his burger and took a couple big bites. Cob experimented spraying but David intervened.

"You gotta shake it more, then hold it further away to get it even." It went on better, but when he was done it seemed thin.

"Another coat, you think?"

"Wait'll it dries—don't put on too much. Keep it mysterious."

"Right." Cob ate some gorp.

David wolfed the rest of his fries then crumpled the bag to toss on the ground.

"Don't," Cob said. "The world's not a trashcan."

"Just markin' my territory."

"Think of Earth as an extension of our bodies."

"OK OK." He dropped it in the storage pannier. "Got water?" Cob tossed over his bottle, David drank then crossed to join him. "Oh hey, I like it from here. That's not too thin—it's good."

"Yeah," Cob agreed. "It's subtle."

"That's how Stream was—floatin' through Santa Cruz like a divine ghost." As the small patch of sky dimmed David looked at him closely. "You're wounded man."

"Part of me's with her—she doesn't seem dead."

"When I come up next weekend with my buddies, you better not be around, OK?"

Cob nodded, appreciating the brotherliness behind his threat.

"Once a month max," David warned.

"Yeah. Thanks."

"Take care man," and kicked his cycle to a blast of noise, raising gravel as he roared off. As the stillness returned, the hurrying water its only interruption, Cob spread his plastic on a flat spot near the sculpture, folding the heavy sheet in half lengthwise, closing the foot end with sturdy clips he'd swiped from the lab. He slid his pad and sleeping bag inside the fold and clipped the head-end to his pack frame to keep it off his face. He did sun salutations slowly, focusing as he stretched, feeling his right forearm bind and pull, sending thought and breath into the scarred muscles, coaxing length from them. The cosmos had used Len to punish him—for bringing her home? Keeping her there? Loving her not enough, or too much? Loving Laura? The questions in his head blended with voices in the water till he slept.

In his dream Stream was the butterfly sculpture, then with a quick movement freed herself, flitting, alighting on him the way the monarchs had. "Take yourself lightly," she said, her wings like solidified air—invisible, weightless, but lifting her. "I left because it was time to go."

"Didn't you love me?" he wailed.

"I do love you. Rise with me. It's not my death you're mourning it's your guilt."

In gray daylight it was raining, dripping off high branches. He looked through his transparent shelter right up into water falling at him, flinching at first then coaching himself not to. He lay there watching drops come at him, listening to them *thwock* the plastic, splat the rocks, hiss into the creek talking its way around obstacles on its short journey to the Pacific.

Time crawled and he had little to look at or think about but the rain and the shiny sculpture with drips falling off its wings or through them. Stream was right—something in his grief had turned from her to himself—time to move on.

PART THREE

Karma
Satisfied

CHAPTER 20

Sue

I n early April, Laura's high school friend Sue flew west to check out the Bay Area, find housing, and meet some of her research contacts. A five-day visit should be long enough to settle the basics before she drove out with her stuff six weeks hence. She took BART from the airport, then a bus put her in Laura's neighborhood. Duffel on one shoulder and her purse on the other, she read house numbers, coming up onto a porch where a John Lennon look-alike was talking to a dazzling woman she recognized with a jolt as her old friend.

The guy didn't skip a beat, including Sue in his rap—he introduced himself as Steve, and explained he needed volunteers to distribute literature for a ballot initiative.

"Whoa," she said, reading the leaflet he'd thrust into her hand, "I had no idea Berkeley's got a reactor—"

"Doesn't matter how small it is," he said. "Just the fact it's here supports the myth of benign nukes—that whole 'atoms for peace' BS. The timing's perfect to shut the thing down—with the Three Mile Island accident two weeks ago, then Tom Hayden and Jane Fonda here promoting *The China Syndrome,* people are waking up who never really thought about what could happen when something goes wrong."

"Yeah, that is scary—I'll put leaflets on doors," she agreed. "Give me a pile."

"And a territory," taking a neighborhood map and pad from the box at his feet. "You can do these four blocks—should need about a hundred. I'll leave more in the living room in case you run out. Let me know if you don't finish so I can assign somebody else." He wrote down block numbers and streets, rubber-banding the note to a stack of leaflets he handed to her. "Now what about the raffle—you want to win a ki don't you?"

"Of pot? 'Win'?"

"We're trying to make marijuana law enforcement the lowest priority for the police. Who knows if pot will ever be legal, but in the meantime we'd rather the cops spent their energy catching muggers and rapists—putting smokers in jail doesn't make anybody safer. The guy who wrote the initiative is funding his ads through a Win-A-Kilo raffle. I've got tickets here."

Sue shook her head in disbelief. "So there's a drawing?"

"Right after the election April 17th."

"I won't be here—how would I claim my prize?"

"How will anybody?" Laura challenged—she'd stood by silently while Steve made his pitch. "If the guy doesn't announce the winner publicly, how do we know he really gave it away? And if he does, whoever wins gets arrested—some prize!"

"Oh, he's thought about it," he assured her. "There's going to be a secret testimonial by the winner—"

"Which he could be making up—"

"Which authenticates the giveaway. He can't explain now, but the winner will get the stuff."

"Don't you think the police will buy tickets?" Sue asked. "What if they win?"

"The law prohibits possession," he said. "If the prize is at a neutral location and the winner's told where, he or she's the one in violation—be funny to bust a cop, wouldn't it? Imagine the flap at the trial when he says 'the Department paid for it.'"

They all laughed, but Sue declined to sell raffle tickets.

"That's OK," he said. "Thanks for helping with the leaflets—I'm off to my next drop." Balancing the box on his shoulder he headed down the street.

"Not even in the door and I've already been drafted." Laughing they hugged then went in. Laura gave her the Grand Tour; in her room Sue set down her bag, looking in vain for signs of male presence. "Isn't Walt here?"

"He lives sixty miles down the coast." At her puzzlement, Laura breezed, "I see him—we just spent a week together. How's Eddie?"

"He was talking about coming out with me."

"Why didn't he?"

"No money."

"As usual." They laughed. "But you're making some."

"This research job pays pretty well," Sue said, "and I think it'll be interesting—I laid the groundwork last month. How's grad school?"

"It's great—this program's exactly what I wanted."

Sue's brow knotted. "But why isn't Walt—"

"When we checked it out, every time I said 'this is perfect,' he said 'I can't live here'—so he doesn't."

"Guess I thought I'd see him too. Anybody else I should meet?"

"Well there's Cob."

"'Cob'?" Laura'd stopped as though there was nothing more to say. "A male swan."

Sue considered her inward-facing smile. Laura used to confide in her but since moving to California, nada—it had been easier to assume she was too busy than to wonder if she cared. But who was this new woman? Maybe Walt would know. "Show me around campus."

Grabbing jean jackets they went out. Laura walked her through the Biology building and peeked in the grad lounge; continuing down the hall they met a man in his forties wearing jeans and a warm-up jacket, his hair combed forward to hide a receding hairline.

"Oh, hello Laura," he said, eyes on her like hands—god, he was creepy.

"Dr. Dolph, my friend Sue—she has a research fellowship in anthropology."

"One of our rivals," adjusting his leer into a respectful smile. "Very often students start with us, then take a class with one of those dynamic professors in Anthro and we lose them—excellent department."

"So I've been told," Sue said.

Laura steered her on their way and when they'd rounded a corner, told her a story: the as-yet-unexplained Cob, her fellow student, worked in the Biology stat lab, and one dead Friday afternoon in the last ten minutes of his shift Dr. Dolph had showed up, interrupting them in the middle of a kiss to dump a huge pile of data he expected Cob to input and run for Monday morning. She left and the prof followed her, asking her out for a beer, persisting despite her refusals.

"Sue, it was awful. He was abusing his authority—he's on my thesis committee, and besides I think he's married—what the hell was he doing trying to pick me up?"

Sue didn't know what to say—was it possible Laura was unaware of the sex vibe pouring off her like a teenager's dose of cologne?

"Anyway, Cob caught up with us by Sproul Plaza. Dr. Dolph was pissed and said if Cob didn't need the income he'd give that job to somebody else, Cob said the department wouldn't pay overtime so he quit. Dr. Dolph was bluffing but Cob wasn't—he used to be a campus janitor, and his old supervisor hired him on the spot. But that wasn't the end of it—Dr. Dolph went to the dean and Cob sort of barged in on their meeting, and told Dr. Cohen his colleague had been hustling me. Well, the dean takes the heat if anyone in his department gets out of line, so he called me in and said to report any problems directly to him—and then, get this, when I told him my thesis was in Dr. Dolph's area of expertise and I needed him on my committee, Dr. Cohen said he'd serve on it too."

Then Laura with a look halfway between sly and smug explained, "Dr. Cohen has almost nothing to do with students—teaches one postgraduate seminar and oversees faculty research—nobody could believe it when they found out he's my adviser."

"I can see how a professor could get himself into trouble," Sue murmured. The directions Laura's self-assurance had grown were unsettling—if she cost Dr. Dolph his job she'd get an ego boost, not out of meanness but as affirmation of the new power her attractiveness gave her. A girl from Carling, Colorado, a *femme fatale?*

"WHAT IF WE get a place together?" Sue suggested at dinner.

"Well, I like this house, and apartments usually cost more, and there's less people to split utilities and phone—"

"You don't want to." That hurt—they'd always talked about sharing a place.

"Maybe a room will open up here."

In the morning after walking Laura to class, Sue visited the Anthro building where she met with one person in the lab, made a Wednesday appointment to see another then had a long chat with the department secretary who gave her the lowdown on everybody. Meeting people she'd be working with restored her optimism—maybe Laura was keeping her at arms-length so she'd establish her own base here and not be dependent. With a bounce in her step she wandered down Telegraph Avenue taking in the sights—sidewalk vendors were hawking everything from bootleg record albums to hash pipes to radical buttons and bumper stickers. She spent an hour in a four-story used bookstore, picking up one unusual title after another—what bounty. Pledging to fill some shelves once she moved here, she considered the stack she was carrying and finally bought Italo Calvino's *Cosmicomics*.

She was on Laura's porch reading when a guy went past her and inside—not Steve or Jack but he didn't hesitate—she had a feeling he was in Laura's room. She went upstairs, book in hand, wondering if thieves were that brazen here—he stood by the dresser, holding an undershirt to his nose. He turned swiftly when she came in, hand dropping away from his face.

He asked, "Who are you?" before she could.

"Laura's friend Sue, visiting. You?"

"Cob." As though that explained everything.

"What's with the shirt?"

He cocked an eyebrow. "Really want to know?"

"Yeah. I thought you were ripping her off, but nobody steals dirty laundry."

"This could be worth taking—a scent that could save a man's life, or kill him."

"Will it?" She moved further into the room noticing his broken nose, aware now of his energy like a force-field.

"Maybe." He pressed his lips together, eyes darting to look her over.

"She's changed a lot since I saw her more than a year ago. Because of you?"

"Partly, yeah." Doubt clouded his eyes. "Didn't she tell you?"

"I got the feeling she didn't want to."

"Well, it's complicated—can't really blame her."

"Will you tell me? She's a close friend, and I'm moving here in June for a year."

"Really? She never mentioned that. You know Walt?"

"I met him, last time I saw her. But she said he's not in Berkeley."

"We went camping—he just went home a week ago."

"'We'?"

"Law and Walt and I."

"That's what I thought you meant. So she has two lovers?"

"Apparently," he said, eyes bright again. "But she wants space this week."

"Then what are you doing in her room?"

"She's teaching this afternoon."

"So you come smell her shirts when she's not around?"

"No, no," he said softly. "When I hold this I can feel her skin right inside. And when she wears it, maybe she'll feel me touching her."

She'd never heard anyone say such odd things. "When did she— become—"

"Beautiful? Oh, it's such a long story, we should sit. Let's go to Argo." He flashed a high-wattage smile, she found herself smiling back, setting down her book.

HE DROPPED HIS jacket on a table and tilted two chairs against it, joining her in line where her gaze was drawn to the guy working the machine: a black man who looked like he owned this big room and every vibe in it—his eyes suddenly locked on Sue's, not the stare of an ogler but the cold fixity of analysis, and between one blink and the next she felt she'd been photographed then filed with children and innocents in a bottom drawer. At a distance she'd filtered Berkeley's politics and personalities through an idealist lens—now she saw she didn't know the place at all, and felt exposed, defenseless.

Cob bought them espresso, and once they were seated with small white ceramic cups and saucers, he began to talk. As he explained about anticipation she felt her skin tighten, her nipples harden—the combination of his intimate tone of voice and the single-mindedness of his attention was thrilling, even as a story—she could imagine its effect on a woman he was hustling.

Without offering specifics he made clear he'd done something wrong and wanted to atone, but when his look began to feel like physical pressure on her face and upper body she set her eyes to wandering—so this was a coffeehouse. The only espresso in Carling was at the Mars Hotel and Blues Café, but that was a relaxed friendly place—in here everybody seemed old, canny and humorless, as though joy had mummified and they were studying the remains.

"I'm surprised Law didn't tell you about me," he said finally.

"Why do you call her 'Law'?" He'd referred to her that way several times.

"Because she is—not written law, which I don't respect, or social law which I break whenever I can get away with it, nor physical law, which only fools defy. To me she's Cosmic Law, the way the universe operates—I have no choice but to obey."

"Except when she's not around, huh?"

"I won't come over again this week, but you're welcome to visit me." He wrote his phone number and address, pushed the slip across the table.

"We used to be close," she said regretfully, pocketing the paper then tilting her cup's dregs onto her tongue.

"You can be her reality check—she needs one. Walt's not grounded anymore." He stood so she did too, and on the sidewalk just outside as she paused to orient herself, he gave her a light sweet kiss while running a finger from the part in her hair to the hollow at the back of her neck. "Good to meet you Sue." Then he moved easily but fast down the block; she watched, frozen by tingles rushing over her scalp; under the coffee a hint of maple syrup lingered on her lips.

"Met your friend Cob today."

"Oh," as though that wasn't in the plan. "How'd that happen?"

"He came by," at Laura's pained look adding, "We went out."

"Hm." Dissatisfied, but not elaborating.

"He told me why you look the way you do."

"Did he come on to you?"

"No. But he's a sexy guy," Sue's eyes crinkled.

"I know," Laura said flatly. "Thought he was done with those games. Plan to see Walt?"

"Maybe Thursday. Cob said I can use his car."

"Then you better do a test-drive first," handing her the keys.

Out front they got in an ancient clunker whose paint was baked to nothing by decades of sun. Sue said, "This thing runs?"

"He's a good car—name's Rusty."

"Should be Dusty," running a finger across the dash.

"Smells like home, doesn't it?"

Sue inhaled deeply. "Yeah, it does." She looked at Laura. "You miss it?"

"Some things—the big horizon, thunderstorms you can see coming for a hundred miles, people with nothing to do besides watch them."

"And don't forget the big suspense," Sue reminded her: "Who'll land the cashier job at the Circle K and get that extra fifty cents an hour over minimum wage?"

They laughed ruefully—that was about the extent of Carling's opportunities.

THURSDAY MORNING SUE went to Santa Cruz, driving in thin fog that burned off by the time she arrived. Walt came to his door smiling wide, offering a hug.

"Want to go somewhere?" he asked.

"Anything I should see?"

"Mama Pacifica—let's walk." They buttoned their jackets against the cool air, out by Lighthouse Point slowing to observe a few surfers in wetsuits sitting on their boards waiting for swells. One paddled and caught a wave, then she wanted to watch so they found a bench in the sun and sat.

"I met Cob," she said.

"He tell you about Stream?"

"No—which one?"

He recounted a brief sad story about a flower-child who'd killed herself at Cob's apartment. "I never met her, but her death really did a number on Cob—and Laura too. They won't talk about it."

"He wasn't kidding when he said explaining was complicated."

"He tell you about his arm?"

"What about it?"

"Or my leg?"

"No," she said, truly baffled now. "He talked a long time."

Walt told her about a car accident he'd been in, making it sound as though Cob had something to do with it. She couldn't see the connection, but guilty or not, Cob got paid back in spades when he was attacked by a bat-wielding neighbor. As Sue listened she leaned into Walt, he slipped an arm around her shoulders, and pretty soon they were kissing.

She'd thought about him sometimes—at her Christmas party before he went to California she'd liked him, finding him as transparent as Laura was opaque—they balanced each other well. These kisses were friendly, more appealing than Cob's which had the taint of conquest. But Walt was still Laura's boyfriend, as far as she knew.

"We shouldn't," she said, pulling away.

"Cob kiss you?" he asked, and at her assent nodded, "So you can kiss me. It's all one."

"What about Laura?"

"She's the One we all are. Don't worry."

"People say things are loose out here—is this what they mean?"

"Possibly." His eyes half-closed. "Could you do that again?"

She tried to think of Laura but the image that came to mind was Cob, his eyes like x-ray vision becoming the eyes of that guy at the espresso machine who'd pegged and dismissed her so quickly. People in Berkeley were territorial and strong—as she and Eddie would say, she'd been dodging bulls since she arrived.

When she was thirteen she'd decided one spring day to observe a great blue heron that visited ponds in the area, and tracked him on her bike to a pasture several miles from town. She hadn't lived on the Colorado prairie very long—nobody told her about bulls. She was a good quarter mile inside the barbed-wire fence when the first one heaved his bulk upright and lowered his head her direction. She kept walking, slowly circling away from him toward the road. Then the second and third ceased chewing their cuds to watch. They became interested enough to stand, and hearing a basso grunt she saw the fourth, between her and the fence, walking. At first she'd thought maybe they were steers, the castrated beef cattle she'd been teased about mistaking for bulls, but these animals' heads and necks were oversized, their bodies immense, and now she could see their balls hanging between their hind legs in front of frayed-rope tails.

They were as big as rhinos. She'd come alone, still trying to get used to the idea of living in the sticks, not fitting in at school—she had no idea what to do. If she yelled or threw rocks she might goad them to attack. The only tree was by the pond, a broken ratty-looking willow with its main trunk leaning 45°—from here she wasn't sure if it was tall enough for her to climb out of range, but it was closer than the fence and the opposite direction from the bull that was moving fastest. He could probably outrun her so she forced herself to maintain her pace but she could hardly see, her heart bounding inside her ribs the way her legs wanted to across the wide flats, her mouth parched and palms sweating.

Finally she broke into a sprint, thuds gaining on her, and scrambled up the trunk as fast as she could, the ground jarring as the bull arrived only paces behind her. From her perch she looked down at brown eyes with bloodshot margins, smelled his male reek under the cattle odor she was getting used to and the dust he'd stirred up. He actually pawed the bare dirt under the trunk with one huge forehoof, snorting, his rib cage arching out then down from his exertion, and knocked his head twice against the tree which shuddered alarmingly—she had to clench the bark not to tumble onto him.

Some animals considered eye contact a threat so she stretched upward, searching the fields for signs of civilization—a house, a truck, a silo—far off she could see a cluster of buildings but there was no way to get their attention. Once her pulse subsided she realized she was stuck, so she got as comfortable as she could in a crook of the tree while not only that bull but the others settled underneath to chew their cuds. It was the longest afternoon of her life—the heron must've taken off when she was running for the tree, because she never saw it—but as the sun neared the horizon and its slight warmth dwindled, a pickup made a dust cloud out in the pasture. The bulls lumbered to their feet, plodding toward it, and when she decided they were far enough away she climbed down and jogged briskly back to the fence. Safely outside, she still had to walk half a mile to her bike then pedal back to Carling in the growing dusk, shaking from hunger and fright.

She needed to know how much danger she'd really been in; as she noised it around at school everyone had the same pop-eyed expression— she'd been lucky, but behind her back she guessed they were discussing how stupid the city girl was. That day Eddie introduced himself. With his long thin hair and frayed clothes he'd seemed too derelict to talk to, but he came up to her after school and looking her in the eye told her she was rash but showed mettle, keeping her head. His choice of words surprised her, so she confided the full story of her terrifying afternoon, which he made more dire by telling her about bulls stomping drunks—the only people dumb enough to go in their pasture. "Except me," she said, and laughing he said, "Indeed, but you kept your head—that's why you still have one." And on the basis of the mutual respect discovered that day, they became friends, coining the phrase "dodging bulls." Though the brazen stares of strangers weren't as bad as that bull thundering after her, her shocked realization was the same—she'd blundered unawares into a threatening place.

Walt by contrast was laid back and easy—she'd found out more talking to him than from Laura and Cob combined—finally she could let down her guard. So she kissed him again. He shifted her onto his lap, one hand parting a button to slide inside her jacket, moving on her breast. But when she felt his hard-on pressing her thigh she stood up, buttoning against his intrusion.

"Let's go back," she said firmly, gaze fixed on the great blank arc of ocean, level as a pasture. A guilty flush climbed her cheeks. Or maybe she was turned on.

"Sorry," he said, standing, "That was forward of me. I wonder if something simple and straightforward could untangle some of my knots, that's all."

"What knots? What's simple?"

"Nothing is."

She studied him, surprise fading into disappointment—he was one more libido-off-the-leash, in a place where they seemed the norm.

"There's a memorial for Stream I can show you," he suggested. "We'll take both cars, because it's on your way back."

She got to Berkeley midafternoon, and instead of going to Laura's, called Cob from a pay phone. He gave her directions; when she knocked on his door he opened with a flourish, bowing her in.

"Welcome."

"I just saw Walt—he told me about Stream, then we visited the butterfly. That's the kind of headstone I'd like."

"He's the right person to explain. Law and I can't really tie her up with words and push her out into the light of day without doing her injustice. We keep her here—" hand to his breastbone. "But it's good you know."

"I'm starting to see—"

"Why'd you come over?" cocking his head to one side, eyes offering no retreat.

"After what Walt said, I thought maybe I should talk to you again."

"Mm. He tell you about my arm?"

"And his leg."

"So now you know everything."

"Do I?" Didn't seem likely.

"Well no, but enough to spare me further explanations." Then bold as could be he spread his hands on her back and moved in for a kiss. As her mind told her to leave, her mouth was marveling—why'd he taste like maple syrup?

"Tell me to stop," he murmured, lips continuing to her jaw, down the side of her throat as his fingers rippled up and down her back. Laura obviously loved him amid a tangle of other feelings—curiosity overcame Sue's indignation. He bent his knees as he kissed down her front, one deft hand sliding up inside her shirt to unhook her bra and lift it free of her breasts. Raising the shirt he took one nipple in his mouth, her hand in his hair now, fingers plowing his scalp.

"D'you have birth control?" he said.

"I'm on the Pill. Do you still—"

He straightened to look deep into her eyes. "A year ago I'd have stopped with this, and when you came back in June you couldn't get over here fast enough. But I'm reformed. Now you can have what you want, as soon as you want it. Do you?"

He could set a record for seduction. But maybe Laura would make sense—

"Yeah I guess."

"Aaah." He unbuttoned her shirt, helping her out of the sleeves. In one swift shrug he had off his t-shirt, then unzipped her. She nudged off shoes, wriggling her hips so her jeans slumped. He slipped his fingers beneath the elastic of her undies, sliding them down. She unbuttoned his jeans and let them drop—nothing on underneath. He moved to the bed, hands on her ass, then he laid her down. When she was breathing fast he rammed her then slowed, and when he rolled her on top, she rested a forearm on his chest and looked at him.

"Interesting. I've never been laid so fast."

"Well, you know a lot about me—why should I be the only one naked?"

"Are you?"

"Yes ma'am. Under the microscope."

Well, that was true. "Do I need to apologize to Laura?"

"She's gonna marry Walt."

"You sure about that?"

"Yep."

"Do you mind?" she asked.

"Can't I keep any secrets at all? Who are you, rifling my closets when we just met? I tell you stories of my shame, lend you my car to go visit someone who'll tell you the sadder stories I still can't talk about, offer my sex when you don't even care, and now you want to poke around in the ruins of my heart? You got some nerve, woman."

"I—I'm sorry."

"Don't be sorry, be honest. Who are you?"

"You sound like Laura," she said with a little grin, and saw he was touched, grinning back. "I've known her since ninth grade. I moved to Carling from Chicago—like landing in the nineteenth century. I tried out groups at school—the cheerleaders, the fast girls, the athletes— then I met her, a kindred spirit. We were in plays together, there and in high school, and went bicycling and hiking. She showed me everything Chicago wasn't, so generously I didn't mind being there. We made some friends together and a lot of us are still close, but Laura opened the door. Spring of senior year everyone was about to split different directions, and we wanted to link to each other in a way we wouldn't lose so we went camping—seven of us—and smoked a lotta grass, did silly things and laughed a lot, and when we came back to town we were friends for life."

"Sounds good. So now I know more about Law. What about you?"

"I studied Anthropology at a state school, and when Laura told me she'd applied out here I wrote to the Anthro department about research positions. I was amazed they accepted me, but Laura was too, when she got in."

"She's an excellent student—why wouldn't they admit her?"

"Berkeley always had this mystique for us—unattainable."

"Well, mystique or mistake, here we are," turning onto his side.

"Are you always so aggressive?"

"The word 'always' has lost its meaning—I just do what makes the most sense."

"THAT GUY'S A trip," she exclaimed, coming into Laura's room.

"Walt?" puzzled or worried.

Sue decided not to say he'd come on to her. "Cob."

"*That's* where you've been," as though she could see Cob's sweat on her skin. "All day?"

"No. I went to Santa Cruz, and Walt told me about Stream, and broken bones."

Laura shook her head. "What's your verdict?"

"I think Cob's the most self-centered person I ever met." With Laura a close second, followed by Walt.

Laughing, Laura said, "Could be."

"He ticked me off, moving on me so fast."

"He would've stopped if you told him to."

Sue was floored. "My god, you're just like him. I don't know what's worse: 'slam-bam-thank-you-ma'am' or hearing you defend him."

"Forget it. You found out too much too fast."

In Laura's embrace her confusion came out in sobs. "How could you go through all that, and not tell me?"

"I couldn't even tell Walt everything." She petted Sue's shaking back. "It's all right. You could go back to Cob's and spend the night—you might feel better."

"Are you kidding?" She'd heard it called Berzerkely—it was.

"You're only half-laid—shouldn't you finish?"

"It doesn't faze you at all." But Cob had said she should be Laura's reality check—how could she shed any light from this fog?—maybe—"Would you—talk—"

"Sure sweetie." She wiped Sue's cheeks and they went downstairs.

CHAPTER 21

A Berkeley Welcome

When Sue got to his apartment, Cob was spooning avocado out of a rind.

"Want some?"

"No thanks—a couple crackers maybe."

"I don't have those, but look around, help yourself."

She opened the fridge and the cupboard. "Where's your bread?"

He told her about his fruitarian diet. Treating plants and animals as equals sounded like folk religion—not what she'd expect of a scientist. She improvised a meal of walnuts, plain yogurt and an orange.

"I have to study," he said. "Pick some music if you want, or something to read."

"I should've brought my book." This always happened—she'd lug a book around all day and never find a minute to read, then as soon as she went someplace without it, slack time appeared.

"Help yourself to mine." He arranged papers on his table while she scanned his shelves; though she worried about distracting him he ignored her completely. Picking up *The Tin Drum* by Günter Grass she sampled a few paragraphs then snuggled into his broad armchair with it. The room was quiet except the hollow thump of his pen on the card table, paper shuffling, pages turning. She'd read several chapters when he stood up, packing notes and a book into his backpack, setting that by the door. She glanced at her watch—eleven—early, by her standards.

"Hate to be a party pooper but I get up at five," pulling off his shirt and tossing it onto the heap in a corner.

She remembered Laura's story about him undermining her professor's threat by jumping ship for a menial job. "You don't mind grunt-work?"

"Nope—as long as I keep the place looking good my supervisor leaves me alone, and in a crunch I can study. Beats the hell out of being jerked around." He switched off the overhead bulb, his eyes reflecting the lamplight. "Anyway, if you care to join me—"

"That's why I'm here," she said, half to herself, marking her place in the book and turning off the lamp. Naked he stood by the foot of the bed, stretching as she watched in the dimness. When he turned to her she stood frozen, baffled about Laura—why had she sent her here? Was she even still her friend, or just coasting on habit? But Cob moved his hands, warm electricity filling the space where his palms almost touched her skin. She sank into her body as though she was stoned, touching his smooth torso, observing the motion of his hard-on as he stepped back against the side of the bed, coaxing her closer.

"I will completely respect you," breath warm in her hair. "Anything you don't like, speak up. If you want me to do something, tell me—otherwise, I'll take your body's word for it. OK?"

"OK." *I'm out of my mind*, but as her brain began to chatter, the flavor of his kiss summoned her awareness back into her mouth and skin. Sitting on the bed he pulled her, she lifted one knee then the other to the mattress accepting him incrementally while his fingers traced crescents on her back, ass, thighs. He planted one hand to arch her spine so his teeth could play her nipples, his other supporting her head. Lifting her upright he got some bounce going, riding into her then out on the impacts, then she laughed which opened all her nerves to him, bathing her in energy fast-moving and gone as meteor tracks. They lay back, rolling up the bed and down, each laugh a fresh surge as though a waterfall ran through her from thighs to scalp, icy water and heat in layers that didn't blend. Her skin was turning on and off, her awareness of contact coming and going with every rapid breath. Lying still finally, holding him inside, she met his kiss instead of simply receiving it.

"Better now?" he murmured.

"Mmm," smiling. "You shouldn't be so arrogant."

"If I wasn't I'd be somebody else."

For Laura to tame this guy she must be as egotistical as he was.

SHE WOKE TO the smell of frying, squinted toward the stove where he stood in his t-shirt, his small round ass bare. The lamp was on, the overhead light off, he sang "Tangled Up in Blue" softly, inserting *da da da* where he forgot lyrics. Wrapping a thick sock around the handle he lifted the skillet off the stove, eating from it with the wooden spoon. A kettle whistled, he poured steaming water into a cone. At the scent of coffee she sat up; he came over with the skillet.

"Corn mush?" extending the spoon.

She took a grainy scorching bite, he bared his lips taking the next, when she tried again it was cooled enough to eat without burning her tongue. He held the skillet away so he could kiss her, then returned to the stove to get his coffee. He creamed it and sat beside her to share.

"Why doesn't Laura mind?" she said.

"She can have me anytime—we're like DNA: endlessly chained together."

"And Walt?"

"Him too." He dressed quickly and slugged the rest of the coffee, put on his jean jacket and backpack, and grabbing an orange from the fruit bowl came over, resting his hand lightly on her shoulder.

"The door locks when you shut it, just make sure it's closed. Take the book if you want. Say hi to Law." He kissed her quickly, pressing her nipple between thumb and forefinger. "It's been a pleasure Sue," he smiled wide, then left.

She showered in the tiny stall then dressed, combing out her long fine brown hair thinking maybe it was time to get it cut, then in the armchair returned to *The Tin Drum*. But her head was buzzing and she couldn't concentrate—Walt would've laid her too only she'd stopped him—why not Cob? Because Walt was Laura's intended—off-limits. So didn't that make Cob the man she really loved, since he didn't fit her plans but stood right in the middle of them anyway? Yet she'd practically ordered Sue to come back over here. Spending the night with him was as different from that speed-bang as if he was two people. And what an oddball—"fruitarian" sounded like something he'd made up just to be different. Too much to absorb—suicides, broken bones, this love that seemed both completely open—both men hitting on her shamelessly, with no resistance from Laura—and so tightly sealed she'd never glimpse what was inside.

She gave up trying to read and looked out the window. It was past dawn but streetlights were still on, fog glowing over what she guessed was the Bay—it looked chilly. Deciding a walk would clear her head she put on her jacket, wedged the thick paperback into her purse, and checked to make sure she had everything—she was flying out in the afternoon.

Strolling down the block, she was debating whether to leave the book in Rusty, when something struck her. She spun trying to keep her balance as a ragged-looking youth dashed away, her purse in his hand. Yelling she gave chase, at the end of the block he darted around a corner; when she got there he was out of sight. Reaching the alley she saw movement—a homeless woman wearing layers of clothes, two hats stuck over her matted hair, was standing on a pile of stuff in a shopping cart, poking in a dumpster with a broom-handle. Sue jogged over.

"Excuse me."

The woman ignored her, intent on her exploration.

"Excuse me, did a young man just run by? He stole my purse."

The woman turned. Her creased weathered cheek was smudged, the reek of urine and old sweat rolled off her, stronger with each movement. Her milky blue eyes squinted down at Sue.

"Whachu say?" her voice as ragged as the hemless plaid skirt she wore over a pair of stained pink sweatpants.

"A teenager just stole my purse. Did he run past here?"

"T'day?"

Every passing minute reduced her chances of getting her purse back, but this woman had no obligation to help her. Impatience would turn her off. "Just now. Did he run this way, did you notice?"

"Oh." She peered ahead as though the dumpsters were signaling. "He ran by."

"Thank you." Sue dashed down the alley, at the end of the block looking around—if he had a place to go he was headed there, if not he'd probably zig-zag. In the next block she pulled herself up to sit on the edge of a dumpster to see further, and heard a low growl—below her stood a German-shepherd-sized yellow dog, teeth bared.

"Go away," she scolded, but as she moved her foot the dog jumped at it. Crouched on the corner of the steel container she looked for something to throw, then carefully lowered herself in, the trash halfway up her shins when she stopped sinking. She picked up an athletic shoe with its sole torn half off, then as though her vision cleared, suddenly saw not "trash" but objects people had discarded—rags, a vacuum cleaner bag, a toaster, Kleenex, pill bottles, cereal and cracker boxes covered with bright pictures too upbeat for a dumpster. And as she mused on the American propensity for using things then pretending they'd ceased to exist, she saw it: her purse lay on a pizza box, in a splat of canned spaghetti. Scraping off what she could of the orange sauce with a cracker box flap, she checked the purse's contents. Cob's paperback was gone—probably fell out somewhere—and her wallet too, but not her plane ticket or travelers checks. Her address book was still in here, her checkbook—why hadn't she left that at home? A crumpled napkin was dissolving among the pens, paper clips and coins in the bottom—she pulled that out to wipe off the rest of the spaghetti. She habitually chose purses that were too small—hoping their size would limit what she felt compelled to drag around? In the store they looked sleek and elegant, their flimsy straps designed to carry the minimum, but filled with her stuff they bulged like footballs.

"No more dress purses for me," she vowed. Back on the rim of the dumpster she realized she'd forgotten the shoe to throw at the dog—but the animal was gone. Dropping to the greasy asphalt she laughed—that mutt had helped her—otherwise she'd never have found her purse. She walked back to the corner and along the street looking for the book, and got clear around the block before spotting it on a storm-drain grill, cover torn but otherwise intact.

Returning to Rusty she dug in her jeans for the keys—not there. She rummaged clear to the bottom of her purse—only her apartment key. Damn, would she have to root through that dumpster? She went through her pockets one at a time, jeans then jacket, even the breast pockets though she never put keys in there. No. She pictured herself parking the car, taking the key from the ignition, buttoning her jacket—she'd put them down to button. There they were, on the seat—she'd never been so spaced out. This visit was rattling her badly—Laura being so changed, and hard, and Walt's kisses, then Cob… She leaned against the car, two breaths from tears. No, that wouldn't do. She had to get into this car and go back to Laura's. Returning to the alley she walked after the homeless woman, now halfway up the block.

"Excuse me, thanks for your help," she smiled. No response, but as Sue moved in front of her cart the woman stopped. "Do you have a coat hanger?"

"No closet honey," she wheezed—might be laughing.

"I locked the keys in my car—I could use a piece of wire," taking a quick look at the junk in the cart—filthy clothes, a rolled-up piece of pitted polyurethane foam, soda and beer cans scattered through the mess. Lots of street people took care of their stuff but this cart was a miniature dumpster. She looked into those lost eyes.

"Whachu want?" the woman snarled defensively.

"Never mind." Walking back up the alley she found a hanger and returned to the car, doing up the bottom two buttons of her jacket to tuck her purse inside against her waist—not so easy to grab now. The window was all the way up so she slid one looped end of the unfolded hanger between door and frame, bending the wire to curve around the door as she lowered it to the flared tip of the lock knob. She wiggled the loop over, lifted—it slid off. She grimaced, trying again.

"Locked out huh?" A boy about fifteen stood a few feet away, watching. "Ever do this?"

He put his hand on the back door latch, testing. It opened, and reaching past her dangling hanger he lifted the knob. "That easier?" then walked away laughing. Face burning she opened the door and retrieved the keys. Nobody wanted this car—that's why it was still here.

CHAPTER 22

Visitation

When Sue left Carling the Tuesday before Memorial Day in her Datsun station wagon, Eddie accompanied her, intrigued by her Berkeley report and inclined to see for himself. They planned to spend the long weekend at Laura's—one housemate was out of town. Sue hadn't found housing on her April trip so she'd have to settle that now. They arrived Thursday night; as they pulled up out front, Laura came to greet them.

Eddie's hands checked out her new shape as they hugged. "You've become a siren, Reiner—how'd that happen?"

"Sue must've told you."

"She wasn't exaggerating—you're magnificent."

"I'm still me—don't get weird OK?" He detected a clench under her bantering tone. She aimed him at her housemate's room then helped Sue bring her stuff upstairs—they'd share her room again. With things stashed they met in the kitchen. "Hungry?"

"Buzzed, actually," Eddie said. "Got any beer?"

She plonked a six-pack on the table, they each took one. Laura shot her bottle-cap at the trashcan and ricocheted it in. "Bank shot," she crowed.

Eddie aimed too high, his bounced onto the floor, Sue lobbed hers, a foot short. They all laughed.

"You could've been Carling High's center—why did we never suspect?" he said.

"I've had practice. At this distance I seldom miss." They clinked bottlenecks and drank, looking each other over.

"You missed the fun," Laura said. "The jury let off Dan White for murdering Mayor Moscone and Harvey Milk—he won with the Twinkie Defense."

"The what?" Eddie said.

"His lawyers claimed eating too much junk food unbalanced him—basically he pleaded irresponsibility—a watered-down insanity defense."

"That *is* insane," Sue said.

"No, what's crazy is the jury that bought it."

"They put Manson in a hospital for the criminally insane," Eddie said. "What happens to this killer—is he sentenced to diet rehab?"

"Not even that—he's off virtually scot-free. Monday there were riots in San Francisco—started out as marches but by nightfall they were smashing things in the Castro. I suggest staying out of the city while you're here."

"Californians are different, aren't they?" Eddie said. "Or should I say 'aren't you'?"

"Same people," Laura shrugged, "just without the constraints they'd feel elsewhere—this is truly the land of self-invention."

"What about the marijuana initiative?" Sue asked. "Did that pass?"

"Yeah, by almost sixty-five percent—but the turnout was a historic low—Berkeley's not the political hotbed it used to be. Steve gets worked up over local issues but most people couldn't care less."

"So who won the ki?"

"Only the winner knows—wasn't me."

Eddie sat back. "Sue tells me you've broken the chains of coupledom."

"Feels more like I'm coupled twice: a boxcar with an engine on each end."

"What happens when they pull opposite directions?"

She gave him a hollow look. "They are. We're goin' nowhere, with enough friction to melt the tracks. I think we'd all be better off not knowing each other."

"Oh no, you're our pioneer, into the land of sexual freedom."

She laughed shortly. "I've concluded people can't be free."

"Not even in the moment of ecstasy? I always thought that was the true reason humans enjoy nonprocreative sex—to slip the bonds."

"And come back to more? Maybe it's our circumstances, Eddie. If Cob hadn't—" The thought died unspoken. "If Stream—" Again, she faltered. "Sorry."

He watched her, gauging whether to probe. From what Sue had told him, she'd been through some ghastly experiences. He couldn't offer insight if she wouldn't unburden herself, but her beaten-down look suggested wounding too severe and recent to respond to the balm of confession. He changed tack. "Is Walt coming over?"

"He has long shifts all weekend—he'll be here Tuesday."

"Does he want to see me? At Sue's party—" remembering how Walt shied from engaging in debate, as though repartee was personal animosity not the clash of ideas.

"Sure, we'll all do stuff together."

"What about Cob?"

"He's around—he'll be TA-ing once summer school starts. He has this weekend off but he's been working full-time since finals."

"Sue said he's—what did you call it?"

"Fruitarian," Laura said. "I tried it a few months. He'd be happy to explain it if you're actually interested, not just prying into his habits thinking he's weird."

"But he *is* weird," Sue said.

"We all are, Sue—haven't you noticed?" she said testily. "If nothing has to die for him to live, he prefers that."

"Nothing?" Eddie challenged. Laura elaborated, but the diet sounded impossibly restrictive. "Sure he doesn't sneak hamburgers?"

But instead of answering, she got a malicious glint in her eye and said, "Sue, did you tell Eddie about laying Cob?"

Startled and hurt Sue set down her beer, looking beyond Laura at the fridge, the sink, then picked up the bottle again, peering into it. "A little bit."

Turning back to Eddie, Laura demanded, "What'd she tell you?"

Taken aback by that flash of hostility, he stumbled, "She—ah—said he set a speed record getting her in bed."

"And didn't say she went back to spend the night?" Laura's eyes narrowed at Sue who looked away, face sagging into unhappiness.

"Ah, no, she didn't actually."

"Be honest Sue—you don't have to like Cob, but don't misrepresent him."

"The two of you put me in a situation I shouldn't have been in."

"And gave you plenty of opportunities to back out. That's more than we had."

"So your bad experience justifies—"

"I didn't say that. But maybe I have a different threshold now." Laura leaned forward and set her beer on the table. "Sue, Berkeley's not a kind place. If you can't handle what happened with Cob, maybe you don't belong here. Stream didn't, and now she's dead."

"I didn't mean—Laura, you're so—"

Laura took a slow breath, her face softening. "Guess I've developed a thicker skin, living here. I apologize." Their eyes met, Sue's injured, doubting. Laura came around the table offering a hug, her friend holding back. Eddie didn't get it—why so bellicose? There were other ways to be truthful.

Laura broke the tension by telling them about Walt's house Entirely Surrounded By Water while they finished the six-pack. Sue yawned and declared she was ready to sleep. As she headed upstairs, Laura called, "Be right there," then turned to Eddie. "Can we talk?"

"Certainly." She seemed to have lost patience with Sue. That was lamentable, but if she'd confide in him perhaps he could broker a reconciliation.

"Hang out," she said. "I'll be back."

While she was gone, one of Laura's housemates came in. Having learned Eddie's connection with her, Jack asked, "So, you know Cob, the Check-Out King?"

"I thought he was a janitor—"

"'Check out' as in 'bye-bye cruel world,'" Jack said.

"I know only anecdotes—"

"Some of us have been a little closer to the Master of Havoc."

WHEN LAURA GOT back downstairs Jack was opening beers.

"Your housemate seems to know Cob," Eddie said, accepting a bottle.

"Not like he thinks he does—Jack's knowledge is strictly second-hand."

"You know how dangerous mother bears are, when you get near their cubs," Jack said snidely.

"Be accurate if you're gonna badmouth people," she snapped. "Where's Larry?"

"Out."

"Something happen?" she persisted.

"Is it your business?" Jack shot back.

"If you're going to sit around picking Cob apart, I'm entitled to be nosy."

"Fuck you," he said, and stormed out.

"What was that?" Eddie asked, not sure he should laugh.

"Jack can't stand Cob—I don't have to listen to that."

"Your reaction seems disproportional—"

"Eddie, there are things I can't talk about. Cob and I helped each other, and now we're tied together, like it or not."

"Walt as well? *Ménage à trois?*"

"That makes it sound romantic and sexy—Eddie, there's so much pain."

"My mother was at her happiest with two men."

"Maybe they were just fucking."

"That was my impression."

"There's no way back from where we are now."

"Sorry to hear that, but why mistreat Sue? Have you lost your empathy?"

"She ticked me off, talking about Cob like he's a sideshow freak—know why he's studying Biology? Because he respects living things."

"Other than people…"

"Not true—he's been very generous—even after I told him 'hands off' he studied with me, and helped me with a paper—he didn't have to. And he helped me see Walt."

"I'd very much like to meet him—tomorrow?"

"Yeah, for FAC—we'll go to a bar for drinks and loud music."

"Which limits conversation—"

"Sometimes it's easier to meet people with distractions around—not so much like a police grilling."

"You're familiar with those?"

She told him about spending an afternoon detained and interrogated; when she was done he nodded, setting his empty bottle on the table. "Well, much has changed for you. But it sounds like you're too busy to humor me if I make a pass at you."

"Don't do it Eddie. Really. I'm up to here," touching her hairline.

"So which one do you like better, or is that a fair question?"

"It isn't."

"Summer is upon us—what are your plans?"

"Walt and I are going to Montana for a couple weeks, camping."

"Two weeks do not a summer make. No work, no school?"

"I might start my research—that's what I should do."

"So once you get back, Walt goes home and Cob comes over?"

"Pretty much. He'll give me space if I ask him to."

"Come back to Carling with me, return in the fall with a clear head."

"That much time'd be a desert I'm unequipped to cross—we'd all just go nuts."

He stood, weaving slightly. "Well, after three beers I think the floor has ceased to vibrate. I'm ready to attempt sleep."

"We'll talk again Eddie. It's good to see you."

"You too." As she walked past him he grabbed at her even though she'd told him not to, but that third beer sabotaged his balance—she sidestepped, he kept falling. On the floor he rolled onto his back, grinning. "I know, I know. No more passes."

CHAPTER 23

Full Circle

ob had called Friday morning, instructing Laura to meet him at
the Econ building at noon, wearing her diaphragm. As she climbed
the steps he pushed the door open—most buildings were locked
between terms, only people with keys could get in—faculty and janitors.

"These are the cushest offices," ushering her down the empty corridor, its only light filtering through transoms, the plop of their feet
preceding then passing them on the echo's way back to the wall behind.
Selecting a key he unlocked a door, inside setting the latch so no one
could walk in on them. Mullioned arched windows welcomed bright
day into the high-ceilinged office whose tall built-in shelves showed off
leather-bound books. The dark wood floor was buffed to a glow, a large
handsome walnut desk with inset leather blotter was graced with art deco
accessories—fountain pen and bottle of ink, silver letter opener, lamp
with two-tone etched glass diffuser. The desk chair was upholstered in
black leather, its padded arms burnished brown by long use, and in front
of the radiator beneath the tall windows stood a handsome antique sofa
with carved wooden legs, upholstered in fine glossy fabric—narrow white
stripes dotted with small pink roses, widely spaced against a deep blue

background. Facing the desk was an armless chair on casters, upholstered in burgundy corduroy.

Cob nodded at that last piece, "Looks fun, don't you think?" shedding his clothes. This made her nervous—if someone walked in, he'd not only lose his job, they might both get kicked out of school. "I've cased it—the prof's in San Luis Obispo for a week with his aged mother. Nobody's coming in here."

She draped her things on the radiator, glancing out the window—trees behind—seemed private. He'd parked his trash cart in a corner, with spray bottles, several rags and the handles of brushes visible in its array of pockets, a feather duster on a hook, the plastic bag neatly folded over the top of the frame, knotted at one corner to keep it there. She could smell cigarette butts—he'd told her that after emptying ashtrays he finished up by spitting in them then wiping them out with used paper towels or Kleenex, whichever was handy.

"That's gross," she'd objected. "Shouldn't you use a rag?"

"And have it stink up my office? No way," which had brought home to her the difference in their status—she prepared for recitations in the grad lounge with its comfortable old furniture and big windows, but his "office" was a mop closet in the library, its shelves lined with rolls of toilet paper, cans of cleanser, stacks of orange bars of soap, gallon jugs of window cleaner, bleach, floor wax. He'd parked a desk chair missing a caster next to the floor sink, and by the light of the bare overhead bulb studied in there sometimes, surrounded by the smells of chemicals, the drying mop-head, treated dust-rags. Thinking that looked like exile, she'd suggested he try to get his job back at the stat lab—he just laughed.

"My supervisor respects me—wish I could say the same for Dr. Dolph—when I met with him in his office he smoked nonstop, even after I said it bothered me. Why shouldn't I spit in ashtrays? Nothing I put in 'em is as filthy as a cigarette butt."

"Sounds like poorly disguised animosity," she observed.

"So what if it is? I'm not picking fights with anybody. Don't you have negativity to blow off?"

"Not that much—sexual release frees me, I guess."

He grinned and sat in the armless chair, hard-on rising to greet her. She stepped over the seat to take him but her legs were too short—all she could do was sit on his thighs as the well-oiled casters moved, Cob extending his legs with his feet planted. Again she tried to stand over him, he bent his knees pulling the chair forward, sloping her to touch his dick, then straightened his legs—the chair moved back, his hard-on just out of reach. He beamed with blissful mischief as he bent his knees again, she nudged the floor with her toes—all the purchase she could get—inching toward his lap, making contact before he stretched his legs again, one hand on her back, the other to her hot spot. When he bent his knees higher she got him a little way inside, squeezing with her inner muscles while his finger coaxed heat, then when he let his legs fall she kept him in, leaning forward so mouths could meet, and he raised his knees, propelling her into his lap. Fully on him she got tiptoes on the floor, the chair tilting slowly back. She leaned away and it righted.

"Great chair huh?" he laughed. They rocked and rolled, pushing off with toes to spin in a circle, the warm air rich with the smells of wood and leather, dizziness compounded by their contact. Collapsing into a long embrace they cooled as gravity took hold again, then he propelled the chair over to the sofa, offering his bandana so she wouldn't stain the prof's furniture.

"Lie down facing me." He moved a rose and white throw-pillow to one end to cushion her head, she stretched out against the dark blue, the roses matching her skin as though ecstasy had shaken loose little dots of her. "Wish I could paint," he said. "You're dazzling."

She felt wonderful, his admiration like a heat-lamp. He kept tilting his head to meet her eyes, finally lying on his side on the floor. After a while she rolled onto her back, he stood so he could look down at her, and she sensed the tension between adoration and ownership in his gaze: he still harbored a yen for power, and putting her in this environment he'd chosen teased that. Impressed at his control even as she worried about it slipping, she extended her arm, he knit his fingers with hers and let her pull him down, kneeling now, head to her belly. Her free hand played in his hair while his fingernails brushed one nipple then the other, she sat up and still on his knees he held her for a kiss, when she lay back he lifted one thigh for her to hug between hers.

"This is breaking my knee, y'know," he said.

"Lie down then." She pressed against the sofa back, he levered himself up and scooted till his hips were more-or-less flat then she draped over him, his fingers tapping a rhythm on her butt while they kissed.

"My turn," she said eventually, moving to the chair to look at him. His body had gone from being just a decently built guy, to a frame and upholstery she liked very well—no, *loved*. Might as well be honest. Wherever it was going to take them, or prevent her going, she loved him—not the wide warmth that included Walt, but focused desire for one person to merge with, cherish, walk the world beside.

He turned onto his hip so she could see him better, smiled at her pleasure and perceived the shift, the balance slipping toward him. His dick rose again, she stood over him a moment possessive and hungry, then clearing the desktop's accoutrements to the floor she lay back across the blotter. He pulled her pelvis to him, working his way in then with his hands cushioning her from the edge, jammed hard, his force moving them onto the desk. She thumped him with her heels, howling as he thrust, and forgetting himself he howled back. They finished with a whoop and lay breathless, grinning at each other.

When they floated back into the continuum of time she asked, "Is lunch over?"

"Long gone. I'm playing hooky now. Kiss me please."

She obliged. "We better move—I'd hate to ruin this beautiful desk."

"I'd hate it too—take me years to pay off." He lifted her away—one little smear on the leather. She wiped the blotter quickly, then him, then herself, and tucking her clean bandana to her crotch she put on undies.

"You're going?" As though their time wasn't up.

"You have work, remember? So are you coming tonight?" She'd told Eddie and Sue they'd all be going out for FAC.

"Really want me to?"

"Sure." Clothes back on, she stepped to the desk where he stood, still, naked, and hugged him, but as though his batteries had conked out he didn't respond. At the door she paused. "Shouldn't you dress?"

He shook his head, lost. "I think I'll spend the afternoon in here crying."

"Don't get fired."

"I don't care. If you're leaving, go."

He meant it—he really was going to stay here in the company of his tears while the rest of his shift passed unattended. His will extended like a magnetic field to bring her into his zone, keep her here. She moved the button that locked the office from the inside, opened the door and looked up and down the corridor with its segmented shadows. This sunny doorway lit the wall opposite, dust motes floating in the brightness like a projector's beam—*Walt*. She'd betrayed him at last. And as soon as he saw her he'd know. Thinking about driving to the airport to kiss him made her angry with herself, and she pulled the door shut and walked down the hall, leaving Cob to his afternoon without her. She looked through the glass before opening the outside door, and once the coast was clear, slipped out then eased it shut, going quickly down the steps and away. If she went around behind the building she'd see Cob at the window—didn't want to. But she couldn't go home now—Sue and Eddie meant well but their questions were crowbars. She needed solitude.

Stopping off to buy a bottle of wine she walked to Cob's apartment, let herself in, poured a glass and flipped through his tapes—here for some reason was the one Walt had made her. She put it on, at the first *I want you* her tears began, and all the way through the tape they ebbed and increased as she thought about Walt, about Cob. She wrote:

Walt my dear one—

This is the crappiest thing I've ever done. Through wonderful times and awful ones I've been yours and you mine, and that's kept me going. But that is no longer true. I love Cob. I am so so so so sore sore sorry. Oh babe I know I'm the dashboard that broke your leg, the blues that flew you away. If I hadn't made you come back would I be hurting you today?

All I have for you I've already given—the box of rain has filled with dust. I'm crying for you, for me, for our dragons and Greeks, for Onion in the snow.

—*Laura*—

TUESDAY, AFTER A holiday weekend that stretched far too long, Sue started looking for a room, Eddie going along to help her evaluate. Cob hadn't showed up and Laura said nothing, reluctant to drag her raw feelings into public, which even her kitchen seemed to be now, these visitors like window-shoppers curious but not buying. The whole weekend her duties as host had kept her from Cob but all she could think of was his heart, his energy filling her completely. She didn't even call because it wasn't words she wanted to exchange. If he wasn't at work she'd be with him today. When they came back Sue and Eddie wondered why Walt hadn't showed, making her phone his house in the late afternoon, then again that evening. No one answered. They got worried—she finally had to say something.

"I told him not to come. I need a breather."

"But I thought we'd get to see him," Eddie objected. "Doesn't he want to?"

"It's me he doesn't want to see."

"What changed?" he pressed, dissatisfied.

"I'd rather not explain." She studied the wood-grain on the kitchen table. "From now on people have to figure out things on their own."

"Not that we have enough data to draw an inference," he said dryly.

"If you're going out for dinner it's time." She hated being so blunt but their attempts to draw her out with high school nostalgia had become oppressive.

"Aren't you coming?" Sue asked. "You don't have to eat, but come with."

"Just go. Here, take my key. I might be out when you get back."

"Out where?" Eddie asked. "With Cob?"

She nodded.

"For the evening?"

She didn't respond.

"The night."

She nodded again.

He took the key. Laura watched them head up the street. Her past was a pair of people she once knew, walking away, her future demolished in an envelope. Cob was all she had left. She got in Rusty warming him up, choking him down, driving over. Upstairs she pulled out her key, wondering if she should knock first, and while she stood deciding he opened the door, wearing only his jeans. She extended the key, pressed it gently to his navel, turned it, he stepped back pulling the door wider. She came in, he shut it—as soon as she crossed the threshold she knew she was in trouble—Randy Newman sang "Sail Away," a lullaby to slavery.

"You shoulda come sooner," he rasped.

"I wanted to."

"That's not good enough." His eyes were obsidian.

"Where's Stream? What about Love's Body?"

"She left."

"No, no—"

"Now it's just us. Or, more accurately, *justice*."

"Justice?"

"For the wronged. For the used and abused."

"When have I—"

In a sneering falsetto, "'Gimme some more, but don't forget I'm holding out for him—we can all live happily ever after if you don't mind bein' a side dish.'"

Where was the man who'd spent Friday lunch with her in that beautiful office? "I gave you whatever I gave him."

"No you didn't. You've been bankin' on him the whole time."

"Not anymore. I sat in that chair," she pointed, "after I left you Friday, and wrote him that's over because I love you. How can you stand here and spit on that?"

"Hm." He smiled, ironic and superior. "What a coincidence. Over this extremely long weekend I decided I had all the boot-heels on my heart I could tolerate. I cried every tear I possessed Friday, then for three days while I sat here trampled you didn't come. You didn't call. Nothing. Now I'm done with you."

He said it with such smug satisfaction, a line delivered perfectly after extensive rehearsal—he knew it would hurt, and she could see how much he liked that—as much as he liked the sex they'd shared, maybe more. He still craved dominance—sacrificed even love for it. But he was too self-absorbed to see her amazement condensing into fury.

She'd been a slave—not again. Picking up the wine bottle from the card table she swung it hard, striking his temple. His eyes flew wide an instant before his gaze dulled and he sank. At first she thought it was blood all down her arm and side, but he wasn't bleeding—that was wine. She let the bottle slide from her grip, it thunked to the floor landing upright. While time stalled she stood stupefied, then swallowed and bent to touch his head where beneath the skin blood was purpling, a lump growing from the impact. She reached further down, to the artery under his jaw. Heartbeats. Remembering when she'd found Stream, she held a pan lid in front of his mouth and nose. No breath steamed it. First aid—pulse but no breathing: mouth-to-mouth resuscitation. He was in a heap so she pushed him over and pulled his legs, arranging him flat on his back then pinching his nose and locking her lips over his, blowing into his mouth, feeling the air push back, not going in. *Oh, the head.* She had to tilt his head. Hand on his forehead, the other under his neck, she angled it. That was better. She pinched his nose and blew again, looking saw his chest barely move, and letting that breath seep out, blew in the next.

She continued while the clock registered fifteen minutes, then befuddled with dizziness sat back. She thought she should check for a pulse again, and now there wasn't one. Picking up his telephone she dialed the police.

CHAPTER 24

Karmafornia (Reprise)

I t was in the mail Tuesday with the holiday backlog, and Walt almost didn't look—he was packed, ready to drive to Berkeley. But his hands tingled as he sorted—his housemates' stuff—both out of town—the electric bill, the union newsletter. The thin envelope. He sat on the short couch on the porch, holding the letter between finger and thumb, wondering if he could absorb what was written here without his eyes having to find out, finally pressing his nails together, sliding them down, sliding again, again down one end of the envelope, creasing till the paper parted a few fibers at a time, reaching in a finger to coax it open, tilting it to shake out the trifold piece of paper. Even the blank was hurting him. He unfurled the bottom third—empty. Taking a long blink he lifted the top.

It seemed he'd been reading these words since September—no news but the intensity of the pain. Expecting this so long, shouldn't he be ready for the punch?

A piece of paper marked on and mailed—was he supposed to write back—*Ms. Reiner—regret to learn this heart didn't fit—return it in the original packaging for a full refund?* Or phone her, and have some conversation a hundred times worse than this note, with the same answer? Or make her look him in the eye and tell him to disappear, she was done with him, thanks but no thanks—if she could? But if she couldn't, then what? It took courage to write this, to face her certainty, consciously spare him the slow death. This was her "clean break," which was what the doctor called his femur fractures—"good clean breaks." Was the crisp parting of bone so good it didn't matter those ends were supposed to be a middle? Memories like mosquitoes swarmed, raising welts—his September visit when he'd first glimpsed Cob's influence on her. Thanksgiving. Her drive down in the rain after his accident. Her kiss at the airport.

If Stream hadn't killed herself, if Cob had never been born, if Onion had trapped them like the Donner Party—*if if if.* "What if" was an empty gas tank, stranding him: "if" had become "now." Now she loved Cob, now she was through with him, really through, not just waiting for her piece of paper in a couple years. She loved Cob. What a sucker, going to Yosemite, playing the "we're all friends now" game. At isolated moments that seemed possible, even right; those moments were his claim to pavement on Highway 17, given a karmic shove.

He'd expected to see Sue and Eddie, but they had no connection—without Laura he was just an ex, an X, the mark of an illiterate or a slave's descendant whose branch had been lopped from the ancestral tree. Cob was stronger—he'd summoned and dismissed her, changed her body, changed her mind. Walt didn't like Berkeley but she went anyway, he didn't want to be her man-in-the-sack but she'd compelled him there. Every step his direction was on her own behalf—her love, her needs—and now she'd turned, swallowed into Cob's sphere. It was the story of Kallia again, choosing Arkhilos over Phoros. Again it was the spearman ending the dragon's life. Cob's larger hands took more, grasped more—not selfishness: karmic entitlement. *How long have I known?* he asked himself. *From the moment we met, not willing to believe it, refusing to see the pattern in the lines? How long will I be howling?* beginning to howl.

Late in the afternoon the phone rang. He let it jangle then finally stop, some lonesome bird taking its mating call elsewhere. He remembered Laura finding the box of rain under this jasmine bush—assurance that everything was—then—all right. Down the steps he parted the branches and looked—the box had sagged apart, its layers of cardboard buckled and dry, but in the bottom, green sprouts: toothed sunburst leaves of marijuana. Mugged by love and left for dead, he was revived by this tickle of cosmic absurdity—*psst!—just kidding.* With Laura cutting him loose, he'd battled his karma to a standstill; a nomad without past or place, he was free to invent a future.

Note on the kitchen table—*I'm gone—help yourself to whatever I left—Walt*—he packed a milk-crate with books, collected his tapes, pulled his blanket off the bed, filled another crate with food and a mug, plate and silverware. He assembled his camping gear, loaded his car, locked the door and pushed the key through the mail-slot, then gently moved the disintegrating box from under the jasmine to the passenger-side floor.

Up by Stream's butterfly he planted the spindly eight-inch seedlings, with cupped hands watered them from the creek then took a drink himself, sprinkled drops in his hair, slapped his cheeks with cold wet palms and said goodbye. Pushing *American Beauty* into his tape deck he sang about that box of rain as he turned east—time to retreat from Karmafornia, rediscover the interior.